WILDE FIRE

A FOREVER WILDE NOVEL

LUCY LENNOX

Cover Art by: AngstyG www.AngstyG.com

Cover Photo by: Reggie Deanching of

www.RplusMphoto.com

Cover Model: Blake Sevani

Editing by: Hollie Westring at www.HollieTheEditor.com

Beta Reading by: Leslie Copeland lcopelandwrites@gmail.com

SERIES NOTE

All Lucy Lennox books are written to be able to stand alone. However, if you prefer to read the series in order, begin with Facing West, an enemies-to-lovers romance featuring a bad-boy tattoo artist and the goodie-two-shoes doctor who thinks he knows what's best for him. Either way, happy reading!

ACKNOWLEDGMENTS

(IT SERIOUSLY TAKES A VILLAGE.)

Leslie Copeland for sending me the song "Never Seen Anything 'Quite Like You'" by The Script and suggesting I write a childhood friends to lovers story.

Sloane Kennedy for telling me to stop fighting the story and let it happen the way it needed to happen. And for reading it in one day so I would know whether or not it needed to be chucked in a dumpster and set on fire.

Chad Williams for helping research submariners and naval accidents.

Reggie and Blake for creating the gorgeous cover image.

AngstyG for making the image into a smoking hot cover.

Hollie Westring for editing like a boss and explaining why "navy" isn't capitalized (see *The Chicago Manual of Style*).

THE WILDE FAMILY

Grandpa (Weston) and **Doc** (William) Wilde (book #6)

Their children:

Bill, Gina, Brenda, and Jaqueline

Bill married Shelby. Their children are:

Hudson (book #4)

West (book #1)

MJ (subplot in book #5)

Saint (book #5)

Otto (book #3)

King (book #7)

Hallie

Winnie

Cal (book #8)

Sassy

Gina married Carmen. Their children are:

Quinn

Max

Jason

Brenda married Hollis. Their children are:

Kathryn-Anne (Katie)

William-Weston (Web)

Jackson-Wyatt (Jack)

Jacqueline's child:

Felix (book #2)

.

PROLOGUE

OTTO - ALMOST TEN YEARS AGO

"That's a mighty fine cock you got there, boy."

The voice, as familiar as my own heartbeat, washed over me. I closed my eyes for a brief moment and let out a breath I felt like I'd been holding all summer.

Walker was back.

"Round these parts, we call them roosters, shithead," I said with a grin, turning from my spot at the fence to see my very best friend in the world sauntering lazily toward me down the dirt drive. Long, skinny legs were wrapped in worn blue jeans, and a faded Hobie 4-H T-shirt was snug enough to show off his rounded shoulders and narrow waist. The late August sun beat down on his golden skin, making him look even more like a mini-god than he already did.

"Now that I've seen your cock, you gonna show me that fine ass I know you're hiding around here somewhere?"

There was a sparkle in his blue eyes, and I noticed he'd grown another inch, maybe two, since I'd seen him last. The guy had been slow to grow, but he was finally getting taller and more muscular with each passing month it seemed. Now that we were both eighteen, I wondered if he was ever going to come close to catching up with me when it seemed I might just keep growing forever.

"Debbie Gibson finally bit the dust," I said with a laugh. "Sassy is trying to get Grandpa to buy her a mule to replace the old bitch. In the meantime, no ass."

I waited, butt leaning against the fence and arms crossed in front of my chest, for him to come to me. Every nerve jangled under my skin, and my heart thundered in my chest. I was afraid if I took one step toward him, I'd lose my composure and fling myself at the guy with a guttural sob.

As Walker got closer, I saw the crooked eyetooth of his lazy grin. I noticed the familiar cowlick that sent his white-blond hair flipping the wrong way above his left ear. But as he came near, I also saw the telltale signs that all was not as easy and happy as it seemed with my best friend.

Faint worry lines etched his young forehead, and there was the faintest wobble to his chin.

"Seth?" I whispered as he got closer.

"Fuck," he croaked. "Fuck, I missed you, Otto."

We were Walker and Wilde. Neither of us used first names unless something was terribly wrong, and the sound of it on his voice nearly dropped me to my knees.

I uncrossed my arms and held them open as I stumbled toward him. His body crashed into mine, and our arms went around each other as tight as barrel bands.

"Oh god," I groaned into the side of his neck, inhaling his scent like a drowning man taking his last desperate breath. "Thank fucking god you're back."

We held each other like that for long minutes; the entire lengths of our teenaged bodies pressed up against each other as if maybe, if we were lucky, we could just crawl inside of each other and become one person.

I sent up a prayer of gratitude for Walker's safe return from a summer spent at his grandparents' house, and thought I might never survive another absence of his again.

But then that fucker opened his mouth and broke my heart with three little words.

"We're moving away."

PART I

REIGNITING OLD FLAMES

CHAPTER 1

WALKER - ALMOST TEN YEARS LATER

Dear Walker,

Well, today sucked donkey balls. First day of senior year and where the fuck are you? Goddamned Minnesota, that's where. I'll have you know I had to sit next to Carrie-Anne in AP History, and she was wearing so much perfume I almost hurled. How in the world did we ever go for that?

Shit. Gotta go. Coach is starting practice. It's hot as fuck here. Wish I had your sweaty ass to maul after practice. I'm horny as fuck without you here.

Miss you, jackass.

Wilde

OTTO WILDE IS BACK in Hobie.

All I could do was repeat that sentence in my head over and over again.

Otto Wilde is back in Hobie.

Nerves coiled in my gut as I returned to the sheriff's office after lunch with my dad. He'd heard it from Liddy at the insurance office, who'd heard it from Cheryl at the supermarket, who'd talked to Doc Wilde at Sugar Britches, who, of course, knew where his own grandson was.

Ten years. Ten years since I'd last seen the other half of myself, the boy I'd loved since I was eight years old and had fallen into the pond between our properties. I'd been fishing alone which was, of course, against the rules. As soon as I'd gotten sleepy out there in the sun, I'd let a stupid fish yank me right into the drink. The next thing I knew a pair of arms was around my waist pulling me up onto the grassy, muddy bank.

"Holy cow! How big was that fish if it yanked your butt in the lake?" the boy had asked with genuine excitement. As if the Loch Ness monster itself had been responsible for my tumble off the little wooden dock.

"Uh, pretty big, I think," I'd lied. "Did I lose it?"

Bright green eyes and messy brown hair had framed a face full of freckles. "Must have. Your pole's gone and everything. You okay?"

You okay?

He'd ended up asking me that a million times over the next ten years.

After I'd broken my arm on a skateboard wipeout. "Shit, man, you okay?"

After I'd gotten back that horrible grade in Señor Miller's Spanish class. "Fuck, dude, you okay?"

After my first horse died. After my grandmother died. After my grandfather made me shoot a buck. Every single goddamned moment of my childhood from that point on was Otto Wilde by my side making sure I was okay.

After we both lost our virginity to Carrie-Anne Clapper at the same time, but locked eyes on each other instead of the poor girl throughout every single moment of it. After both of us realized that we would have been a thousand times happier had Carrie-Anne not even been there that night.

Seth, you okay? Are we okay?

Fuck no.

I hadn't been okay in ten goddamned years.

"You just gonna stand there all day or what?"

My head snapped up to see our receptionist-slash-dispatcher

8

sitting at the desk eying me over her bright red reading glasses. They hung from a purple-and-turquoise beaded chain and perched on the end of her nose when she was on the clock and matched her artificially red hair that had been teased up into some kind of beehive hairdo since about 1910.

"Sorry, Luanne. Guess I was zoning out there for a minute," I admitted, trying to shake off distracting thoughts of Otto Wilde. "What do you have for me this afternoon? Anything?"

"You're talking to the youth club at three, but that's about it. Oh, did you hear about Saint and Otto Wilde quitting the navy? They're back on the ranch with their grandads for the time being, but I heard Saint wanted them to go to Dallas and find jobs. Says there's a firehouse that's trying to get Otto to come work for them since that's what he did in the navy. Not sure what Saint plans to do."

"I thought he worked on submarines?" I asked without thinking. I'd kept my ears peeled for any molecule of news about Otto over the years, and when I'd learned he was stationed on a sub, I'd panicked. He fucking hated small spaces.

"Yeah, fires are a big deal on those death tubes. But maybe that's why they train their firefighters so well. Anyway, supposedly the Hobie fire chief is desperate to get him on board when Nathan retires this spring. Don't know if Otto'd be willing to wait around that long though. I'd sure hate to lose him to a Dallas station. Surely Doc and them want him to stay in Hobie, right?"

"Yeah. I'm sure they do. What about Otto's parents? Aren't Bill and Shelby still living overseas?"

"Singapore, I believe. They seem awfully happy to stay there, but I don't understand how they can stand to be so far away from those kids this long."

I let her prattle on with gossip about some of the other Wilde kids. Hudson lived in Dallas; West was newly settled with a partner and a baby here in town. Some of Otto's sisters lived in Dallas too, but I was pretty sure a couple of brothers and his youngest sister were still in Hobie. It was hard to keep track since I'd only been back a few weeks myself.

"Hey, Lu, any idea where Otto's staying? He at the ranch, you think?" I asked. "Or his parents' house maybe?"

She put her pencil eraser against her chin while she thought. "Bill and Shelby's house has been buttoned up for years. In fact, I think at one point they were going to sell off that corner of the Wilde ranch land. Don't know what ever happened to it, but you might ask your dad about that. I'd imagine Otto's at the ranch with his grandads. Why you ask?"

I pulled out my phone to check the time. "Oh, no reason. I just might drop by later and say hey."

She studied me for a minute before her face widened in a grin. "You two were thick as thieves, weren't you? I'd forgotten all about that. Wasn't it you two who got caught skinny-dipping in the lake on Easter morning one time?"

I felt my face heat. "Yes, ma'am. But please don't remind me."

Luanne's laughter was hearty and familiar. "Sheriff Walker, even the baby Jesus was laughing that morning. Nothing like seeing two preteen hineys hotfooting it across the docks in the early morning sunrise to make you grateful the Good Lord died for our sins."

I couldn't help but chuckle. She was right. While it was humiliating at the time, it had turned into a pretty damned good story after a while.

"How were we supposed to know Pastor Carlisle had a whole big baptism thing going on that morning at the waterfront?" I asked through my tears.

I heard a woman's voice behind me. "You talking about that time my brother begged God to save his ass, and not in the salvation kind of way?"

I turned around and saw the almost grown up version of a young woman I hadn't seen in years. "Sassy Wilde? That you?"

She held out her hands and twirled. Her long hair was pulled back in a ponytail and her dimpled face was covered in a light smattering of Wilde freckles. She wore faded blue jeans, a hot pink hoodie, and worn-down cowboy boots. "The one and only," she said.

"Holy crap," I said before I could stop myself. "When the hell did you grow up? Jesus, woman." I stepped forward and pulled her into a hug. "God, it's good to see you. You were tiny when I saw you last, all chicken legs and buck teeth."

"Gee, thanks, sweet-talker," she replied with a laugh. "Here I thought you'd turned into someone mature enough to be our new sheriff. Must be mistaken, right, Luanne?"

Lu shot Sassy a wink. "He's doing okay despite being a newborn baby. How're you, sweetheart? How are things at the doctor's office? Goldie said you'd been helping out manning the reception area for West."

"Yeah, fine. Not super-thrilling, but it's just temporary anyway. Enough about me. Walker, when are you going to come by the ranch for family dinner? I know everyone's dying to see you. Your dad's been about to bust a gut ever since you took the job and moved back."

"Um, your brothers back yet? I heard they got out of the navy," I said, trying to be cool.

Sassy narrowed her eyes at me. "Otto got in last night, and you'd better go see him soon before he whips himself into a frenzy."

My stomach churned with nerves. "What do you mean?"

She rolled her eyes. "Soon as he found out who the new sheriff was in town, his eyes just about bugged out of their sockets. My brother plays his shit pretty close to the vest, as you know, but damned if he didn't blush the color of Miss Luanne's eyeglasses at the mention of your name and Hobie in the same sentence."

I closed my eyes for a second and breathed. Otto Wilde was somewhere nearby waiting for me. My hands shook so violently I prayed I wouldn't have to show them to anyone anytime soon.

I opened my eyes again and looked at Luanne. "What time did you say I have that youth club thing?"

I wasn't sure I'd ever been so terrified of seeing someone in my entire life.

He was going to hate me. And rightly so.

CHAPTER 2

OTTO

Wilde Man,

It's only October and I think I might freeze to death. You ever had to wear a parka? They suck. There's nowhere to put the damned things. And everyone is stupid friendly here—it's annoying as hell. Everywhere we go, someone's mom is serving something called Hot Dish. It's basically tater tots mixed with whatever the fuck. Gross.

You know how I always loved my brother Ross and looked up to him? Well, I hate him now. Mom and Dad said we moved up here to stay close to Ross while he was in school. Can you believe the reason for the move is my fucking brother? I hate him.

Okay, fine. I still love him. But he's an ass.

Some girl named Mo keeps making flirty eyes at me, and every time I come around her and her friends, there's this big giggle fest. I'm biding my time before making The Big Gay Announcement. Wonder what poor Mo will think when I tell her the only tits I like sucking on are yours?

Miss you, fuckface.

Walker

. . .

It hit me completely out of the blue. After returning to Hobie, I'd expected to see the same old faces—mostly my crazy family. But then someone mentioned the new sheriff, and I almost dropped my beer all over Doc and Grandpa's kitchen floor.

"Say what now?" I croaked, barely escaping falling on my ass when I whipped my head around to find out who'd said it.

It was Christmas night, and Saint and I had gotten into Hobie too late to join in on the presents and the big meal. We were all sitting and standing around the huge open kitchen and family room picking at leftovers and dessert.

My brother Hudson repeated himself. "Yep, Sheriff Walker. And don't think we haven't already made all kinds of jokes about Texas Rangers."

Everyone laughed about it while my entire fucking world lurched.

"He... what? When? Walker? *Seth* Walker?" I'd stammered. "*My* Seth? Here in Hobie? Right now?"

Doc was the only one who noticed my freak-out. He came over and put a hand on the back of my neck. "You okay, son?"

I felt my hands begin to sweat and my knees shake. It hadn't even occurred to me that Walker would ever set foot in Hobie, Texas, again, and that I'd get the chance to reconnect with him after so long.

"I think I'm just wiped out from the trip," I said.

Doc wasn't stupid. He saw right through me, and I could tell from Grandpa's glance at us across the room, Doc wasn't the only one.

Doc's hand squeezed the back of my neck gently. "Why don't you get some sleep? Felix's cabin is free and might give you some privacy."

"Where's Felix?" I asked, wondering where my shy, bookish cousin had gotten off to.

"He's studying some special stained glass in Europe. Won't be home until after the New Year. I'm sure he wouldn't mind you staying at his place, Otto. Otherwise, it'll be hours before this crew gives you any peace."

I looked around at the room filled with Wildes—aunts and uncle, cousins, siblings and grandfathers. There were girlfriends and boyfriends now, and even a baby. It was everything Doc and Grandpa had always wanted—a full house of happy people coming together for each other and celebrating life's moments. I wondered, not for the first time, why in the world my parents had been so hell-bent on moving overseas once all their kids were out of the house. They'd said it was the perfect time to go adventuring—after the kids were grown but before grandkids started coming—but now there was a grandchild in the mix, and Pippa hadn't even met any of her grandparents yet.

I sighed and looked at Doc. "Have you talked to Mom and Dad today?"

He nodded. "They called this morning and talked to everyone on speakerphone. Said they're hoping to come for a visit this summer if your dad can work it out with his schedule… They asked why you and Saint had decided to quit the navy."

I swallowed and looked away. That wasn't an easy question. "What did you tell them?"

"That it was none of my business, and I was just happy to have you home. As hard as it is for us to accept sometimes, you're a grown man, Otto. You can choose your own path and no matter which one you pick, I'll be happy as long as you are. I'm sure Bill and Shelby feel the same way."

"Thanks, Doc. That means a lot."

"You know what you want to do with yourself? I hear some firehouse in Dallas is trying to get you to sign on with them."

I thought about my buddy Tanner who kept trying to get me to come join his station. I'd served with him briefly a couple of years before and kept in touch via email. It was a good offer, but I hadn't been sure about moving away from Hobie. Now, with the news about Walker being in town, I was even less sure.

"Yeah. We'll see. I need some time to think, I guess."

Doc smiled. "Sure. Well, in the meantime we've got a few horses who'll be happy to see you tomorrow. Why don't you go on now and get some shut-eye?"

I leaned in and gave Doc a big hug. "Love you. Merry Christmas."

"You, too, son. So happy to have you and your brother home safe where you belong."

I made my way to Felix's little cabin across one of the paddocks on the ranch property. After showering and sliding into bed, my thoughts went straight to the slender boy who'd left me without an explanation all those years ago. I had no idea what I would say to him when I saw him, and I had half a mind to ditch out of town before first light to avoid even the chance of seeing him. But my body knew my heart was spouting bullshit, and it finally dragged me down into a deep sleep that held me tight well past daybreak.

THE FOLLOWING afternoon I lingered a long time in the barn after a mid-day trail ride with Doc, Grandpa and my aunt Gina. I rode my favorite horse, Gulliver, and enjoyed the fresh air and wide open spaces despite the cold nip in the air. When we returned to the barn, I'd offered to untack and brush all four horses myself so I could remain outside moving my body after all the long travel the day before and the endless months cooped up on a sub before that.

Once I stored all the equipment and got the horses settled in their stalls with some treats, I sat on a dusty wooden bench in front of one of the stalls and stared off into space. The warm smell of horse and hay was intoxicating, bringing back memories of my childhood and the familiar comforts of home.

I wondered how long it would take me to get up the nerve to go find Walker.

What would he say? How would things be between us?

Would he even want to see me? Did he think about me as much as I did him? My stomach was tied in a thousand knots, and I couldn't for the life of me think of what in the world I was even going to say to him.

"Wilde Man?" The voice was deeper but familiar, and just the sound of it released something in me that had been caged up for a decade.

I lifted up my eyes and saw a masculine frame silhouetted in the big open doors of the barn so I couldn't really make out his features. I

16

saw enough to know a grown man stood in place of my childhood friend. He wore a khaki sheriff's uniform, including a gun belt and the whole deal. Even though he hadn't grown much taller, his shoulders were broader, and I could make out the delicious curves of muscles in his arms and legs through his snug-fitting uniform.

"Walker?"

"Make a Texas Ranger joke, and I'm drawing down on you right here," he said, moving into the barn. I stood on shaky legs and walked toward him.

His face was open and friendly with a big smile, but as he got closer, the nerves were clear as day in his sky blue eyes. Seth Walker was just so fucking beautiful; I wanted to cry like a goddamned baby.

"Hey," I managed to choke out.

"Hey yourself."

Despite ten years of hating him for leaving me, I wanted him with a desperation that left me breathless. I didn't know what I would do if I opened myself up to him again and he rejected me once more.

"I-I..." I tried. "I..."

He shook his head. "Uh-uh. No way. We're not starting with all that shit. Fucking come here."

It took me two strides to get there, and then I was holding on to him as if my life depended on it. I felt every single tremble of both his body and mine, and our blood nearly sang with the rightness of being back together again.

"Oh god, Walker," I breathed into his hair. "Damn, you feel good."

"I missed you so fucking much. I don't know whether to shoot you or fuck you," he growled into my neck.

My dick jammed hard against my zipper, and I felt his growl in my balls.

"Do I get a vote?"

Walker's lips were on mine before I even finished getting the words out. After that it was lips and tongue and teeth and hands.

Everywhere.

I heard his gun belt hit the bench behind me as my hands went for his shirt, yanking it out of his pants. Then his trembling hands were in my hair and mine were on his ass as if they'd never left. I grabbed rounded, muscular cheeks fuller than they'd been before and even sexier if that was possible.

I wanted to touch him *all over*.

"Get naked," I demanded in a harsh tone. "Right now."

My shirt was half rucked up and twisted around my armpits already. Somehow my belt was open, and the buckle was pinned between my hipbone and his stomach. I pulled his uniform shirt apart so fast buttons went flying into the wood slats of the stalls making little *plik-plik* sounds.

I had no patience for this clothing bullshit. "Get this mother-fucking shirt—"

His hands grabbed mine and squeezed. "Hey. Hey. Slow down. There's no hurry, baby. I'm here. You're here. We're here together now, okay?"

Seth Walker calling me "baby." Fuck, my heart couldn't take it.

"Seth," I whimpered, resting my forehead against his. I slid my hands around his bare back and pulled him in tight.

His hands came up to cup my face. "Shh, Wilde Man. Take it easy. Shh."

Walker's lips dropped soft kisses all over my face as his palms slid down over my shoulders and chest to my stomach. I was dizzy with desire and wondered how in the hell I had survived ten whole years without this man in my arms. As I struggled to catch my breath, I realized what he was doing.

Walker followed his hands down my body with open-mouthed kisses until he landed on his knees on the dusty floor.

So much for catching my breath.

CHAPTER 3

WALKER

Seth,

I don't know if I can really do this, I miss you so much I feel like I'm going to be sick all the time. Thank god we agreed not to video chat or talk on the phone because, I swear if I saw your beautiful face or heard your sweet voice, I might crack into a million pieces.

I thought I'd be able to make it through this year, but tonight was bonfire night, and you weren't here for the first time ever. How am I supposed to do this, Seth? I can't stand it. Please tell me you miss me as much as I miss you.

I love you, beautiful boy,
Otto

I COULDN'T THINK. The minute I saw him, my entire brain went on the fritz. Had I been quizzed on my own name right then, I would have had to phone a friend.

The man was goddamned glorious—about fifty times more stacked than when we were kids and seemingly covered in ink. I was surprised my dick hadn't gone off already. It wanted to. It really, really wanted to.

"Lemme suck you off," I begged unnecessarily. I fumbled into his open fly and pulled out his fat cock. It was just as giant as I remembered, if not thicker. I looked up at him. "Really? What did they feed you in the navy, boy?"

His sheepish grin was adorable as hell, and the weak winter light streaming in through the open barn door illuminated freckles that hadn't all disappeared.

"You're so beautiful," I breathed.

We locked eyes for a moment—me with his thick, hard shaft in my hand and him with his fingers threaded in my hair. Dust motes floated through the silent air, and I had the sense that if I didn't grab hold of him now, I was going to lose him forever.

Nerves rustled in my stomach as reality tried pushing in. There were things that needed saying between the two of us, but I'd be damned if I was going to stop touching him long enough for talking before I got him in my mouth.

I licked a fat stripe up the length of his cock without taking my eyes off his.

The groan that came out of him came from deep within, and I was desperate to make him do it again. My mouth enveloped him, sucking and slurping and devouring.

Strong fingers tightened in my hair and his hips began to pump into me. He remembered how much I loved it when he fucked my mouth.

My hands moved to his ass, and I pulled him in even tighter, encouraging him to go deep. I wasn't a virgin teen anymore, but to this day, I'd still only tasted Otto Wilde's cock.

Otto's eyes widened as I took him deep in my throat, but he didn't have time to think about it before his balls drew up, and he gasped out a warning.

"Gonna come."

I sucked him harder and felt his cock jerk against my tongue as he exploded into my throat. My hands squeezed his balls gently and ran up the furry trail of his lower abs, appreciating every hair and bump along the way.

Finally, when I had slurped and licked and cleaned every inch of him, I looked up expecting to see the blissed-out relaxed face of the only man I'd ever loved.

His entire face had gone ashen and was creased with confusion and shock. He stared at something and I followed his gaze to the hand I held against his abdomen.

There, in all of its damning glory shined my thick gold wedding band.

I blinked at it and back up to him, realizing he'd have no idea what it was all about.

"Wait," I blurted. "Wait, Otto. Let me explain."

"Are you married or not?" His eyes begged me to deny it. "Yes or no."

I couldn't. "Yes. But—"

"Are you separated?"

"No, but Otto, listen. If you'll just—"

He jumped back from my touch and nearly stumbled onto his ass. After yanking his jeans back up his legs and scrambling around to find his shirt, he dropped his face in his hands and made a sudden sobbing keening noise I thought would completely break me once and for all. It was the kind of noise I'd only ever heard when giving death notices to next of kin.

His words were broken. "Come find me when you're no longer married, Seth. Until then, stay the fuck away from me."

I didn't even realize I'd started crying too until long after he'd run off and left me kneeling half naked on the barn floor regretting the day I'd ever met Jolie Prichard.

My wife.

WHEN I WALKED through the front door of the house, I almost got run over by a skinny little girl.

"Whoa there, Tishie-poo," I said with an attempted smile, reaching out to wrap my arms around her when I realized she'd come to give me a welcome home hug. Just the feel of her familiar embrace was enough to take the edge off what had happened between Otto and me. "What's the hurry?"

"Uncle Seth! Mom let me make a cake from the cookbook you got me for Christmas, and we're having it for dessert. So you have to hurry so we can eat dinner first. C'mon, we've been waiting for you! Where the heck have you been?"

I thought about being late to my family dinner because I had another person's genitals in my mouth and felt an uneasy jangle in my gut. It hadn't been cheating... not really. Jolie and I weren't together like that. She'd known from day one that I was gay. But I'd still always respected our marriage vows anyway, out of simple respect for her reputation and Tisha's.

"Just saying hey to an old friend, Tish," I explained. "He's got horses, if you can believe it. Hopefully I can take you out there sometime soon and let you see them."

I knew full well Otto wouldn't be there, but I wondered if Doc and Grandpa would welcome my family and me to the ranch. Would Otto tell them what had happened between us? Had they heard through the grapevine that I'd moved back to Hobie with a wife and child in tow?

I followed Tisha back to the kitchen where I smelled onions and garlic enough to make my mouth water. I'd always teased Jolie about becoming some lucky bastard's housewife one day with her cooking skills, but she'd always answered with a wink and the same phrase...

I already am.

She glanced up at me from the oven where she was pulling out a glass dish of chicken breasts. "Hey, Sheriff. I hope you brought your appetite because I made one of your favorites."

I looked at the woman cooking me dinner in my home. *Our* home. She was different from the first time I'd met her all those years ago. More mature and relaxed, not quite so terrified of being abandoned and alone.

She was a beautiful woman. My brother had always had exquisite taste. Her long blonde hair was pulled back in a messy ponytail and she wore leggings with one of my old SPPD Academy sweatshirts that swamped her small frame.

"Hey, beautiful," I said out of habit, but this time the word tasted like poison on my tongue. I wanted to pull it back and keep it for someone else, someone whose word it should have been all along. But the time for that decision had long passed, and I'd been the one to make the choice willingly.

She stepped forward and pressed a kiss to my cheek, pulling me in and wrapping her slender arms around my waist. "How was work? You look exhausted. Did something happen?"

I shook my head, throat filling with the unsaid lie. "Work was fine." At least that part was true. "How did things go here? Did you and Tisha finish any more of that puzzle?"

She nodded as she began dishing out food onto three plates. "Your mom and dad came over and worked on it for a bit. They seemed to be having fun. I think they're happy we're here, you know?"

I blew out a breath, realizing just how shortsighted my move back had been. When my parents had decided to move back to Hobie, Tisha had been devastated. She'd already lost her best friend to Hobie a few years before, and losing my parents to Hobie as well had sent her into a downward spiral. She and my nephew Cody were bosom buddies. They were only a year apart in age and thick as thieves. When even Jolie had expressed a desire to move near my family, I'd thought it would be for the best. After all, Otto was in the navy, and from all the gossip I'd heard through the grapevine, he was planning on staying in for the full twenty.

But now he was back. He was back, and I was stuck between a rock and a huge goddamned boulder.

I felt my chest tighten and my eyes smart.

There was no fucking way this was going to end well. Regardless, I had to find him and tell him what the hell was going on.

But first, I needed to have a serious conversation with my wife.

It was time to bring this marriage to an end once and for all.

It took about a week and a half before Luanne began calling me the Ghost Sheriff. She'd told Jolie and my mom the other day I was there but not there, just like the Maberley sisters in that haunted inn she'd read about somewhere up north. I floated around doing what needed doing but never really came down to earth long enough to interact with mortals.

She wasn't wrong. I felt about as hollow as a ghost. Worn thin and flimsy as hell, not to mention aimless.

Otto had run.

He'd taken the first opportunity and not only split town, but left the goddamned country with Doc and Grandpa. Motherfucking coward was what he was. After everything we'd ever had between us, he couldn't stick around for five fucking minutes to let me explain?

Shit head. Jackass. Asshole cocksucker.

"What did you just call me?"

I whipped my head up from my desk at the sheriff's office to see a young man with spiky pink hair and a leopard print apron over some kind of bright yellow jumpsuit. He stood in front of the empty reception counter with hands on his hips and a knowing smirk on his face. I thought I recognized him from the bakery in town.

"Not you."

The guy looked around at the empty space and back to me with a raised eyebrow.

"I promise I was talking to myself. How much did you hear?"

"Asshole cocksucker—which, let's be honest, sounds like a recipe for a damned good time."

That got a laugh out of me. The kid was clearly snarky and bold as hell.

"What's your name, and how can I help you today?" I asked.

"Stevie Devore, and I'm here because I work over at Sugar Britches bakery, and we've been having a problem we could use your help on."

"I thought Nico Salerno owned the bakery now?"

"He does, but he's... ah... well, let's just say he was going to come talk to you but got distracted upstairs in the tattoo parlor. Playing doctor. With a doctor. So, you know. Legit."

His sprite-like face crinkled with laughter, and I couldn't help but smile even though I still felt hollow inside. "What kind of problem have you guys been having over there?"

"The bakery has become the cool kids' hangout when they don't want to be at home around their parents. Which is fine for the most part when they're buying coffee and sodas and cookies or whatever. But we have a crew of kids who've started not buying anything. When we politely ask them to give up their tables to our paying customers, they hassle us and then loiter right outside the bakery windows with their vape clouds in our customers' faces."

"That sounds annoying as hell," I agreed.

"Right? We just need a nice, strapping officer of the law such as yourself to come hang out with us one afternoon and help scare the little rapscallions away." He batted his eyelashes at me before adding, "Pretty please with handcuffs on top? Ooops, I mean, cherries on top?"

I nodded. "Sure. Let me find my dispatcher, and we can head over right now. I could use a latte."

Stevie hopped and clapped his hands. "Perfect. Whatever you want, Sheriff, is on me." He tilted his head for a split second and barked out a laugh. "I just said *Sheriff is on me*. I was wrong earlier, now *that* sounds like a recipe for a damned good time. Am I right?"

I held up my left hand out of habit to reveal my wedding band. "Sorry."

Stevie's face fell, but then he shrugged and winked at me. "Damn, shoulda known. All the cute ones are taken."

"I sure could use some new friends though. Especially ones who know how to make a decent coffee and a pastry. That sound okay to you?"

The cute guy held out his pinky finger. "To new friends. Nice to meet you Sheriff Walker."

"Nice to meet you Stevie Devore." I linked my pinky with his and shook on it.

While he wasn't exactly the man I'd been hoping to get to know

now that I was back in Hobie, I allowed myself to enjoy Stevie's easy company on the walk over to the bakery.

CHAPTER 4

OTTO

O,

We only have eight months left. We can do anything for eight more months and then we'll be together when we get to college, okay? In the meantime, let's concentrate on avoiding blue balls. Send me dick pics please. It's been way too long since I saw Big O. I miss that beast.

But seriously, baby. You can do this. Know that I miss you more than words can say. Always remember, it could be worse. You could be taking ice hockey lessons like a certain person you know and love.

I love you so much Wilde Man. You and me together forever.

S.

Oh, and did I mention I was cold as fuck? Also, Ross has a new girlfriend who Mom and Dad can't stand. I kind of feel sorry for her. I think it's just because she's poor. Kind of like how they were when John was dating Candice, remember? Why can't they just be the loving Christians they always claim to be? That poor girl can't help it if she doesn't have money or family to help her.

IT HAD BEEN eight weeks since I'd seen Walker in the barn and discovered his dirty little secret. I wasn't stupid; I'd known there could have been an explanation that made what we did somehow not cheating. Maybe he'd lost his husband and was still wearing the ring in mourning. Maybe he was in the middle of a divorce and hadn't gotten up the nerve to remove the ring yet.

But none of those things were true.

When I'd crashed my way through the door to Felix's cabin, Grandpa had been there dropping off a few containers of leftovers.

"Hey, big guy, what's after you? You about threw that door off its hinges," he'd said with a frown.

"Did you know Walker was married?" I'd asked, my voice sounding way less sane than I'd hoped.

"I didn't until this afternoon. I ran into his father when I stopped to get the mail, and he told me about how happy he was that Seth and his family had finally moved to Hobie."

I'd felt like the whole world had gone insane.

"His parents are back too?"

"Oh, yeah. His parents moved back a little over a year ago. John and his wife, Beth, were already here. They've got three kids if I'm not mistaken. Seth was the last to come back. I guess when the sheriff's position opened up, it was the sign he'd been waiting for. He was in law enforcement in St. Paul," Grandpa had said.

"And he's married? To whom? What's the guy like? And his family's just okay with him being married?" I'd asked incredulously. We'd always been out to my family, but not as much to his. I knew he'd told his family he was gay at some point, but they sure as hell hadn't been happy about it.

Grandpa's hand had come down on my shoulder. "It's a woman, Otto. Her name is Jolie, and they have a little girl."

"No," I croaked. "This can't be happening. He's gay, goddammit. What the hell? Did he just decide to play along with his parents' bullshit?" My voice had gotten louder, and I'd stepped away from Grandpa enough that I could run my hands through my hair without elbowing the man. "Who does that? I don't understand."

"Talk to him, son. I know you two were tight until they moved away. Give him a chance to explain."

But I hadn't.

Because I knew—had always known, really—that I couldn't be anywhere near Seth Walker and not touch him.

So I'd run away like the fucking coward I was. There was no way in hell I was giving him another chance to break me.

I went to Europe to see my cousin Felix in Paris, and then I traveled to Spain to meet up with an old fuck buddy I'd served with. We spent four days of his leave time naked and fucking every which way we could in a hotel room by the ocean. I pretended not to think about a certain Texas law enforcement officer every time I shot my load, and my buddy pretended not to give a shit the one time I accidentally called out Seth's name instead of his.

When it was time for my friend to return to duty, I'd had to nut up and go home. I couldn't allow Seth Walker's life decisions to cheat me out of being around my own damned family.

If Walker wanted to marry a woman and play Happy Hetero, then that was his fucking choice. But I wasn't going to shed one more tear over the asshole.

I made my way back to Texas and joined my friend Tanner at the Dallas FD in late January. After laying low for several more weeks under the guise of having to put in some extra time at work, it was finally time to get back to Hobie for a family dinner night at the ranch.

Since I'd bought myself a motorcycle, I accepted my sister Hallie's offer to ride with her, Winnie, and Saint in Hallie's big SUV. Saint had taken a job in personal security and had been lucky enough to get the same night off. We hadn't seen much of each other in the past month, despite sharing an apartment in the city, and I was looking forward to spending some time finding out how his new job was going.

Once we were in the car, my sister Winnie turned to talk to me from the front passenger seat. "I heard Chief Paige is going to be at the ranch tonight to try and talk you into taking Nathan Hearst's place at the Hobie firehouse after he retires this spring."

"I already have a job," I mumbled.

Hallie piped up from the driver's seat. "You wouldn't want to live

29

in Hobie? Come on, O. You know you hate the city. You've gotta be dying to ride Gulliver again. I can't even understand how you've stayed away from him this long."

The thought of my paint horse waiting for a nice long trail ride with me made me antsy. He'd been one of the main reasons I'd finally agreed to run up to Hobie with my brother and sisters for the night. I was desperate to take him out.

"Not much action at the Hobie firehouse, I'd imagine," I said.

Saint turned to look at me with a frown. "I thought you didn't want any more action, brother."

I grunted and turned to look out the window. He was right, and we both knew it. Saint was the only one who knew the shit I'd gone through on my last boat and how I was damned lucky not to have PTSD symptoms severe enough to make me unfit for a career in emergency services altogether.

But so far the job in Dallas had been fine. Nothing too big to deal with, or at least, nothing too serious on my shifts anyway. There had been a big apartment building fire one night after I'd gotten off work. If I hadn't been already over my hours for the week, they might have called me in to help. I'd dodged a bullet with that one because several of my coworkers had gotten injured and had to get medical attention after the blaze was contained. I'd spent the following week putting in even more hours to make up for so many people being out recovering.

Saint knew it was just a matter of time before I had to respond to a fire serious enough to scare the fuck out of me. I could only hope when it came I was up to the task.

When we got to the ranch, sure enough, Chief Paige's red HFD vehicle was parked out front. The dogs came racing out of the sprawling farmhouse hell for leather, jumping up and causing a general nuisance in the front yard. All except Grump who just stayed back on the porch rolling his hound-dog eyes at the little ones.

Grandpa and Doc appeared behind him and waved us in. "Get out of the cold. It's supposed to rain any minute," Doc warned.

Saint and I grabbed our sister's overnight bags as well as our own and made our way into the house. After hugs and kisses and pets all around, we finally walked into the kitchen for a drink. Hudson was out of town for work, but West and his partner, Nico, were there with their daughter Pippa, and Felix was back from Monaco. Unfortunately, he seemed to be off in his glass studio feeling sorry for himself over the loss of whatever dude he'd hooked up with over the holidays.

I approached Pippa and tickled under her jaw in a spot that made her smile and giggle. She was only nine months old, but her tiny little teeth and her ability to giggle at the drop of a hat brought a smile to my face. West was over the top in the number of photos of her he texted to the whole family, but I didn't mind a bit. There had been many times over the past several weeks when I'd needed to see that little innocent face covered in bananas or half asleep in her peas.

"Just the man I wanted to see," Chief Paige said from across the room. He'd been talking to my little sister Sassy, who was looking older and older every time I saw her these days.

"Good to see you, sir," I said, holding out a hand. Chief Paige had known me since he was a rookie firefighter and coached my middle school soccer team. We'd all looked up to him like a god at the time, and I still had to admit the man was hot as fuck. He'd seemed so much older than we were back then, but now that I was twenty-nine, the ten-year age difference didn't seem so important.

"Don't 'sir' me, Wilde. It's Evan," he said with a big smile and firm handshake. "And I assume you already know why I'm here."

"No, sir," I lied. "I mean, Evan."

"I need you at the firehouse, Otto. We're getting ready to be a man short, and I've heard nothing but great things about your training in the navy. We could really use an experienced firefighter who knows Hobie."

"I'm already employed, Evan. I'm working with the Dallas FD," I told him, accepting a bottle of beer from Doc.

"I understand that, but we need you more than Dallas does, and I'm willing to make you a strong offer," he said with a big, friendly smile. "Hobie has something your current situation does not. A soccer team needing a coach."

I closed my eyes and let out a laugh. Someone had found my weakness and given it to this guy to exploit. "And what makes you think I give a shit about that?"

Sassy, sidled up to me. "Come on, Otto. You know this is exactly what you've always wanted. What's your hesitation? Firefighting and coaching soccer in Hobie? Being able to ride Gulliver whenever you want? I'm sure Doc and Grandpa could set you up with a corner of the ranch to build a cabin like Felix did. Or maybe you can even stay in Mom and Dad's old house. Come on. We Hobie Wildes want you here. Screw the Dallas crew."

Evan studied me with a grin. "Yeah, Otto. We want you here. At least give it some serious thought, okay? I'll email you some more details. The job at the station doesn't have to be filled until late May, but the soccer coach is needed here before then. I hope you'll consider it. You and Sheriff Walker sure were a force to be reckoned with on the field back in the old days."

I glanced at him, trying not to choke on the sip I'd taken of my beer. "Walker isn't coaching, too, is he?"

"No. Unfortunately, his job is too unpredictable for him to be able to do it. That's why we need you. Let me know when you're ready to say yes, Otto. Can't wait to get you in the firehouse and show you what we've got," he said with a wink before turning to say goodbye to the rest of my family.

Was that a flirt wink? Was there any chance Chief Paige was gay or bi? God, that would be a dream come true for any number of my brothers and cousins, not to mention myself. I wouldn't mind a roll in the hay with that gorgeous man if it would get my mind off a certain law enforcement officer.

The image of Walker going down on me in the barn flashed through my mind and set my entire groin on fire. I tried like hell to force the image away. I'd never knowingly engaged in sex with a married man, and the fact it was with the person I'd once trusted more than anyone else rankled the hell out of me.

I spent the rest of the family dinner night surrounded by comfortable chatter. Everyone grilled Saint and me about our jobs in Dallas and everyone but Grandpa and Doc seemed to want to get in their opinion about me moving back to Hobie. By the time everyone shut the hell up, it was too late to take Gulliver out on a ride.

After staying up a couple more hours drinking with everyone who'd chosen to stay over in the ranch bunkhouse, I turned in. I slept soundly and got up early in the morning to take the horse out before we had to get on the road back to the city after breakfast.

After greeting and tacking the big old guy, we made our way up past the scrubby forest to the edge of the ranch where one of my favorite trails led to my parents' old house. The sun was just peeking up over the edges of the trees and the cold winter air seemed to make everything around me look brighter and cleaner than usual.

Halfway down the trail I heard a high-pitched squeal that startled both the horse and me. Luckily, Gulliver was smarter than I was and figured out right away we weren't in enough danger to need to bolt or rear. I looked toward the fence off to my right and saw a little girl standing there almost vibrating with excitement.

I waved my hand and smiled, forgetting for the moment that the fence marked the border with the Walker ranch.

"Hey there. Good morning, sunshine," I called out.

"Oh my gosh! Is that your horse? Can I see him?" she cried. "I've never petted a horse up close."

I steered Gulliver toward the fence and hopped off so I could show the little girl how to properly greet the large animal.

"My name is Otto Wilde, and who might you be?" I asked, wondering who was living in Mr. and Mrs. Walker's old place. Then it came to me. The *Walkers* were living in their old place. They'd moved back and brought the whole damned Walker crew with them.

"Tisha Walker," she said proudly, running a tiny hand up the horse's large nose. "Do you live next door? I thought it was those two granddads."

I let out a chuckle. "No, ma'am. Those two granddads are *my* granddads, though. I'm just here for a visit. What about you?"

"I'm here for good. Which means I might be able to have my very own horse. I couldn't have one in Minnesota because it was too cold.

And we lived in a city. But here... well, I keep hoping Mom and Uncle Seth will let me get one."

My heart stuttered a beat when I heard Seth's name come out of her mouth.

"Uncle Seth?" I asked. "Who are your mommy and daddy?"

She tilted her head and shot me a look like I was an idiot. "Jolie and Seth are my parents. I mean, well, *technically* I guess Ross is my dad, but I never met him, you know? So really it's Seth because he's the one who raised me from when I was a baby."

As she continued to babble on, my stomach twisted up and tried to make sense of the words she was saying. Seth's older brother Ross had a child? But Seth had raised her? I looked up to see if I could spot anyone at the house across the expansive backyard. There were two houses on the Walker ranch, or there had been ten years ago last I checked. The main house was up closer to the road and was the house where Seth and his siblings had grown up. This house was more of a guest cottage and had only two small bedrooms with a loft upstairs that had a set of cheap bunk beds in it. Was this where Seth was living with his wife and this little girl?

"Is Uncle Seth around, sweetie?" I asked.

"No. He got called out on a case last night. He's the sheriff, you know."

I couldn't help but smile at the pride in her voice. "Yes. He's very important around here. We're lucky to have him protecting us, don't you think?"

She nodded, messy blonde bangs falling in her face. "Yes. Granddad says it takes a real man to be sheriff, and it's a good thing Uncle Seth decided to become a real man."

I felt my jaw tick. Mr. Walker had always been friendly as all hell most of the time, but damned if he couldn't drop some of that old southern bullshit bigotry he still had.

"Your uncle has always been a real man, Tisha. I promise you that. He's one of the best men I've ever met."

Her eyes flicked up from where they were gazing longingly at Gulliver. "You know Uncle Seth?"

"He sure does, baby girl," Seth said, walking across the lawn in his full sheriff getup. Damn, the man could wear a uniform like nobody's business. "Mr. Wilde and I grew up together."

I felt my skin prickle with awareness as he came nearer. I'd never been able to be this close to Seth Walker and not touch him. Even when we were in class together, we'd have the edges of our shoes touching or our elbows brushing.

I swallowed hard. "Hey."

Walker studied me. "Hey yourself. Haven't seen you around lately."

I stuffed my hands in my pockets to keep from grabbing the front of his jacket and shaking him. "Been in Dallas."

His nostrils flared slightly, and he glanced at Tisha before bringing his eyes back up to bore into mine.

"So I heard."

The awkward silence was broken only by the desperate internal screaming and wailing of my double-crushed heart.

Thank god Tisha spoke up. "Look at this pretty horse, Uncle Seth. Do you think maybe it could have babies so I could have one?"

Walker smiled down at her with a softness in his face I'd never seen. "No, cutie pie. Gulliver is a boy horse, which means he's not having babies anytime soon. I think it's time for you to skedaddle, though, because your mom is planning on taking you to church with Grandma and Granddad."

She huffed out her displeasure and gave another longing glance Gulliver's way before looking up at me with a smile.

"Nice to meet you, Mr. Wilde. Hopefully I'll see you and Gulliver again some time soon!"

I smiled back at her and nodded. "Nice to meet you, Tisha."

Once he made sure she was back in the house, Walker turned to face me.

"Can we talk, please? I need to explain some things to you."

My heart thrummed painfully in my throat as I considered his words.

"I'm not sure there's anything to say, to be honest. You're married with a child. Can't say as I understand it, really, but it's not my place to. It's your business."

"Bullshit," he barked angrily. Gulliver and I both startled and stared at the sheriff. It wasn't like Walker to lose his cool.

"How is it my business, Walker?" I snapped back.

"Because I love you, dammit. I've always loved you. All I've ever wanted is Ottowa Hubert Wilde. It was always supposed to be you and me together forever and now you're fucking saying you don't matter? That it's none of your business? What the fuck, Otto?"

His voice ramped up in tone and intensity until it was almost a sob. Hearing him say he loved me had to have been a hallucination. Seeing him hurt and confused gutted me. It made all the raw parts of me feel even more exposed and vulnerable until I thought I might detonate right there and just be done with it.

"You left me, dammit! Do you remember? Do you remember you were the one who decided it was over? How dare you act like you've only ever loved me and it's only ever been me. *Bullshit.* Don't you for one minute tell me I have a say in who you're with. That ended ten fucking years ago when you chucked my heart straight out the door. Fuck you, Seth Walker. Seriously. Fuck. You."

I turned to get on Gulliver, but I wasn't fast enough. Walker hopped the fence in one smooth move and shoved me against a tree trunk on the other side of the trail. My back hit the hard bark with a jarring thud, and I took a moment to be grateful for the thick coat I had on.

Suddenly, I found myself nose to nose with an angry Walker. His eyes were stormy and fraught with emotion. I thought he was going to yell at me again, but he didn't. The lapels of my coat were bunched in his hands up under my chin, and he tightened his hold before speaking in a rough voice.

"It's over with Jolie. Done. I've already hired Honovi to start divorce proceedings. He says it'll take at least sixty days. Please, please, don't leave me again. I was never in love with her, Otto. I swear to god. I married her because Ross got her pregnant and then got himself killed in a fucking bar fight before the baby was even born."

"Ross is dead?" I asked in shock.

Seth's anger turned to grief in an instant as he nodded. His eyes filled, and I wanted to pull him into my arms to comfort him. But he wasn't mine to console.

"He got beaten so badly in a bar fight when she was pregnant that he was on life support. Before they intubated him, he begged me to look after Jolie, to marry her so the baby had a father. Jolie never had a dad and that's why Ross promised to marry her, so their child wouldn't experience the same fate. He said Jolie and the baby shouldn't have to suffer because of his stupid mistakes. He made me promise, Otto. What could I do?"

I could see the panic and desperation in his face he must have felt back then as a terrified teenager making unfair promises to the brother he'd always idolized.

"What was I supposed to do? She had no one. No job, no insurance, no family." Walker babbled now. His tears streamed freely and his gorgeous eyes begged. "I wanted to tell you, but I couldn't bear it. Please let me tell you the whole story. I need you to understand why I did what I did. And that it's truly over."

My head swirled with all the information he gave me, and I didn't even know where to begin processing it. I could see the truth in his eyes and feel his need for me to understand.

We had a lot to talk about, but now wasn't the time.

"I've got to go," I said, pushing him back as gently as I could. His face dropped, and I reached out to tilt his chin up. "Look at me. We're going to talk, Seth. But not right now. Right now I've got to go back to Dallas to work, and you've got to handle things with your family. I don't feel right being alone together until your divorce is final. But after that, I'll come back, and we can hash through it, okay?"

He let out a breath and nodded. "Thank you," he whispered in a shaky voice. "I thought I lost you. I can't lose you again, Otto. I can't."

I thumbed the tears off his face and looked at the most beautiful human being I'd ever known. He was perfect inside and out, and him marrying Jolie to help her was just like him. He'd always been selfless and sweet, the kind of guy who'd give you the shirt off his back. How could I have ever thought he'd changed so much that he'd ditch me to marry some random woman?

"I wish you'd told me," I said, fighting back my own prickling eyes. There was really only one thing on earth that had the power to make me cry like a baby, and it was this man right here. "I would have..."

"Don't say you would have understood, dammit. You and I both know you would have flipped your fucking lid and hitchhiked to Minnesota," he said with a weak smile. And he was right.

I smoothed the familiar wrong-way curl of blond hair by his temple. "Maybe."

Walker stepped back and tried to shake himself off, wiping his cheeks roughly with his palms. "I'll call you as soon as it's final, and we'll talk."

He hopped the fence and took a few steps away while I got back in the saddle. Before I turned Gulliver's head back to the trail, Walker spun back around.

"Be safe, Wilde. Promise me."

The lump in my throat was too hard to speak past so I just nodded.

Seth Walker still loved me, and I would wrap myself in bubble wrap if that's what it took to get back to him in one piece.

CHAPTER 5

WALKER

Walker,

    I sent in my applications to the schools you told me to. I guess now we wait and see who wants both of us. Just thinking about sharing a dorm room with you makes me horny as hell. My poor hand is getting so tired, even Carrie-Anne is starting to look cute again.

    Just kidding. But I sure could use some video sex with you. Are we sure it was a good idea not to Skype? I think I just need a quick peek at your dimpled cheeks. Oh, and also your face ;-)

    Saint announced he was signing up for the Navy. Grandpa and Doc are beside themselves trying to talk him out of it. I think after their experience in Vietnam, they're none too keen on any of us putting ourselves in danger like that. I gotta tell you, it's hard to imagine letting him go by himself. I think if I didn't have you, I'd consider joining up too, just to keep my eye on him.

    So thank god I have you. Because going into the Navy sounds like a whole lotta not fun if I'm being honest.

    As for Ross's girlfriend, I gotta say I'm impressed Ross is willing to go out with a girl from the wrong side of the tracks. Remember when he wouldn't date Wren because she wore rubber flip flops to the homecoming dance? Maybe your big bro is growing up finally.

    Until next time,

Wilde XOXO

AFTER WATCHING OTTO RIDE AWAY, I returned to the house with a heart lighter than it had been in a long time. *Finally, after ten years, I might get a chance to make this right again.*

Jolie hadn't taken the news of the divorce proceedings well, which did *and* didn't surprise me. Even though she'd known from the beginning I hadn't been promising her forever, it had always seemed like she'd hoped for it. She'd tried to talk me out of the separation, even going so far as to bring sweet Tisha into the conversation.

"It's too much change all at once, Seth. How can you expect a girl her age to understand her parents divorcing? She doesn't even have any friends yet, for god's sake, and you're going to put her through this?" she'd railed.

"First of all, I promised you five years. I said I'd stay long enough for you to stay at home with her in the early years to give her a strong start, Jolie. You agreed when it was time for her to begin school, you'd go back to work, and we'd separate. Secondly, she absolutely has friends and you know it. She has her very best friend, Cody, as well as at least four other kids who've been begging her to play for the last two months. I never see her alone at school, and I swing by there all the time to check up on her."

Jolie had narrowed her eyes at me and crossed her arms in front of her chest.

I said the last but most important thing in answer to her tirade. "And don't call us 'her parents' like I'm her father. I'm not. My brother Ross is her father. I am her uncle. This is exactly why I kept fighting you when you said you wanted me to be her daddy. I never wanted her to get the wrong idea about you and me."

"Your parents aren't going to be happy," she'd warned.

And she was right. I'd wanted to wait until the initial paperwork was filed before telling them, but now it was time.

Later that night I went up to the main house to talk to them alone, I was torn up with nerves. For some reason, when it came to Jolie and

Tisha, my parents had always had the ability to turn my words around and make me feel like shit even though otherwise they were the nicest people around.

"Hey, Sheriff," my mom said with a big smile. I had to admit to getting a kick out of how proud she was of me. Being able to parade around her hometown as the mother of the sheriff had made her feathers puff up pretty significantly. It was kind of cute.

"Hey, Mom. How are you? Sorry I haven't been up here in a few days. Work's been nuts."

"I heard about the vandalism in town outside the hardware store. Did they find out who did it?"

Mom led me through to the kitchen where Dad sat at the kitchen table with a cup of decaf coffee. He gestured to the mug and raised his eyebrow in offer.

"I'll fix it. You stay there," I said. "No. There's surveillance video, so we know it was a bunch of kids, but we haven't been able to identify who yet. I think some of the stores are going to need to upgrade their video equipment if they expect to actually be able to identify criminals with it."

I helped myself to the coffee maker before joining them at the table. "We're also doing some of the prep work now for the Hobie Hootenanny festival. I didn't realize what a big deal it was. When I was growing up, it was just a summer weekend you could get away with hanging out at the lake without your parents realizing how late you were staying up," I said with a wink at my mom.

"As if we didn't know what you were up to. Hobie is tiny. That's partly why we wanted you two to bring Tisha here to grow up. Let her have a whole town looking out for her like you did. It's nice knowing your neighbors. Not like that place you lived in St. Paul."

She'd hated the little rental house we'd had in South St. Paul, but it had a backyard with a little play set for Tisha, and it had been only fifteen minutes from the precinct where I worked. It was a good thirty minutes from my parents' place in Edina, but I hadn't been able to afford anything nicer on my cop's salary at the time. Once my parents decided to move back to Hobie after my dad bought out the Hobie office of the insurance company where he worked, I knew it wouldn't be long before we'd move back with Tish, whether I liked it or not.

Despite how hard it would be to live here without Otto, I knew it would be a good place for Tisha to grow up and for Jolie to get a fresh start. In a tiny town like Hobie, it would be easier for her to support herself and be able to get to and from Tisha without long commutes or traffic. Plus, she'd have my extended family and me to help as much as she needed.

Okay, fine. Maybe I agreed to move back because I hoped like hell Otto would leave the navy and come home. And we could finally, somehow miraculously, be together.

"I agree. It was the right decision to move here, and I can't tell you how much we appreciate your help with Tisha," I said.

Mom and Dad smiled at me. "She's a good girl," Dad said. "I was proud to see her good manners in church this morning."

"Jolie does a good job with her," I said, always trying to sell Jolie to them out of habit. They'd absolutely hated her in the beginning, blaming her for getting knocked up and then blaming her for the bar fight that had ultimately killed my brother. It was one of the main reasons I'd stepped in to take care of her.

"Mpfh," my mom scoffed. "Seems to me you do most of the discipline around there."

"That's not true, but I didn't come here to argue with you."

My dad raised an eyebrow. "Why did you come here? What's going on?"

"Jolie and I are separating," I blurted. *Might as well just get it out there.*

As soon as I explained we were ending our marriage, my father lost his friendly face.

"No, you're not."

I wanted to laugh.

"I most certainly am. When Jolie and I married, it was the only way to do right by Tisha. She needed a home and family, stability, insurance. But now that we're here in Hobie, we can afford two places. She and Tish will stay here in the little house on the ranch, and I'll—"

"What makes you think we'll let Jolie live in that house without you?" my father cut in.

I stared at him. "Because it's my house, and I own it outright. You gave it to me when we moved here."

"We gave it to you and Jolie, so you could live there together, just like we plan on giving the main house to John and Beth when we're gone. We most certainly did not give it to you so you could settle her there and take off like some deadbeat father."

I laughed at that and looked incredulously at my mother who'd remained conspicuously silent. "If you think after all this I'm capable of becoming a deadbeat dad to that precious girl, where the hell have you been for the past nine years?"

I left without another word and spent the rest of the night scouring Hobie rental listings to see if I could find a small, cheap place to live that would be close enough to work and to Tisha for me to keep up my two biggest commitments. I found a little cabin on the lake I really liked, but it was for sale, not lease, so I was going to have to take some time to be sure about it before making such a big decision.

After peeking in on Tisha to make sure she was sleeping peacefully, I ignored the light still on under the door to the other bedroom and made my way upstairs to the loft.

Things were getting ready to change around here, and I had to admit to being half excited and half terrified. It was hard for me to think of anything other than when I would see Otto next, but I knew I had two months to get through first. It was the reason I hadn't run after him when he moved to Dallas. He was too principled to mess around with me while I was still married, and maybe I was too scared to have the important conversations with him until I knew I could act on my feelings toward him.

I had a lot to explain to him and time to figure out how to go about it.

Time was going to crawl until then.

~

THOSE TWO MONTHS passed even more slowly than I'd expected. By early May the divorce still wasn't final. I'd been pestering Honovi for special treatment in the courts, but he'd just laughed and accused me of trying to bribe an officer of the court.

"It'll be less than three weeks now, Seth. Quit your whining," he'd said over lunch the previous day. "What's your hurry? You got another lady lined up I don't know about?"

I debated whether to be real with him, and I quickly realized I'd known Hon for years and had always felt an easy camaraderie with him.

"Not a lady," I'd admitted.

His eyes had widened and his lips had curved into a mischievous smile. "Let me guess… a certain Wilde child, perhaps?"

I'd felt the blush to the tips of my ears. "Yeah. If he'll have me."

"You two were something else in high school before you moved away. I thought for sure you'd end up together forever."

"I did too. Sometimes things happen though," I'd said with a shrug.

"They sure do, Seth," he said softly, reaching across the table to squeeze my arm. "They sure fucking do."

Late that night, I awoke to the sound of my phone blaring with the tone for dispatch.

"Walker," I answered.

"Sheriff, Doc Wilde is trying to get a hold of you. Says it's some kind of emergency with one of Bill and Shelby's kids. Can I patch you through?"

My stomach dropped as I rubbed my face and glanced around for my clothes. "Yes, of course."

"Seth, that you?"

"Doc, what's going on?"

"Otto's been sent to fight the Amarillo wildfire. Is there any way you can use your connections to find out if he's okay? We can't get a hold of him."

I looked at my watch. It was after one in the morning. His words sank in, and I felt my vision go dark around the edges. "Jesus, Doc. What the hell is he doing up in Amarillo?"

After putting the phone on speaker, I quickly threw on some jeans, a T-shirt, and a hoodie before finding my running shoes.

Doc's voice was ragged. "They needed extra hands and he volunteered. He sent us a text two days ago saying he was headed up there and might not be reachable while he's fighting the fire. We haven't heard from him since, and he's not answering his phone. They've already announced fatalities, Seth. We're beside ourselves."

"Grab a pen, Doc, and let me give you my direct number," I said, running down the stairs of the loft and grabbing my service weapon from the lockbox before finding my wallet and keys. "Better yet, you want me to pick you up? I'm gonna head to the station and see what I can find out."

A beat of silence before a sigh of relief. "Yes. God, yes. We'll meet you there."

It took me only five minutes to get to the Hobie PD, but it took hours before we got news of Otto. The hospital called Doc's cell phone to notify him Otto was in the emergency room with blunt force trauma. He'd been felled by a heavy dead branch they referred to as a "widow maker" and rushed to the hospital. Within minutes of getting the update, the three of us were on the road to Amarillo with our hearts in our throats and the emergency lights flashing the whole way.

CHAPTER 6

OTTO

Wilde,

I think it's best if we break this off. What we had was kind of a high school thing anyway, right? So it probably wouldn't have lasted the way we always thought. I've met some great people here, and I think it'll be easier for me if I concentrate on the here and now instead of some future dream plans that may or may not happen.

I guess what I'm saying is... things change, Wilde Man. And I need to move on.

I'm sorry.

Walker

IT TOOK me forever to remember how the hell I'd ended up in the hospital. When I woke up, I felt groggy and confused. My head was pounding and my shoulder felt like it was throbbing to the beat of my heart. The smell of woodsmoke permeated my nostrils, and when it registered in my brain, the memories flooded back.

The Amarillo wildfire.

God, I was an idiot for volunteering. What had I been thinking?

You know what you were thinking. Anything to keep your mind off Walker.

I coughed and felt my throat scream in response. Why was my throat roughed up? Hadn't I had my SCBA on? My brain scrambled to remember what had happened.

There had been tons of volunteers and crews from several different Texas fire departments like ours. We'd been organized by the incident commander and sent in with one of the strike teams to manage one quadrant of the blaze. We'd been clearing debris with chainsaws and trying to create part of the fire line when it happened. One of the branches high up in a tree being cut hadn't been attached to the trunk. So, instead of falling over with the tree, it fell straight down on top of me when the tree pulled away from another one nearby.

Fuck.

The flash of pain ignited in my memory as I recalled how the heavy branch had landed on my shoulder before knocking me over and pinning me down by my hip. Thank god it hadn't been my head. No helmet in the world would have protected me from the concussion that would have caused. I tried to move my hurt shoulder and nearly passed out from the pain.

When I finally got up the nerve to open my eyes again, they stung.

My SCBA mask had come off when I fell. I remembered that part now too. The hot smoke had burned as I'd sucked in breaths against the pain. I noticed the throbbing pain in my hip and wondered what the damage to my body was from the stupid incident.

Totally preventable. If only the guy cutting the tree had fucking communicated to clear the area before the tree had come down.

After pressing the nursing call button, I closed my eyes against the pain.

Once a nurse came in and explained nothing was broken, it was just a couple of horrible hematoma, she told me to be patient a little longer to be discharged. I was still in the hospital gown waiting for a set of scrubs a nurse had promised me so I wouldn't have to put my smoky uniform back on. My turnout gear sat in a pathetic heap in the little room where I waited and the familiar smell of smoke permeated the entire area.

I was fighting the sedative effects of the pain medicine they'd given me when I made out a familiar voice raised in frustration out in the corridor. "Wilde! W-I-L-D-E."

"Doc?" I croaked, craning my neck to see if I could spot him. "I'm back here."

The man who shoved the curtain back wasn't my grandfather, though. It was Walker.

His eyes were wild and frantic, and his pale hair looked like he'd been scraping fingers through it all night.

"Jesus Christ, Otto," he blurted, lunging forward and wrapping his arms around me. He smelled like coffee and the slightest hint of Irish Spring soap. The scent brought back a flood of memories of sneaking into the shower together at his house as teens and washing each other with the familiar green bar of soap until both of our cocks were hard.

"What are you guys doing here?" I asked, spotting Grandpa and Doc over his shoulder and trying my hardest not to wince at the pain in my own.

Walker pulled back and stared at me with his hands on my face, drawing his eyes all over my body as if looking for evidence of injury. "Where are you hurt?"

I leaned to one side and pulled the gown away so they could see the large mottled bruises all over my hip. "Big-ass tree branch nailed me in the shoulder and hip."

Walker's hand came down to caress my skin near the ugly bruises, and it took my dick about half a second to realize he was incidentally touching my bare ass cheek.

We both seemed to realize it at the same time because our eyes locked before he quickly removed his hand.

"You okay otherwise? Smoke inhalation or anything?" he asked as if trying to cover the awkward, intimate moment.

I shook my head. "Not too bad. You guys didn't need to come. I'm fine."

Doc approached me and ran his cool, dry hand across my forehead as if testing me for fever. His face was a combination of concern and relief.

"Glad you're okay, son. We were worried. On the news they said it was bad and that there were casualties."

I felt Walker's hand sneak into mine and thread our fingers together. My head spun with mixed feelings. Embarrassment that they'd come all this way for just a few bruises, relief they hadn't come for something more serious, confusion about how things stood between Walker and me, and an overall sense of wrongness that the four of us were in Amarillo instead of Hobie.

"The casualties were from some of the houses involved," I explained. "When the fire started, it was the middle of the night. Rescuers found the bodies, but they think the victims had been dead already since the night before."

Grandpa shook his head and frowned. "Those poor families." He stood at the foot of the bed and reached out to squeeze my leg through the blankets. "Thank goodness you're okay. When do you get out of here? Can we take you home to Hobie?"

After getting my prescription for pain meds filled and waiting while Grandpa, Doc, and Walker grabbed some lunch in the cafeteria, we got on the road back home. I lay in the backseat of the big SUV with my head on Grandpa's lap. There wasn't even a moment's hesitation before I used him as a pillow. Grandpa had taken care of me more times than I could count in my lifetime. Even though Doc was usually the one to nurse us through our injuries and illnesses, Grandpa was steadfast and present whenever we needed him, always.

I slept to the sounds of their murmured conversations and tried tuning in whenever Walker spoke. But the medicine they'd given me for the pain kept me dull and dozy, so I wasn't able to comprehend anything I heard. When we finally made it back to Hobie around dinnertime, Walker dropped us off at the ranch.

"I have to get some sleep and get back to the office first thing in the morning. Can I come check on you tomorrow after work?" he asked as he held the car door open for me.

"Yeah. I'm going to be doing a whole lot of holding down the sofa in the family room, I think," I said with a smirk. "I need to call my chief at the station and find out when they need me back in Dallas."

Walker hesitated before frowning and nodding.

"What?" I asked softly. Grandpa and Doc had already gone into the house ahead of me to greet the dogs.

"Do you have to go back? Can't you stay here and take the job at the Hobie FD?"

His jaw was set, but his eyes were pleading. I leaned in and rested my head on his shoulder for a moment. "I'll think about it, okay? Come over tomorrow and let's talk."

Walker's hand came up to caress my cheek and sift through my short hair. "Thank fuck you're okay," he whispered roughly. "When I heard you were in the hospital, Otto…"

I wrapped my arms around him for a full hug. His body felt like it was made to fit with mine like that, and I struggled to swallow the groan trying to come out.

"I'm okay, Seth. God, I was so happy to see your face in that hospital room—you don't even know. Thank you for coming to get me," I murmured. "And for bringing the guys."

He pulled back and brushed a kiss across my cheek, almost, *almost* touching the corner of my mouth. My lips itched to feel his in a real kiss.

"I will always come to you when you're hurt, Wilde Man, but I'd appreciate it not being something that happens often. Can you think about that next time you go walking into danger?" He winked at me, but I could see the truth of his concern in his eyes.

"I could ask the same of you, Sheriff," I said, stepping back and letting him go. "See you tomorrow."

Once he was gone, I entered the house and let Doc and Grandpa fuss over me. They got me settled on the sofa and turned the TV on something or other. I dozed on and off the rest of the evening until it was time to move to the guest room and let myself fall completely under for the night.

I needed the sleep badly, because, unbeknownst to me, the following day I was going to finally meet the woman Walker left me for.

CHAPTER 7

WALKER

Seth?!

Are you joking? Please tell me this is some horrible prank, you jackass. Surely you aren't giving up on me when we're only a few months away from finally being together? Are you crazy?

What's going on? What's the real reason for your letter? Talk to me, baby. Please tell me what has you running scared. I'm worried about you.

I love you,

Otto

I RETURNED HOME after dropping Otto and his grandfathers off and ran right into trouble before the Amarillo dust was even off my boots. Jolie was fuming mad, and Tisha was nowhere to be found.

"Hey," I said, entering the kitchen and stowing my service weapon in the lockbox on a high shelf. "Where's Tish?"

"I sent her to your brother's house for a sleepover so we could talk," Jolie said. I tried not to sigh. After over ten hours of driving in the past twenty-four in addition to the stress of not having known whether Otto was okay, I was dead tired.

"Let me shower and change, and we can go out to eat." I didn't wait for a response before making my way to the hall bathroom and shutting myself away for a long, hot shower.

When I couldn't stall any longer without feeling like a selfish prick, I dried off and got dressed in nice jeans and a short-sleeved button-down shirt before joining Jolie in the kitchen again. Jolie was still in yoga pants and a workout tank top, and I wondered if this might be a rare night I could get away with taking her somewhere less fancy than normal.

"Ready to go?" I asked, reaching up to get my gun out of the lockbox again.

"Leave it. I ordered delivery," she said before sitting down at the table. "Why don't you grab a beer and have a seat?"

My stomach began to twist with nerves. She'd made no secret out of the fact she opposed our separation. I'd finally convinced the owner of the little lake house I liked to let me sign a lease-purchase agreement to give me a little bit more time to be sure I wanted to buy it. Once they found out I was the Hobie sheriff, it hadn't been a problem. I was due to move in the following weekend.

Jolie had made every effort to talk me out of it, even going so far as to say that me spending money to rent a separate place was taking food out of Tisha's mouth. Whenever she got like that, I shut down completely and just avoided her altogether. I spent as much time with Tisha as possible, but Jolie had become nothing but a ball of stress and pressure on me whenever I was around her. I counted down the days until I moved out, and the knowledge it included leaving Tisha wrecked me.

Instead of a beer, I fixed a tall glass of ice water and sat down at the small round wooden table we ate our meals on. There were three red-and-white-checkered placemats, and I fiddled with the edge of one while I waited for her to speak.

"I got a job," she began.

I glanced up in surprise. I'd been nudging her to get a job for months. "Really? That's great, Jolie. Where? Doing what?"

"Your dad hired me to take Liddy's place at the insurance office."

I blinked at her. "Where's Liddy going? She's answered the phones there since I was a little boy."

She shrugged. "I think your dad realized it was more important that I have the job than an older married woman. At least she has a husband who can help pay her bills."

The words came with such toxic barbs, I almost recoiled. Surely my father hadn't let Liddy Freeman go after all her years at the company just so Jolie could get a paycheck.

"Well, ah… that's great, I guess. When do you start?"

"Tomorrow. Since Tish will go to school with Cody, I'll have extra time to get ready and get there early."

I nodded. "Good." I had no idea what else to say.

Jolie pulled the elastic band out of her hair and ran her fingers through the thick blonde strands. She tossed her head back and forth and fussed with her hair a bit before giving me what I'd come to think of as her "are you sure you're gay" look. I hated when she got this way.

"Seth, I'd like you to stay here a little longer while Tisha gets used to me working full-time," she said in a soft voice. "She's going through a lot right now and becoming a latchkey kid is going to crush her."

I wanted to laugh. "Jolie, we talked about this. Mom and Beth have both offered to keep her after school until you get home from any job. There is no reason whatsoever she needs to come home to an empty house."

She shook her head. "I don't want someone else raising our child, Seth."

I felt my teeth grind together. "Having Tisha stay with her aunt or grandmother for two to three hours a day is hardly having someone else raise her. If you don't want her with them, then you can put her in after school care or find a job with different hours. I've already told you I'm happy to adjust my hours to try and cover some of that time, but I can't promise anything. You know how unpredictable my job is."

"And that's another thing," she said, her voice rising in frustration. "Where the hell have you been? You lit out of here in the middle of the night, and all I got was a text that said you were headed to Amarillo? What was in Amarillo that was so important?"

I wanted to tell her it was none of her goddamned business, but I didn't. "I got word Otto Wilde was hurt in a wildfire near there, so I volunteered to take his grandfathers to the scene."

"Is he okay?" Her brow was wrinkled in concern, and I let out a breath at the reminder she really was a kind person most of the time. It was only about Tish and me that she got a little strange.

"Badly bruised mostly. I'm going to go check on him tomorrow night." I felt my cheeks heat and wondered if it was weird talking to my wife about the man I hoped like hell would soon be my boyfriend. If Otto and I were going to make a go at a relationship, Jolie deserved to know about it.

Before she had a chance to say anything else, I spoke again. "About Otto... um... there's something I need to tell you."

I forced myself to meet her eyes as she looked up at me.

"What?"

"As soon as the divorce is final, I'm hoping to start seeing him," I confessed. "Well, that is... if he can bring himself to forgive me for leaving him."

There was a beat of silence while the words floated in the air between us.

"Say what?" she asked. "You're hoping to start seeing him? As in *dating*?"

"Yes. Dating."

"Are you fucking kidding me?"

I felt my jaw open as I stared at her. "No. Why would I joke about this?"

"You're just going to jump out of a decade-long marriage with me and into bed with the first guy you meet?"

Her voice was rising again.

"No, Jolie. In case you don't remember, Otto Wilde is the guy I left for *you*. The guy I've *always* been planning on spending my life with. I told you all about him in those early days, so I have no idea why you're acting all surprised by this now."

"I thought that was over. I thought it was just high school bullshit. People don't marry their childhood sweethearts, Seth. Especially gay guys who're just fucking the local cowboy, for god's sake," she snapped.

My heart was banging around in my chest, and I felt anger crawling up my neck. Resentment, above all else, threatened to suffocate me. "Are you kidding me? Do you have any idea how that makes me feel? Like I don't know my own heart? I have loved that man since I was a kid, Jolie. A *kid*. And there hasn't been a single moment I've stopped wanting him in all this time. How could you begrudge me a chance to build a life with him now that we're both full grown and back in the same small town? *How?* After everything I've done for you and Tisha."

I realized I was on the verge of crying like a baby. I tried so hard not to ever make her feel like I'd sacrificed anything in order to take care of her. I'd told her a million times she and Tish were worth it. But I deserved a chance to have someone to love me more than just friends. I deserved to feel the loving touches of a man who cared about me holding me when times were tough or when times were good. Plus, I'd told her from the get go that this was a temporary thing —only long enough to give her a chance to get on her feet.

"Is this why you dragged me back here to this godforsaken place?" she asked, standing up and moving to the sink to look out the window toward the driveway. I wondered at what point the food delivery guy was going to turn up and whether he would see World War Three happening when he did.

"What? You're the one who begged me to move back here! I was perfectly happy staying in St. Paul, and you know it."

"Yeah, I wanted to move back here because I thought I could finally have more time with you. Like we could finally make a go at being a real family, Seth. Your parents, your brother and his family, and you having the sheriff's job... all of those things just felt like the perfect chance to finally give Tisha the life she deserved."

Now she was pulling out the sniffles act, which only incensed me more.

"In case you forgot, I'm gay!" I snapped. "What on god's green earth possessed you to envision we were going to be some kind of regular family?"

"Pfft. You're hardly gay, Seth. Bisexual, maybe."

I wondered if my eyes would bug completely out. "Wrong. I'm gay. Fully gay," I corrected her.

"You've had sex with me more than once," she reminded me with a raised eyebrow.

My stomach turned. "Yes. I have. And you and I both know those were stupid mistakes made by lonely-ass people."

"I wasn't lonely. I love you. I had sex with you because I wanted you. I *still* want you," she said, her voice taking on a note of pleading I absolutely could not stand.

There were so many things I wanted to say, but I knew none of them were going to make this better. All the words had already been said even if she refused to hear them.

"I'm sorry, Jolie. I'm sorry I can't give you the marriage you want. Our divorce will be final soon, and I hope after that, you find someone better than me. Someone who can take good care of you and love you the way you deserve. I love you, Jolie, but not like that. Never like that."

I stood up and made my way to the door, pulling out my wallet and dropping a couple of twenties on the counter to cover dinner.

"I have to go."

I didn't look back. I strode out to my vehicle and drove to my new place on the lake. Even though I didn't have legal rights to live there for a few more days, I already had the key and knew the place was empty. I spent the rest of the night on the wooden floor of the main room wrapped up in an old blanket I kept in the back of the SUV.

My nerves were raw and my emotions were all over the place. I was tired as hell from the jaunt to Amarillo and back, but the wooden floor beneath me made it hard to fall asleep. At one point, I even considered driving over to the Wilde ranch and begging mercy to sleep in the bunkhouse, but I didn't want to wake them.

Tomorrow would come soon enough, and I could finally tell Otto everything.

And hope like hell he was crazy enough to forgive me.

CHAPTER 8

OTTO

Seth

I still haven't heard back from you and you won't answer my phone calls. Even your parents won't let me talk to you. What the hell is going on?

I know something happened. This isn't you. You wouldn't do this to me... to us. Talk to me, beautiful boy. If this is because I said being apart was hard, you have to know being shut off from you altogether is fifty thousand times worse.

My heart is shattered until I hear from you again. Please don't make me beg.

I love you,

Otto

WHEN I WOKE up the next morning, I felt much better. The bruising was just as ugly on my shoulder and hip, but the pain in my side had lessened noticeably. After breakfast, I ventured out to the barn to visit the horses and help Grandpa with some of the chores. Despite his constant nagging at me to take it easy, I enjoyed the time spent feeding and caring for the animals.

My baby sister had been right. I'd always pictured myself living and working in Hobie so I could be around the ranch. I missed the animals and the slower pace of Hobie.

"I think I'm going to take the job with Chief Paige if it's still available," I said across the fence to Grandpa while he walked one of the horses in the ring on a lead.

He stopped what he was doing and walked over to me. The calm chestnut mare he'd been leading followed him dutifully despite Grandpa dropping the lead rope. I reached out a hand for her to nuzzle.

"I'm certainly happy to hear that, Otto. Do you want to talk about it?"

I shook my head. "No need. I've been avoiding Hobie because of Walker, and now his divorce is almost final…"

Grandpa's eyes crinkled as he peered at me. "Does that mean you two…?"

I shrugged. "Hope so. He says that's what he wants."

"And is that what you want?"

I took a deep breath and blew it out. "I've wanted that guy since I was thirteen, Grandpa."

Grandpa's face softened. "I always thought you'd end up together. What ever happened? How'd he wind up married?"

"Ross got his girlfriend pregnant after they moved to Minnesota and then he up and died on her. I guess Walker felt like he needed to step in and be a goddamned white knight or something."

Grandpa stared at me. "Whoa."

I barked out a laugh. "Yeah."

"He's a good man, Otto."

"You don't have to tell me that, Grandpa. I already know."

We spent the next hour exercising the horses and taking care of what needed doing out in the barn. When it was time for lunch, Doc announced we were going into town to have lunch at the Pinecone.

"Never been there," I said. "Never even heard of it."

Doc nodded toward the house. "You'll like it. New bistro that does salads and sandwiches for lunch and fancier stuff at dinner. Go on and shower and get dressed. We can stop and see Chief Paige on the way to tell him the good news."

I didn't even ask him how he knew what I'd decided since he hadn't been standing there when I told Grandpa. I'd learned long ago that Doc and Grandpa had a sixth sense when it came to their family. I simply nodded and smiled before following him back to the house to get ready.

We decided to stop at the firehouse after lunch and headed straight toward the bistro first. It was a new modern-looking storefront right on the town square. I was surprised at how many people were out and about in the little downtown area and realized Hobie must have had a growth spurt while Saint and I were away.

"Lots of new people and places," I said to Grandpa as we walked across the grassy square toward the bistro from where we'd parked on a side street.

"I forget you haven't been around in quite a while. A bunch of people got together to try and wrangle the town's development into some semblance of organization about five years ago. Seems to finally be making a positive difference," Grandpa explained. "New business owners have moved in, and now the lake tourism is not just in the summertime. I think it's been helped by more and more people being able to work their jobs from home. It means they don't have to live in the big cities anymore."

Doc reached out and took his husband's hand. "What Weston's not saying is that he is on the development board and has worked his ass off helping this town thrive when similar small towns were going out of business."

As we walked, several people waved or called out greetings to Doc and Grandpa. I recognized one of the women I'd gone to high school with and gave her a quick smile and nod of recognition.

"Kelly Tucker still lives here?" I asked. "I thought she'd moved to Seattle after high school."

Doc and Grandpa looked after her as she strolled toward the bakery. "She did. Met and married a nice woman named Nina. When they had their first child, they decided to move back here to raise him.

The two of them own a plant nursery out on Ashby Road and have two kids now."

"She's gay?" I blurted. "She dated the biggest jock in school."

Grandpa raised an eyebrow at me, and I felt my face heat up. "I'm just surprised, that's all," I muttered. "I would have pegged her as a straight-up homophobe."

"You should know better than to judge—"

I held up my hand to stop him. "I know. I'm sorry. Forgive me. Maybe Hobie's gotten more open-minded since I left."

Doc reached out to squeeze my shoulder as we approached the restaurant with a stylized pinecone logo on the front. "It definitely has, Otto. And Sheriff Walker's been an unexpected part of that change. The sheriff we had before that was a jackass."

"I heard," I said as I reached out to pull the door open. I tried not to look four doors down the street toward the sheriff's office where I knew Walker was most likely fighting sleep deprivation from his jaunt to Amarillo. Hopefully, I only needed to be patient for several more hours until I could see him again.

A female voice called out from our right, startling me. "Excuse me, are you Otto Wilde?"

I turned to see who'd called my name. The woman speed-walking toward me was an attractive blonde-haired, blue-eyed fashion plate, dressed in a starched pink blouse tucked into a trim gray pencil skirt. She had a designer handbag of some kind under her arm and a pair of sunglasses perched on top of her hair.

"Yes, ma'am," I responded automatically. "Can I help you?"

When she got close enough for me to make out her features, I saw tight lips and flared nostrils. She was lovely but pissed. Her eyes flicked from me to my grandfathers and back again.

"May I have a word with you in private, please?"

"Sure, can I ask what this is about?" I inquired, racking my brain to figure out if I was supposed to know her. I stepped to the side and let Grandpa and Doc go ahead into the restaurant before gesturing for the woman to join me on a nearby bench.

"My husband," she said in a clipped voice. "Seth Walker."

My throat tightened in shock, and I simply gaped at her.

I couldn't stop staring. She was a beautiful woman. She looked a bit like a famous actress who was in all the perfume ads. Why the hell had someone this attractive and poised settled for a sham marriage?

"You must be Jolie," I said in a voice low enough to keep our conversation private despite it taking place in the town square.

"Yes. You've heard of me then?"

"Of course. I met your daughter a couple of months ago while I was riding my horse near my parents' old house. She seems like a delightful little girl," I said as politely as I could. My brain scrambled to fit this woman's face into every missed moment of Walker's life for the past ten fucking years and with each new image, a little part of me died inside.

"You've met Tisha?" she asked, clearly peeved by the news.

"By accident. I was trail riding on my grandfathers' ranch when she saw my horse and called out to me," I explained. "Seth was there. He can tell you."

Why was I trying to reassure her I hadn't been alone with her daughter?

Because she's making you feel bad for talking to her child.

I clenched my mouth shut and forced myself to allow her to steer the conversation.

"How long have you and my husband been seeing each other behind my back?" she asked.

A gasp sounded from behind me, and I turned to see a petite man in a whack-a-jack outfit. Purple pleather pants with a floral button-down blouse of some kind and giant yellow-framed sunglasses. I ignored him to focus on the hellcat in front of me.

I looked from Jolie's angry face around to make sure no one besides the strange little guy had overheard her accusation.

"We haven't been," I answered between tight teeth. "Until last night, I've been living in Dallas, and before Christmas, I was overseas in the military for years."

"Yet you still managed to screw up my marriage?" she hissed. "How exactly did that happen?"

I couldn't help but glance in the direction of the sheriff's office and notice the floral-shirted man racing in the front door all aflutter. *Oh shit.* "I think you should talk to Walker about this," I began. "It's not my place to—"

"I tried to talk to Seth about this last night," she interjected. "But then he bolted and went to shack up at your place. So now I'm asking you."

I looked at her in surprise. "I haven't seen Walker since he dropped me and my grandfathers off at the ranch last night before dinnertime. And I haven't been alone with him more than about fifteen minutes in the past ten freaking years. I don't know what your agenda is here, but it sounds like something that's between the two of you. Now, if you'll excuse me..."

I stood up, but before I could offer her a fake polite goodbye, I noticed the door to the sheriff's office open and a familiar uniformed body rush out.

Uh-oh.

It took him about two seconds to spot us, and when he did, his eyes got comically large. I couldn't help my petty jealousy of the woman in front of me, so I made a big production of waving to him with a giant smile. His approach was hesitant, but there was no denying the blush that crept up his neck when he looked at me. Just the sight of it made me want to close my eyes and say a prayer of thanks to the baby Jesus for Walker's fair skin betraying his attraction to me.

"Uh, hey..." he began. "I didn't... I mean, I didn't realize you two... Ah... what's going on?"

I held his eyes and asked the question I'd asked him a million times. "Everything's fine. Walker, are *you* okay?"

His face softened just the briefest amount, and his shoulders released some of their tension. "Yeah. Yeah, Otto. I think I am."

"Good." I grinned. "I'm going to have lunch at the Pinecone here with Doc and Grandpa. Would you two like to join us?"

Jolie quickly stood and looped her arm possessively through Walker's. He furrowed his brows at her before glancing apologetically at me.

"We can't. We're having lunch with Seth's parents," Jolie said before Walker could say anything.

"We are?" Walker asked.

She shot him a look, and I swallowed a chuckle.

"Well, I'd better get in there. Nice to meet you, Jolie. See you tonight, *Seth*," I said, caressing his first name in the deep voice I knew would go straight into his uniform pants to plump up his cock. Walker seemed to shudder the slightest bit, and I noticed Jolie's eyes widen.

"Y-yeah," Walker said before swallowing. "Tonight. I'll swing by around six."

When I got inside the restaurant and was shown to my grandfathers' table, I realized they had a perfect view of the bench where Jolie and I had been sitting.

"What did you say to Walker there at the end?" Grandpa asked with a snicker. "Looked like you let slip you were wearing a sequined jock or something. Was that a nightstick in his pocket; or was he just happy to see—"

Doc elbowed his husband with a laugh. "Stop. That's gross."

I grinned. "I can't help it if he gets a thrill out of hearing me say his first name."

"You ain't playing fair, boy," Grandpa snickered. "I need to send Stevie some flowers for alerting Walker you two were out there."

I remembered the guy in the purple pants worked for my brother West and his partner Nico over at the bakery.

"Nosy little thing," I murmured, picking up the menu.

"Nah. He and Walker have become friends the past couple of months. I'm sure he was just looking out for him by letting him know you were in the crosshairs," Doc said.

I snapped my head up. "Friends? What kind of friends?"

Both of my grandfathers began laughing, and I caught several heads turning in our direction.

"Don't worry, son. I'm pretty sure Sheriff Walker has about all he can handle between his wife and you," Doc said through his chuckling.

"Soon-to-be *ex*-wife," I grumbled.

Grandpa took a sip of his sweet tea before locking eyes on me. "You know he's moving out to that lake house on Shady Cove, right?"

"He is? Wait. He's not staying in that cabin on the Walker ranch?"

"No," Doc interjected. "He's leaving Jolie and Tisha there."

I nodded and gave the approaching server my order before looking back at my grandfathers. "Do you think I'm doing the right thing by moving back here?"

Grandpa was the first to answer. "Moving back here is definitely the right thing, Otto. I think your real question is whether or not you're doing the right thing by getting involved with Seth Walker again."

I lowered my head and began to fiddle with the straw paper between my fingers. "Yeah, I guess you're right."

"Otto, the way I see it, you and Walker are like summer bugs flying around the porch light. Even if you knew it wasn't good for you, you'd still fly dangerously close over and over again."

"I can't stay away from him. I've tried."

Grandpa's smile was sympathetic and kind. "Then maybe it's time to try something else."

I looked up. "Like what?"

"Acknowledging you love flying into the light and just go for it."

A shrill voice came out of nowhere. "Oh. My. Gawd. Is that Otto Wilde?"

I turned to the horrific sound and saw a noticeably older and pudgier version of the girl Walker and I had lost our virginity to.

"Carrie-Anne? Wow, so nice to see you," I lied, standing up to give her a hug. "How've you been?"

She pressed her significant breasts against my chest and held on several beats past comfortable.

"Mm-mm, just look at you," she gushed. I noticed my grandfathers clamping their mouths against the laughter as Carrie-Anne ran her hands all up and down my chest and shoulders inappropriately. "You sure did grow up mighty fine, didn't you?"

"He sure did," Doc hooted from his spot at the table. I shot him a look that made Grandpa snort. Those two were such kids sometimes.

"What's new with you?" I asked, struggling to think of something to say when all I wanted to do was enjoy a nice quiet lunch with my family. "You're living in Hobie?"

"I am. I work for Leonard Fickle at the accounting firm." Her smile was predatory, and her lacquered fingernails still ran teasingly up and down my shirtsleeves.

Doc leaned around with a grin. "Aren't you and Leonard married?"

Leonard was about as old as the Bible and had been the primary tax preparer in town since before Texas was granted statehood. My eyes widened at her.

"We are," she said with flared nostrils at Doc. "But he's a very *understanding* husband, if you know what I mean." This last part was whispered at me with significant eyeballs.

"Whoa-ho, what's going on?" Walker's voice interrupted Carrie-Anne's flirt attack on me, and I'd never been more grateful for an interruption. "You two having a class reunion without inviting me?"

He reached out and tugged on my shoulder until I stumbled behind him while he gave Carrie-Anne an awkward handshake. It was a pretty smooth move, and I wondered if Carrie-Anne was the only person there who didn't see it as the territory marking it clearly was.

My heart swelled with warmth, and I felt giddy as a schoolgirl watching him "protect" me from the cougar.

"Well, hello, *Sheriff*," she drawled. "Fancy meeting you here. My, my... a sheriff and a firefighter together in the same—"

"So sorry to interrupt, but Walker was getting ready to consult with us on some town plans we need to discuss, and he doesn't have a very long lunch break in which to do it. It was very nice seeing you, Carrie-Anne."

Thank god for Grandpa. I could have kissed the man.

"Oh. Well, I guess... don't be a stranger then, all right?" she cooed. "See you soon?"

Walker and I nodded as she sashayed away. When she was gone, he reached out and squeezed my shoulder, letting his warm hand linger a few beats longer than usual.

"I'm sorry about earlier," he murmured. "I didn't know that was going to happen."

I wanted to pull him into my arms and rest my face against the familiar skin of his throat, but I didn't dare touch him like that in public while he was still married.

"It's fine."

"Why don't you two sit and eat?" Grandpa said, leaning forward and pushing out the fourth chair from the table.

Walker looked at me with a raised brow as if asking if it was okay for him to stay. I nodded.

"I thought you had plans to eat with your dad?" I asked.

"No. She made that shit up. Her jealousy of you was pretty off the charts. I'm sorry about that too."

Once we were both seated, I reached over under the table and ran my fingertips against his outer thigh just softly enough to let him know we were okay. He turned and focused those blue eyes on me, and I saw the pain in them. He was worried Jolie had scared me off.

I smiled at him as reassuring as I could. "I'm really looking forward to tonight," I said with a glance around to make sure no one was within earshot besides Grandpa and Doc.

He let out a big sigh of relief and smiled back at me. God, he was gorgeous. "Me too."

We wound up having a nice lunch with my grandfathers talking about Walker's niece Tisha and what it had been like living in Minnesota. They asked me some more questions about my time in the navy, but I tried to change the subject as quickly as I could. I knew Walker noticed every time I did it because he gave me a funny look. My grandfathers weren't stupid either, but I wasn't ready to talk about it yet.

Finally it was time to finish up so we could let Walker get back to work.

"We're headed to the firehouse to talk to Chief Paige," Grandpa told Walker with a grin.

Walker's eyes widened as he looked at me. Despite my rule against touching him in public, I couldn't help put reach out my finger to lift his chin up.

"Your jaw was hanging open," I teased softly.

Red heat moved up his neck at my touch. Damn, the man was so responsive; I couldn't wait to get him in bed with me again. Just the thought of it made my pants uncomfortable.

"You're really going to do it?" he asked just as softly. "Move back here?"

I nodded and smiled at him. "Of course I am. I'll do anything you ask me to, Seth. Don't you know that by now?"

The big, strong law enforcement officer in all his hardware and body armor looked like he was going to melt into a puddle of goo right in front of me. I wanted to draw him into my arms and reassure him until he really believed that I'd been his all along, regardless of him dumping my ass all those years ago.

But the time for that shit wasn't now, in front of everyone lunching at the Pinecone in downtown Hobie.

"See you tonight, Sheriff," I said before turning and walking out.

Now all I had to do was hope Chief Paige hadn't already found a replacement for Nathan Hearst.

CHAPTER 9

WALKER

Wilde,

Please stop trying to contact me. You're only making this harder on both of us. I didn't mean to hurt you, you have to know that. But I can't be with you anymore.

Please move on and let me do the same.

I truly wish you all the best,

Seth Walker

As soon as Otto said he was going to see Chief Paige, I felt like my whole life was finally getting ready to begin. I walked out of the Pinecone with all my damned peacock feathers spread wide in the sun. I was even pretty sure if a bullet had come for me in that moment, it would have bounced right off and skittered along the sidewalk. That's how amazing it felt to know Otto Wilde was moving home to Hobie to be with me.

Before heading back to the station, I decided to stop in at Sugar Britches and grab something for Luanne. I wandered across the square before entering the cute little bakery and seeing the tattoo-covered owner behind the counter.

"Hey, Sheriff. What can I get you?" Nico called with a smile.

"A glimpse of that chubby-cheeked girl of yours, for one," I said.

Nico's grin got even bigger. "She's sacked out in the pack-n-play upstairs, or I'd let you have a snuggle."

"No, she isn't," Stevie said, approaching from the back of the building where the kitchen and staircase were. In his arms was a sleepy-faced angel whose head was resting on Stevie's shoulder. As soon as she saw me, her eyes widened.

I remembered to take off my hat since that seemed to scare her the last few times I'd seen her.

"Hey, cutie pie," I said, approaching Stevie with my hands out. "Remember me?"

Stevie's sassy grin was accompanied by a wink. "Of course I do, Sheriff. I just saw you a little while ago."

I barked out a laugh. "Shut up and gimme that baby."

As soon as Stevie leaned toward me, Pippa reached out her arms for me and came willingly. She was a very easy baby who seemed used to being passed around among lots of sets of loving arms in town.

"Hey, sweet girl," I murmured, pulling her in for a hug and inhaling the scent of sleepy baby. "Did you have a good nap?"

One of her hands came up to reach for my shiny badge the way it always did when I held her in uniform. I let her put her sticky prints all over it.

"You getting your usual or something for Lu?" Stevie asked.

"Lu. That cold drink thing she likes and whatever cookie or pastry you think she'll want," I said. "Thanks, Stevie."

He went back around the corner to wash his hands and select something for Luanne while Nico helped the next customer.

While Stevie made Lu's drink, he looked back at me. "You gonna tell me what all that was about out there? You lit out of the station so fast, you about set your desk on fire."

I shifted Pippa on my hip and made sure she wasn't anywhere near my service weapon.

"Yeah, uh... Thanks, by the way. For the heads-up, I mean."

He smirked at me. "No thanks needed. I should be thanking you for the show. Been a while since I've seen kitty-cat claws like those. You sure she knows you're gay?"

The customer standing next to me gasped and shot me wide eyes. I recognized Mr. Ritches from the hardware store and smiled politely at him before turning back to Stevie. I wasn't going to keep all this stuff a secret from the town, but that didn't mean I wanted any of it out until my divorce was final either.

I lowered my voice. "She knows. Doesn't mean she likes it."

Stevie's eyes shifted from me to Mr. Ritches and back with a little wince. *Sorry*, he mouthed. I winked at him to let him know it was fine. Stevie and I had gotten to be pretty good friends over the past few months and he was one of the only people I'd confided in about what was going on between Jolie and me and what I hoped was going on between Otto and me.

I blew a strawberry on Pippa's plump cheek before handing her back to Nico and reaching for my wallet.

Nico held up his hand. "I told you. Cops don't pay."

"And I told you it's just a tip."

I dropped a bill on the counter and ignored the eye roll from the guy.

"Hey, Sheriff," Nico called as I was walking out. "When you gonna let me put some ink on you?"

My usual answer was when hell froze over, just to mess with him, but this time I turned around and answered differently. "When I have something important I want to make permanent."

I walked out through the doors to the sound of Nico and Stevie hooting and hollering with speculation about what I'd meant by that.

The rest of the day went by about as fast as a turtle riding a sloth. When it was finally the end of my shift, I passed off my notes on the day to the evening deputy, a woman by the name of Shayna Diller. She was whip smart and ten times more capable than several of the guys on the force in St. Paul I'd worked with, but I knew she still caught hell working as a sheriff's deputy in small-town Texas with the unforgivable trait of being a female.

"Have a good night, Sheriff," she said with a smile as I gathered up my things from my desk. "Looks like you have something to look forward to. Not sure I've seen you quite so smiley before."

"Indeed. But that doesn't mean you can't call me if you need me, okay?"

"Sure thing. I'm sure I'll be fine. Have fun and be safe."

I raced home to what I was quickly beginning to think of as Jolie's house. She wasn't home from work yet, so I swung by my parents' place to grab Tisha.

"Hey there, Tishie-poo," I said as I entered my parents' familiar kitchen. "How was school?"

She looked up from where she sat at the kitchen table reading a paperback book and grinned at me. "Good. Mrs. Alexander let me borrow her copy of *Rump* and it's really, really good. Did you know there used to be a fairytale called Rumpelstiltskin?"

"I did, indeed. Is that what this book is about?"

"Kinda. But it's more like..." She put her finger to her lips while she thought about what she wanted to say, and I almost burst out laughing. She looked so grown up and serious. "It's like *his* story. Not someone else telling a story *about* him. And Mrs. Alexander says if I like it, there are more like this one by the same lady."

"That sounds amazing. Maybe we can read the next one together," I suggested while I gathered up her backpack and gave my mom a quick kiss on the cheek. "Thanks, Mom. I really appreciate you doing this."

Mom's face softened into an affectionate glance toward Tish. "It's my pleasure, dear. She's been nothing but easy-peasy. Isn't that right, Tishie?"

"Yes, ma'am," Tisha said without looking up from her page.

"Eye contact when talking to a human being, baby," I warned.

Her eyes flicked up to my mom and she had the decency to blush. "Sorry, Grandma."

"That's all right. I'll see you tomorrow, then?"

"Mm-hm," Tish said absently, clearly having a hard time not going back to reading her book.

"Come on. I need to take a shower and change out of this uniform. If it's this hot in May, I think I might actually melt come summer."

My mom's smile dropped away and she looked at me with concern. "You wouldn't ever go without your vest to stay cooler would you?"

I shook my head. "No, ma'am. Not a chance. Being hot is preferable to being dea…" I glanced at Tish. "To being dumb."

"Thank god," she said with a sigh of relief.

I grabbed her hand and squeezed it. "Mama didn't raise no fool," I teased. "Thanks again."

While Tish climbed up in my SUV, I stowed her backpack in the rear seat and hopped into the driver's seat. We made the short stretch to the house before getting out and going inside.

Still no sign of Jolie.

I showered and changed while Tisha curled up on the sofa to read more of her book. By the time I was ready to go to the Wildes', Jolie still hadn't arrived.

After trying to call her and getting no answer, I finally decided to go ahead and feed Tisha dinner. I warmed up some leftover chicken and whipped up her favorite rice and peas combination to go with it. She chattered on and on about the book and about school, telling me her cousin Cody had gotten called a "stupid face" by a girl named Bevan. So apparently Cody and Tisha had decided Bevan needed to be shunned for life. I explained that sometimes people made bad choices and had to be given second chances but not necessarily third and fourth chances.

When Tisha was finished, I cleaned up the dishes and tried Jolie again.

Still no answer.

I called Shayna's number.

"Hey, Sheriff, what's up?" she asked.

"Any vehicle incidents this evening?"

"Couple of speeding tickets on Wachett and a failure to yield at that funky spot by the high school. Other than that, it's been quiet. Why?"

"Nothing. Just haven't heard from Jolie, and she isn't answering her phone." I didn't love putting my personal business out there, but I also needed to know if she was hurt in a ditch somewhere.

"Tell you what, I'm close to the insurance office. I'll run the route from there to the ranch and make sure I don't see anything fishy, okay?"

"Yeah. I'd appreciate that. Thanks."

I got off the phone and began the nightly struggle to convince a child to shower and prepare for bedtime. Once Tisha was in the bathroom, I pulled out my phone again and saw a text from Shayna letting me know the route was clear.

I dialed Otto.

"Hey. You running late? Did something come up?" he asked in a kind voice when he answered. Something about the automatic trust and understanding in his tone made my eyes sting.

"Jolie isn't home yet. I can't leave Tish."

There was silence for a few beats before a light chuckle. "She's playing you."

"I know. At least, I hope that's all it is. In my line of work, that's not usually the first thing that pops in one's head, you know?"

"Of course I do. I'm in a similar line of work, Seth."

I blew out a breath. "I know. I'm sorry. I'm just…"

"Annoyed? Pissed? Homicidal?"

"Um…"

Otto sighed. "Sorry, Walker. Maybe I'm projecting. I'm the one who's annoyed. I was really looking forward to seeing you tonight."

"Me too. I… I…" For some damned reason I was feeling teary-eyed like some kind of hormonal kid. "I just need to see you, Wilde Man."

The last part came out in more of a whimper than I'd intended.

"I'm coming over," he grumbled. "Fuck her. If she's going to play this game, then fuck her, Seth."

"You don't have to do that. I didn't mean to lay this shit on you. I just needed to let you know what was going on."

"Baby, if we're going to do this, you'd better plan on laying this kind of shit on me. That's my fucking job, Seth Walker. I'll see you in ten minutes."

I hung up the phone and held it to my chest. God, he was a good man. How the hell was he able to be so open with me after everything I'd done to him?

After a couple of minutes, Tisha came out in her pajamas and asked me to braid her wet hair. I sat her down on the footstool in front of the sofa and began to comb out her long tresses.

"Where's Mom?" she asked. "I thought her job with Granddad finished before dinner."

"I'm not sure, hon. Maybe she had to stay late her first day."

I divided her hair into three sections and began braiding. She knew how much I loved playing with her hair since I'd never had long hair of my own. Growing up, I'd had buzzed short hair because of the Texas heat and then when I got to Minnesota, it wasn't long before I was applying to the police academy and keeping it short according to regulations as a newbie on the force. When Tisha came along and sprouted the same pretty long hair her mother had, it was like having my very own Barbie doll. I learned how to spray detangler, blow it dry with a big round brush, and do ponytails and braids with the best of them. Jolie teased me all the time about my beauty shop skills.

"Did you ask Granddad if I could get a pony?" she asked.

I couldn't help but laugh. "Tish, it's not up to Granddad to decide whether or not you get a horse. It's up to your mom and me. And we need some time to settle in here before making such a big commitment. You know I'm moving to my own house this weekend, remember? That means it would be harder for me to help do all the work involved in keeping a horse."

"Why do you have to move? You could stay here and we could get a horse instead," she pleaded.

"I told you already. Your mom and I only agreed to live together when you were a little baby and needed lots of help around the clock. Now that you're a big girl and can do so much for yourself, it's time for your mom and me to give each other some space. Your mom might want to meet and date a nice man, and I might want to do the same."

"But I still don't understand why you can't just keep each other instead? You already have a wife. Why do you have to find somebody else?"

I took a breath and tried to think about how to help her understand. We'd explained it several times, but I understood it wasn't easy for an almost-nine-year-old to grasp the concepts of sexuality and lifetime commitments.

"Honey, you know your mom and I have never been in love like that. Your mom was in love with my brother, your dad, but then he died. I only moved in to help with money and loving on you as much as I can. But your mom deserves to have a proper husband, one who loves her the way my brother did."

"But you love her. You tell her all the time," she said with a whine.

"I know, sweetheart. And I do. But not the way a proper husband loves his wife. Some men love other men instead of women, and that means they're gay. I don't love your mom like that because I love men, Tisha."

"But Grandma and Granddad always say that's sickening. They say gay is bad even though my friend Jerri at school in Minnesota said her moms were gay. And I met them. They didn't seem sickening."

I wanted to kill my damned parents for being ignorant assholes. For a moment, I thought maybe Jolie was right, and it wouldn't be okay for my parents to keep Tisha every afternoon if that was the kind of shit they were teaching her.

"Being gay isn't sickening, honey. And it's not a choice. I can't help that I love men, just like you probably can't help how badly you want a horse. If I tell you to stop wanting a horse, will you be able to?"

"No. I can't make myself stop thinking about it even if I try real hard."

"Right. So, that's how it is for me with liking other guys."

"So you're going to have a boyfriend when you move into your new place?"

The doorbell rang and I felt my face ignite. "Um. Yeah. I hope so."

I stood up and went to open the door for Otto. He stood on the front porch in a pair of dark jeans and a crisp button-down shirt like he'd dressed up for our evening together. He even looked nervous with his hands shoved deep in his jeans pockets and his shoulders up around his ears.

"Hey," he said, glancing around. "This still okay?"

I heard Tisha's little feet pad across the floor behind me.

"You're the horse guy," she said excitedly. "Did you know we were talking about horses? You musta read our minds!"

Otto's face split into a grin. "It must have been a lucky guess. I wanted to swing by and ask if you were free this weekend to come to my granddads' ranch and let me give you a horse ride."

Her giant intake of breath matched the big wide eyeballs, and I almost laughed.

"Oh my gosh! Are you serious?" She turned to me. "Is he serious? Would you let me? Please, please. I'll do anything, Uncle Seth. Anything at all if you let me go ride a horse this weekend."

"Hmm," I said, pretending to think it over. "Will you clean your room and put your laundry away?"

"Yes, sir. I swear."

"Okay then. I guess I can agree to that," I said with a wink.

Tisha threw herself at Otto and hugged him around his waist. His eyes widened in surprise as he met my eyes and brought his arms around her little frame.

"I'll have to find a helmet your size before then. How big is your brain?" he asked her once he extracted himself from the hug.

"It's big. Really big," she said in all seriousness. "I get very good grades at school."

"Hmm. Size big then. I'll make a note of that."

She turned and jump-skipped her way back to the sofa where she gathered up her brush and extra ponytail holders.

"Can I get on my iPad and tell Cody about the horse ride this weekend before bedtime?"

"Sure," I said. "Tell him he can come with us too. I'm sure Mr. Wilde won't mind."

Otto shook his head. "The more the merrier."

Once she'd gone back to her bedroom, I turned back to Otto.

"Thank you," I said.

"For what?"

"For being a good person. For making her so happy. For showing up here." I sighed. "For not hating me."

He stepped forward and slid his arms around my waist, pulling me into his hard body. My nose immediately sought out the scent of his skin inside his collar.

"I tried hating you really hard, Walker. It didn't take."

I held onto him for dear life and reveled in the feel of his body against mine. If I could have stayed like that for the next sixty years, I would have. But duty called and so did my dispatcher.

"Walker," I said after accepting the call.

"Sheriff, we have a problem."

CHAPTER 10

OTTO

Walker,

You're a fucking coward and an asshole. I can't believe the lies I fell for from you. The promises. You're nothing but a child who wants whatever is in front of him in the moment. So much for long-term commitment. I guess I should be glad I learned about your fickle nature before we built a life together.

If only I hadn't wasted my entire fucking life up to this point thinking you were someone you so obviously aren't.

I hate you,

Wilde

I KNEW from the look on Walker's face it was bad. He reached out his hand to me, and I took it without thinking, threading our fingers together and squeezing to let him know I was with him.

His words were clipped and minimal. "Where?... When?...I'm on my way."

Before he even had a chance to end the call, I was opening my mouth to tell him I'd stay with Tisha, but the door opened and Jolie walked in.

"Oh thank god," I said in a rush. I'd assumed the news might have been about her since she was missing with no word.

Her eyes shot to me and blinked in surprise. "What are you doing here?"

Before answering her, I looked at Walker. "Go. We've got this. Be safe."

I noticed Jolie's eyes land on our joined hands. Her jaw tightened and her eyes narrowed, but she didn't mention it. I quickly dropped Walker's hand out of respect for her feelings. "Where are you going? What's going on?"

"Car full of teenagers went off the road between here and Pelton. Evan's bringing the hydraulics to get them out before the car lights up."

"Shit," I muttered. "Go. They'll need you."

Walker's eyes jogged between Jolie and me. "Otto, come with me? I'm sure they could use an extra pair of hands."

I nodded and raced ahead of him out the door, calling back over my shoulder at the last minute to ask Jolie to please tell Tisha goodbye for me. I didn't stick around long enough to see her reaction.

As soon as we were in the SUV, Walker turned on the lights and stomped on the pedal to get us to the scene as fast as possible. His radio squawked updates as they came in, and we learned only one kid was left trapped in the vehicle. A helicopter was on its way and three ambulances had already joined the EMT first responders on the scene.

"Who is it? Do we know?" I asked, almost not wanting to know the answer. In a town the size of ours, someone knew everyone.

"Shayna didn't know. Says the car has plates from a different county."

I ran my hand over my short hair, feeling the prickly surface of my recent buzz cut. "Shit, Seth."

"Yeah."

We rode the rest of the way in silence until arriving at a scene of red and blue-lighted chaos. Before the car came to a complete stop, it seemed like Walker was out and striding quickly to the incident commander. Chief Paige was there as well as a sheriff's deputy, two highway patrol officers, and heap loads of fire and EMT responders.

I made sure the road was clear before getting out and approaching the fire chief. He caught my eye and nodded while explaining the situation to Walker alongside Walker's deputy. I noticed two fire-fighters in turnout gear at the front of the crushed vehicle, clearly trying to prevent the car from going up before the last victim was extracted.

We'd passed one ambulance racing away from the scene as we approached, and two more already had victims inside. I hoped the only reason they hadn't left yet was because the injuries to their patients weren't critical.

I noticed Chief Paige meet my eyes again a moment later and gesture with his head toward the truck. I scrambled to the truck and helped myself to some extra turnout gear before joining the other guys at the front of the vehicle.

"What can I do?" I called out.

A man who was finishing cribbing the car called out. "Clear debris around the perimeter of the vehicle. Battery's already disconnected, and Daevon is placing a foam line just in case."

I raced back to the truck to find the right tools and quickly made my way back to begin clearing brush from around the vehicle in case fire did occur. Luckily the highway patrol officers had been able to rig up some extra lighting for the scene in addition to the lights from the truck so we were all able to see enough to do our jobs quickly and efficiently.

The sound of powerful hydraulics and metal crunching overtook most of the other sounds around us until they finally went quiet and the last of the EMTs scrambled to get the victim out and onto a gurney.

The helicopter had landed only a couple of minutes before and was ready to whisk the final victim to the nearest trauma hospital. Once the victim and medical personnel were away from the vehicle, Chief Paige and his guys took the final actions to make the area safe. I was impressed with their efficiency and high level of skill, proving

85

they were just as quality a crew to join as any I'd worked with in Dallas or the military.

I overheard Walker giving instructions to his deputy and the two highway patrol officers to notify three of the four victims' families while he announced he'd notify the fourth before heading to the hospital. His deputy would return to the scene and make sure to stay until everything was clear.

Chief Paige pulled me aside.

"Good work, Wilde. Glad you came. You need a ride home?"

I glanced at Walker who was busy on the phone. "I rode here with the sheriff, so I'm not sure yet."

The chief looked between the sheriff and me. "You came with Seth?"

The sound of Walker's first name out of the chief's mouth burned my gut a little. "Yeah. I was at his house when the call came in. He asked me to come along; thought you could use the extra hands."

"Smart man."

"Mm."

We stood awkwardly for a moment as if waiting for Walker to get off the phone. I wasn't sure why things had turned weird all of a sudden.

"Did you call your station chief in Dallas yet?" Chief Paige asked.

"Yes, sir."

"Please call me Evan or Chief, Otto," he said with a smile. "I know it's hard, but we're both grown men now, and you calling me *sir* just feels weird."

"You're my boss," I reminded him. "And don't forget my eight years in the navy. Some of that shit's hard to forget."

He laughed and reached out to squeeze my shoulder. "Good point. It'll take time, but I'll keep reminding you."

I looked at him before deliberately answering, "Yes, sir."

The smile on his face was a nice change from the stressed-out, pinched focus while he'd been trying to save the teenager trapped in the car. We'd both needed the moment of lightness, but when our laughter caught Walker's attention, I regretted it.

He glared at us before going back to his call.

"Uh-oh. We'd better get on out of here. Why don't you let me take you back home since he has to go inform one of the families and then head to the hospital?"

"Um, yeah, sure. Okay," I mumbled. "Let me just tell him he's off the hook."

I walked over to wait next to Walker while he finished up the call. The minute his finger pressed the end button, he turned and hissed at me. "That was one of the kids' parents, Wilde. You really want them to hear laughing in the background of an accident where their kid almost died?"

My stomach twisted at his tone. "Of course not," I said in a low voice. "You know me better than that. You also know how humor works with first responders, Walker. We didn't know you were on with a family, and I doubt they could have heard us from that far away."

He blew out a breath and ran his fingers through his hair. I realized he wasn't in uniform and didn't have his usual hat on.

"I'm sorry, Otto," he said. "I just... I can't imagine how they're feeling right now. What if that had been Tish? Or your brother Cal? Or Sassy? God."

I reached out and held onto his arm. "It wasn't. And those kids are going to be okay. Everything worked the way it was supposed to. You have a really fine team here, Sheriff."

His eyes pierced me for several beats and there was a world of need in them. "I have to go."

"I know," I said. "Chief Paige is going to drop me off at the ranch."

"I'm sorry," he said again. "I have to go tell one of the sets of—"

"Stop. I understand. Be safe and call me tomorrow, okay?"

"Otto..." His eyes were like a set of teeth gnashing against my heart. They were fucking pools of need so deep I thought I might drown.

"Be strong," I said in a rough voice, not quite sure which one of us I was talking to.

I turned and joined the crew on the fire truck for the ride back to the station. Once there, the chief and I helped the crew clean up and put gear away before making our way out to his personal FD vehicle to make our way back to the ranch.

"I heard the sheriff and his wife are getting a divorce," the chief began.

"Mm-hm," I said, looking out the window into the late spring night.

"And apparently their daughter is really his niece?"

"Mm-hm."

"Hm."

More silence.

"Is he gay?"

I turned to face the chief.

"Why do you ask?"

He shrugged and grinned. "He's a good-looking man."

I might have grunted a little. Or growled.

The booming laugh cut through the vehicle. "Relax, Wilde. I was teasing you. I was curious if I might ask Jolie out."

I turned and gaped at him. "You're straight?"

More laughter. "I'm bi. And before you ask, yes, I do think the sheriff is a hot piece of ass. But I also think maybe he's got a little tunnel vision right about now. Am I right?"

"Please ask Jolie out," I said in a rush, ignoring his question. "Jesus, please."

"Consider it done."

"Maybe don't tell her you're bi right away though. She's not all that happy with gay guys these days," I suggested.

He chuckled some more. "I can see why. Did she know he was gay when she married him?"

"You'd have to ask him," I said. I hadn't even heard all the details from him yet, so the truth was, I wasn't sure what she knew.

"In other words, stop asking so many nosy questions, Chief?"

"You can ask them as long as you don't mind me not answering them," I said.

"Touché."

We rode a few more minutes in companionable silence until he pulled his SUV onto Doc and Grandpa's ranch.

"I'm really glad you came tonight, Otto. You didn't hesitate to pick up and do what needed doing. That's exactly the kind of guy we need on our crew. Look forward to you starting as soon as possible."

"Thanks. And in answer to your earlier question, yes. I did call my station chief. He said since I was injured, I didn't need to serve out my notice. I don't need to go back other than to pack up my stuff from my apartment, and even that is pretty negligible."

"Great news. Well, just let me know when you feel up to it and we'll get you on the schedule."

After bidding him a good night, I made my way around back to the bunkhouse so as not to disturb Doc and Grandpa. I found a room with a freshly made bed in it and unloaded my pockets onto the tiny dresser before stripping for a hot shower. I let the soapy water wash away the smell of metal and blood that seemed like it was stamped on my skin, and I tried not to think about what a long road ahead some of those kids would have recovering from their ordeal. I was sure part of Walker's duties involved having the driver tested for substance abuse.

After finishing up, I dried off and slid between the sheets naked since what little clean clothes I had were in the guest room in the house. It didn't take long for sleep to find me and suck me under, but my dreams were scrambled and dark. It was a very normal side effect of responding to a particularly grisly scene, but it woke me up with a sudden gasp. Once I caught my breath, I lay awake, tracing the first hints of sunrise across the ceiling. The bunkhouse was quiet with the exception of a few creaks of wood here and there, and even the animals were still asleep outside including the asshole ranch rooster we all called Pita.

Just as I was finally drifting off again, I heard a door open in the bunkhouse. I assumed it was Doc or Grandpa coming to check on me. When the door to my room opened, however, it was Walker. He looked rode hard and put away wet; his short blond hair stuck out all over the place as though he'd been running hands through it.

I didn't say a word, just held the covers open for him in invitation.

His face looked sad in addition to exhausted, and all I wanted to do was pull him into my arms and let him heal himself through sleep.

"I need to shower first," he murmured in a hoarse voice, putting his gun belt on the small dresser. "I've gotta get the hospital stink off me."

I got up and moved toward him, reaching out to help him remove his uniform without taking my eyes off his face. His eyes were wide and searching and the tiny lines next to them betrayed his continued worry about any number of things.

"Let me take care of you," I whispered.

He dropped his forehead on my bare shoulder while I finished undoing the buttons of his shirt. I pulled it off his shoulders, revealing the Kevlar vest underneath. I was familiar with the soft armor, so I quickly undid the straps and removed it, all while trying to disturb Walker the least. I felt warm lips on the skin of my neck, and I couldn't help but get hard in response. I knew my reaction was hardly a secret since I was buck naked, but I hoped he didn't take it as any kind of pressure to do anything with me. I seriously only wanted him to get cleaned up and tucked into bed so he could rest.

"Come on. Let's move into the bathroom so I can get the water warmed up," I said, reaching for his hand to lead him the short distance.

Once I had the spray going, I squatted down to remove his shoes and socks. All that was left then were his pants and underwear. I thumbed open the button and pulled down the zipper before sliding my hands into the back of his pants and caressing down his ass and legs to get the uniform trousers off. Walker made a small noise of desire in his throat, and when I stood back up, I rubbed my face against his tented boxer briefs. He sucked in a breath.

God, he smelled good. Musky and sweaty and *mine*.

His hands came up to rest on my shoulders, and his eyes became deep pools of need. "Wilde Man," he murmured. "Will you…?"

I cut him off with a kiss to his lips, soft and exploring, slow and tender.

"Baby, I'll do whatever you want. Just tell me."

"I want you to touch me everywhere. I want you to make love to me. I want to fall asleep in your arms and stay there. I want—" When his voice became desperate, I cut him off again with another kiss.

"Shhh. We can do all those things. But first, let's get you cleaned up before you fall over, okay?"

I moved him into the shower and began scrubbing him with the soap and a little shampoo. My hands were everywhere on his bare skin, and I had to concentrate to keep from just dropping the soap and humping him to death.

The man was goddamned perfection. His muscles were fit and defined under honeyed skin and his ass cheeks were plump and full. All I wanted was to press into his body the way I had years ago and feel his tight channel squeeze me to completion. It was all I could think about.

My hands ran up and down his stomach and chest as my cock slid up and down his crease from behind.

"Oh god, Seth," I groaned. "You feel so fucking good."

"Please," he breathed, leaning his head back onto my shoulder to look up at me. "Please fuck me, Otto. I need you."

"I'm not going to last if we do that. I'll blow the minute I get inside you," I admitted in a rough voice.

He turned until our cocks slid together in the warm water running off our bodies. "Then let's get off real quick right here and save the fucking for bed."

Walker's hand was already reaching for the soap and within seconds his slick hands were stroking us together masterfully. I held his hips and bucked into his fists while leaning forward to take his mouth with mine.

"Fuck," I groaned into his mouth. "God, Seth. Fuck that feels good. Tighter… Yeah, just like that."

Walker whimpered and stopped kissing me to drop his head onto my chest and look down at the way he was working our cocks together. Little noises and gasps came out of him until he finally cried out a warning.

"Otto!"

I quickly reached to take over as his orgasm hit him and he lost the rhythm. His hands moved up to clutch at my shoulders, scrambling for purchase and digging nails into my skin as he cried out his release. Watching his cock spurt and his abdominal muscles ripple was enough to make me cry out and shoot.

"Oh fuck. *Aghh!*" I gasped for more air after I ran out, and felt like I'd come enough to bathe him in the stuff. "Jesus, Walker." I looked down to where I was still softly stroking the both of us, and I marveled at how sexy he was standing there naked in the shower with me.

Getting to take a shower with him again was something I'd fantasized about for years, and now it had actually happened. I opened my mouth to say something to Walker about it when I realized his entire weight was slipping against me as he practically fell asleep standing up.

I rinsed us both off as quickly as I could and wrapped him in a couple of towels from the stack on a nearby shelf before grabbing one for myself and leading him back to the bedroom.

He was asleep as soon as he hit the pillow, and I quickly pulled his back against my front and wrapped him up in my arms. We fell asleep that way and didn't move for hours. When we finally awoke, it was to the sound of a woman's screech filling the room.

"What the fuck?"

CHAPTER 11

WALKER

Seth

Please, please. I'm begging you. Explain what is going on. Please, Seth. I can't believe you'd do this to me. To us. Maybe something happened and you can't tell me? Surely you know you can tell me anything? I'll understand, Seth. I promise I will. Just talk to me.

No matter what it is... I need you to know I love you.

And I always will,

Otto

I WAS SO deep asleep when it happened I had no idea where the hell I even was. I was lucky to know *who* I was.

"What the fuck?"

A warm, hard body shifted beside me, and I felt a happy flood of memory wash over me. *Otto.* I'd fallen asleep in Otto's arms. The arms that were now clutching me to him like a vise.

"Ow," I muttered, squirming in his tightening hold before realizing he was trying to keep me covered from whoever was doing the screeching.

It was too late. There was a woman staring bug-eyed at me, and I didn't recognize her at first.

"MJ, can you give us a minute?" Otto snapped in a broken morning voice. "It's rude to barge into a bedroom without knocking, you know."

"I knocked for ten minutes, asshole."

"Wait. MJ? As in your sister MJ?" I croaked.

The woman's shit-eating grin widened. "Yep. That's me. Nice to see you, *Sheriff*."

I felt heat flood my face as I realized I was a very *naked* sheriff in bed with a very naked brother of MJ's.

"Get out," Otto snapped again. "I mean it."

"You have five minutes to turn up for breakfast or else I'm barging in again, and I'm bringing Saint with me."

"Fuck," Otto muttered. "Wait. Saint's here? When did he get in?"

"'Bout twenty minutes ago. We all rode together. Hudson, Saint, Hallie, Winnie, and me. Hudson and Saint found out you were hurt and about went apeshit. So get your ass in the kitchen before they come to give your person an inspection." She raised her eyebrow with a cackle and left the room, but not before chucking a brown paper grocery bag on the foot of the bed. "For you two from Doc."

"Wait," Otto called. "How did he know—"

"Oh please," she called back with a laugh. "The Hobie sheriff's vehicle is parked front and center in the driveway. Everyone knows."

"Shit," Otto huffed. "Goddamned family. I swear to god..."

"It's okay. I should probably, uh... go." I looked around to see if I could remember where I'd put my clothes, but Otto reached out to grab my chin gently and turn my face to his.

"No. You're staying here and enduring the Wilde love posse. You're not leaving me here alone with those fuckers."

I laughed and leaned in for a kiss of his pursed lips. He softened immediately and melted against me for the duration of the kiss. When I pulled back, I met his eyes. "Okay. I'll stay for a little while, but then I'll have to swing by the hospital and check on all those families."

"Deal," he said. "How were they all when you left last night?"

Otto climbed out of bed and reached for the brown paper bag, but not before flashing me a full frontal view of his sexy package.

I gulped.

His eyes snapped up to mine, and his grin was all knowing. "See something you like, Sheriff?"

I nodded.

"A firefighter with a nice hose."

We both dissolved into laughter as Otto pulled clothes out of the bag. I realized quickly they were two sets of dark blue medical scrubs worn soft with age.

"God, this brings back memories," I said, pulling a set on and tying the waist. "That time we fell in the lake and Doc put us in scrubs while he dried our clothes."

"The time we exploded a can of spaghetti all over the kitchen," Otto added.

"Oh my god and when we ate too much at the Hootenanny and both wound up puking our guts out in the back of your grandfather's truck?"

"Thank god for Doc's scrubs," Otto said with a laugh, sliding his own pair on and robbing me of the perfect view I'd had only a moment before.

"Turn around and let me see your butt," I demanded.

He did it without even stopping to question me, and his easy offering of his body made me feel light and free. His ass was high and round under the soft fabric, and I couldn't help but reach out and squeeze a luscious globe.

Otto turned and grinned at me before swatting my hand away. "Hands off the goods, dude. You break it, you buy it."

"I'll buy it," I promised. "Name your price."

I stepped forward until we were toe to toe. Our eyes searched each other in this newness between us.

"For you?" Otto asked softly. "Free to a good home."

I reached for his scruffy face with my hands and pulled him in for a kiss. Our mouths met softly and just sampled each other for a moment before we pulled back and touched foreheads.

"Let's go face the firing squad," I teased. "No time like the present."

"You've obviously forgotten that time they surprised us with one of these interventions after junior prom night," he groaned, opening the bedroom door and running right into two of his brothers. "Holy fuck!"

West and Saint cackled at him, pointing and laughing and giving him noogies until Sassy appeared from behind him and said, "Wait. Junior prom? Isn't that when the two of you stayed out all night and lied about being at each other's houses? You were in so much trouble."

"How do you even remember that?" Otto asked. "You were like, a newborn when that happened."

"It's part of family lore," she said with a straight face. "That and Mom and Dad made me wear a GPS tracker to my own damned proms because of it. Jackass."

I laughed and followed them across the yard and into the big old farmhouse kitchen. It was as familiar to me as my own parents' kitchen because Otto and I had spent way more time here than either of our parents' houses at the edge of the ranch.

"There they are," Grandpa called out from in front of the pancake griddle. "Thought you two were gonna sleep all day. Grab some coffee."

I looked around at all the familiar faces of the Wilde family. Some were familiar because I'd seen them in the months I'd been back; some were less familiar, but still recognizable as Wildes.

In the split second I worried about them hating me for leaving Otto all those years ago, I realized they weren't the type to hold grudges. I guessed if Otto was okay with me, that meant the Wildes were okay with me too. I hoped so anyway.

A baby squawk came from the large wooden table, and I saw Doc holding Pippa while Nico tried spooning something into her tiny mouth. She must have recognized me because she immediately began waving her arms and making baby noises.

"Hey, sweet pea," I called, approaching her and squatting down until I was at her level. "What're you eating for breakfast, hm? Your daddy feeding you some pears?"

Doc held her out to me. "Here, you take over so I can help Weston with the adult food."

I quickly grabbed her from him and took his seat when he got up. Nico went back to aiming the pears at her while I encouraged her with silly faces and baby talk to eat every bite. After a minute, I realized there was silence around me.

I looked up and met Otto's intense stare. "What?" I asked, noticing some of the other people in the room were also staring.

"You're really good with her," Otto said looking oddly vulnerable for some reason.

"He has experience." Nico grinned. "Knows all the tricks."

"Oh right," Hallie said from across the table. "I heard you have a daughter. What's her name?"

"Um…" I looked around again, suddenly in the spotlight. "She's not really my daughter, even though I raised her with her mom. She's my niece. Her name is Tisha. She turns nine this summer."

The room was quiet while I tried to distract myself with Pippa.

"Nine?" This time it was West doing the math. The doctor of the bunch. "That means her mom was pregnant the year that you…" He looked up at me in surprise before looking at Otto. "Oh. Oh, I see…"

I felt my jaw tighten and my eyes prick. Fuck. I didn't want to do this in front of so many damned Wildes. I wanted to tell Otto the story first, without an audience. I felt like the entire room was waiting to pass judgment on what happened—the decision I'd made.

All I cared about was one opinion, though, no one else's.

My eyes searched for him again and found him looking down at his feet. My chest was tight, and I desperately wanted to know what he was thinking.

"Otto?" I asked quietly.

"Yeah," he said, clearing his throat and looking back up at me. A mask of nothingness came over his face before he smiled a generic smile. "You want a cup of coffee?"

My heart pounded in my chest, and I turned to hand Pippa off to

Nico before standing and walking right up to Otto and straight into his personal space. My arms went around his waist, and I looked right into his eyes. I desperately wanted to reassure him this wasn't a flash in the pan thing for me, and I wasn't going to waffle this time.

"I don't want a cup of coffee, Wilde Man. I want *you.*"

CHAPTER 12

OTTO

Otto,

I know I won't send this but I have to at least get the words out before they kill me. Your letters are breaking my heart. I can't even tell you how many tears I've cried for you since my brother died. I can't even call and tell you about Ross because if I hear your voice, I swear to god, I'll break. And I know without a shadow of a doubt, you'll come running. You always have.

I love you so much, Otto Wilde. But I feel like I have to do this, I'm going to marry Jolie and help her take care of her baby, Ross's baby. I told her I planned on giving her five years of support and helping her get through those early years until the baby starts school. But I gotta be honest... I'm scared to death.

I never imagined I'd get married at age eighteen and I sure as HELL didn't imagine marrying a woman. What am I gonna do with a wife and baby, Otto? Mom and Dad are planning on helping us a lot, but... god, I'm terrified.

I applied to a local community college program that should help me become a police officer. You know I've always wanted to go into law enforcement and this way I should end up with good benefits for Jolie and the baby. In the meantime, I just have to focus and work my ass off to try and get through it as quickly as I can.

I think about you every day, Otto, and wonder if you hate me. If you're mad at me or just plain sad. It rips me up inside to know what I did to you, but I hope and pray you can find it in your heart to forgive me one day. Maybe when you find a nice man to fall in love with, you'll realize it was all for the best.

Fuck. I can't even write that without wanting to punch that guy in the face, whoever the hell he might be. But it wouldn't be fair of me to betray you the way I have and expect you to wait around for me.

I love you more than you could ever know, Wilde Man.

Seth

(Unsent)

WHEN I HEARD THE WORDS, I closed my eyes to sear them into my memory. It was no surprise I needed frequent reassurances from Walker that he wasn't going to just ditch me again when his family needed him. I realized after everything that had happened between us back then, it would take me some time to fully trust him again.

I felt him slide his arms around me and lay his head on my shoulder. After pulling him in even tighter to me, I opened my eyes and met his.

"You can have me *and* coffee, you know," I teased before kissing his forehead.

The tension in the room broke at that, and my family began chattering again. A couple of my siblings came up to squeeze Walker's shoulder or pat him on the back. I kept him in an embrace the entire time, though, just to be sure of him. I knew he was most likely feeling judged and nervous about what my family thought of him. He knew the Wildes were fiercely protective and would do anything to keep me from getting hurt again, but I wanted to let him know that things between the two of us were okay.

Grandpa caught my eye across the kitchen island and winked, catching Doc's attention and getting a butt pinch as punishment. "Save your winking for me, old man," Doc teased.

"Come here," Grandpa said, pulling Doc back by a belt loop. He laid a big kiss on Doc's lips and put his big rancher's hands on either side of Doc's slender neck.

I felt Walker shift in my embrace and realized he was watching them too. My lips brushed his ear as I whispered, "You and me in fifty years."

I felt his entire body shudder against mine and his face tucked into my neck. I could have sworn I heard him breathe the words *promise me* against my skin.

It seemed like my arm never strayed from around his waist all through family breakfast. Everyone was lively and chatty as usual. Hallie and Winnie talked about their jobs in Dallas and Nico told everyone about his booming tattoo business now that the guys on the nearby military base had finally started spreading the word about the shop.

"Not about the shop," West said, beaming with pride. "About how talented he is, in particular."

Nico's skin flushed under all that ink, and I thought, not for the first time, about how lucky the two of them were to have found each other despite what an unlikely pair they were.

I noticed Hudson doing his usual thing cutting food into precise size bites on his plate just so. "Hey, Hudson. How're things with Darci?"

He lifted his head up and looked at me like he was surprised to find himself in the farmhouse kitchen. "Huh? Oh. Fine. Her dad's been trying to teach me about their family business, which is beer making. It took me a while, but I think I figured out it's Darci's way of pushing the two of us together. She wants me to bond with her family. Not so sure how I feel about it, but at least the science stuff is interesting. So, I hear you're moving back here and taking that job at the HFD."

"Yeah. I'll miss you guys in the city, but I think it's the right move for me."

He nodded. "Can't argue with that. I've always pictured you here, O. The horses and wide-open spaces... being able to help the people you know and love in your community. It's a good move for you. We're proud of you, brother."

I felt a sudden tightening in my chest at his unexpected words of praise. "Thanks, Hud. I really appreciate that. More than you know," I said in a rough voice.

He reached out and ruffled my hair the way he did when I was five. "I'm so damned glad you're home safe."

I knew he didn't mean Amarillo. Saint must have told him about some of the crap I'd been through on my last boat. I didn't mind, really. It was more that I was a little embarrassed. Like maybe I should have been braver or... smarter or... just plain better. But I couldn't change the past.

"I feel bad running out on the apartment lease with Saint though," I admitted. "He told me he can afford it on his own, but I still feel bad."

Hudson laughed. "You kidding? That kid is a navy goddamned SEAL. He can write his own ticket. Do you have any idea how much he's making in personal security right now? It's insane."

"I still feel bad."

"Nah. He'll be happy to have the place to himself when his job settles down enough for him to have sleepovers," Hudson said with a wink in my direction.

"True enough," Saint said with a laugh, reaching over my shoulder to steal my last piece of bacon. "In the meantime, I gotta catch a flight out tonight from Dallas so we all can't stay long. You want to ride back with me and get your stuff?"

I glanced at Walker who sat next to me finishing his own breakfast. He was obviously avoiding participating in the conversation, but I could see the truth of it in his eyes. He was hoping I'd stay so we could talk.

"Nah. I'll probably drive down there in a couple of days in Grandpa's truck so I can fit my stuff and put the bike in the back. I told Chief Paige I could start after that. Thanks anyway."

Saint winked at me and turned to arrange times with Hudson and our sisters. I turned to Walker. "I told Tisha she could come ride today. Do you want to call Jolie and arrange a time before we do anything else?"

"You sure you're still up for it?" he asked with concern in his face.

I reached up to run my hand through his short hair. "Of course I am. I refuse to be the ogre who crushes that girl's dreams." I chuckled and squeezed his knee. "I'm going to get some dishes cleaned up while you go call. Anytime today works fine for me, and I meant it when I said she can bring anyone she wants."

After sharing dish duty with West, I thanked Grandpa and Doc for breakfast and said goodbye to the Dallas crew. I found Walker standing at the fence to the ring where someone had turned out Doc and Grandpa's favorite trail horses. I wondered if maybe they'd gotten up really early and taken a sunrise ride together.

"Hey," I called to Walker. "Get everything squared away?"

He turned to face me. "I'm going to go pick them up in a couple of hours. And I talked to the Realtor about the house I'm moving into. Today is moving day, but I told her I already had the key and everything. There's no rush since I don't have that much stuff to move anyway. Mostly clothes. I'll have to buy new stuff for the kitchen and family room. Oh, and I checked in with the families of the accident victims. No substance abuse and they're all doing okay."

"Do you want to take a walk and talk or would you rather go back to the bunkhouse?" I asked. Butterflies tumbled in my stomach at the anticipation of finally talking about what broke us apart almost ten years earlier.

"Is there somewhere we can go where no one will interrupt us?" he asked. "I'd offer the lake house, but there's not a stick of furniture."

I thought for a minute and snapped my finger when I came up with it. "My parents' place. Come on."

Instead of going back to the bunkhouse for car keys, we hopped on one of the ranch's electric utility vehicles that was like a golf cart on steroids and made our way out to the far corner of the ranch where my parents' old house was. As I drove, I felt Walker's strong body beside mine, and I reached over to hold his hand. Any excuse to touch him.

It couldn't really be this easy between us, could it? I'd been feeling a little on edge at how smoothly we'd fallen back in with each other. The last time we'd seen each other before we moved back had been when we were getting ready to be seniors in high school. Surely we were very different people now. I worried there would be a time when the differences between who we were then and who we were now would rear their ugly heads and show us the truth of the matter—that this could never really work.

And if that happened, I wasn't quite sure I'd survive it.

We pulled up outside of the closed-up house and got out of the little vehicle. The garage code didn't work since the power was cut off, so I had to search out a hidden key in a nearby planter.

I led Walker through the side door and into the house, noticing how abandoned everything looked. My parents hadn't been gone more than a couple of years, but still the place seemed lost in time. Echoes of our boisterous family dinners seemed to fill the dark and dusty kitchen and the refrigerator still had flyers and photos pinned to it. Since my parents had moved to Singapore, all the furniture and kitchen stuff had stayed here. Walker and I wandered around peering into the various rooms on the main floor as if walking back in time to when we were teenagers running into the house after soccer practice and eating Mom and Dad out of house and home.

"You think our stash is still in your room?" Walker asked with a mischievous grin. It took me a minute to figure out what he was referring to since we were never pot smokers or anything like that.

"The condoms and dildo? Yes. Not that the condoms would be any good ten years later," I said with a laugh. "And I got your dildo right here, buddy." I grabbed my dick and leered at him. He rolled his eyes with a laugh.

"Do you carry a condom on you?" he asked with sparkling eyes. I could see the lines of insecurity in his forehead though, as if he worried I wouldn't be interested in having sex with him. Was he crazy?

"Fuck," I muttered, patting my ass and realizing neither of us had our wallets. "Guess maybe that's a sign we should talk instead?"

"Yeah. I guess," he reluctantly agreed. "Come on. Let's go sit down."

We entered the family room and pulled some old sheets off the giant leather sofas before sitting down and getting comfortable. We sat close and turned to face each other.

"You start," I said. When I heard my voice crack with nerves, I frowned.

Walker reached for my hand and held it between his. "This isn't..." He took a deep breath. "This isn't going to be easy, Otto."

"I understand. But we have to talk about it."

"Yeah. I know." He looked down at our hands and played with my fingers before looking back up at me. His eyes were pinched with worry. "You already know part of it. Ross got Jolie pregnant while he was still in college, and she refused to have an abortion. I didn't blame her. None of us wanted her to even though my parents and her mom thought having a baby that young was going to ruin their lives." He paused and snorted softly. "I guess they were right in Ross's case, weren't they?"

I pulled Walker's hand up and dropped a kiss on his knuckles before he continued.

"So their plan was to get married. Jolie's mom kicked her out of the house when she found out about the pregnancy, and she came to live with us. Ross was living in the dorms, so it was weird. The whole thing really changed him, and I think that's part of why my parents resented Jolie so much. He was so turned around by the unexpected pregnancy; he started fucking up his classes and making poor choices."

I noticed Seth's hands had begun to shake. His eyes darted around the room, not landing on anything in particular.

"Back then, Jolie was like a scared little mouse. She was terrified of my parents and tried to not be noticed in our house. I felt awful for her. It just seemed wrong that she was being judged for making a mistake people have been making for thousands of years, including her own mother. But part of the reason my parents were so rude to her is because they thought her pregnancy was causing Ross to get reckless. He was going out more and drinking more, driving when he'd been drinking and refusing to listen to anyone's concerns.

"We tried to talk to him about it, to let him know he had our support, but he just told us we didn't understand what it felt like to be so trapped. Him going out drinking was his only way to 'unwind.' So I guess we just sort of accepted that was something he needed to do in order to cope with the stress of everything. The pressure to finish school and get a job, the pressure to marry Jolie and be a true family, and the pressure to make something of himself when he really didn't know what the hell he wanted out of life.

"I've often wondered if he picked that fight on purpose. Either as a way of punishing himself or maybe even him having a death wish. He was at a shitty bar one night late when someone apparently made a comment to him about how Jolie probably got pregnant on purpose to get a rich family to take care of her. At least, that's what one of the witnesses claimed after the fact. Ross threw a punch at the guy, and the guy came back at him with a hefty pack of friends. Ross never stood a chance. There was no way to know if he knew the guy wasn't there alone or what. Maybe he did. I don't know. All I know is I still resent the hell out of him for doing it."

I reached forward and pulled Seth closer so I could wrap my arms around him. He leaned his head on my chest and kept talking.

"It wasn't his fault I decided to marry Jolie. I mean, I don't blame him for that. Yeah, he made me promise, but after he was gone, it was my choice. But I do blame him for leaving Tisha. I blame him for leaving Jolie. And I blame him for leaving me."

His voice was hoarse with emotion, and I wanted to tell him to stop. I didn't want him dredging up these painful memories.

"Maybe I do blame him for more than I thought, Otto. Even though I didn't have to honor the promise I made... if Ross hadn't thrown that punch in the first place, I wouldn't have left you." This last part was said in such a broken voice I quickly pulled his head up to kiss him.

"You can't change the past, Seth," I reminded him, speaking against his soft lips. "We're together again, and who knows? Maybe if all this hadn't have happened, we would have gotten together, but something else would have torn us apart. Hell, maybe even stupid youth would have gotten in our way somehow. We can't look back and regret at this point, Walker. We have to just acknowledge the past and move forward."

I kissed him some more, unable to keep from sipping from his sweet lips and enjoying access to him that had been cut off from me for so long.

When I finally came up for air, I met his eyes. "I'm so, so sorry about your brother, Seth. I can't believe you lost Ross, and I wasn't there to help you through that. If I'd known…"

"I know," he said, looking down and then laying his head on my chest again. "It was awful. My poor parents were beside themselves."

"How did your little brother, John, take it? I haven't seen him since I've been back."

"He changed. It was like a light went out in him that never came back on. I always thought maybe he felt helpless being so young when it happened. He was sixteen."

I was surprised at that. John Walker had always been lively and outgoing; so much so he told everyone to call him Johnny just so we could all tease him about his name. "Really? He was the first to move back here, right?"

He nodded. "After college, Dad managed to get him a job at the insurance office here selling policies. He met Beth while he was in school. She already had two sons from a previous marriage—Hal's who's thirteen and Cody, a nine-year-old who's Tisha's best friend. Then together they have a five-year-old daughter named Eliza. I think John was hoping to take over the Hobie office when the position opened, but then Dad decided to move back and take over instead. And now Jolie is working there too."

I'd heard a rumor that Jolie had taken the place of the woman who'd been answering the phones there for a million years, but I didn't say anything. Walker's dad had never been one of my favorite people, and I wasn't surprised he'd fired the woman to make room for Jolie. I wasn't sure I could really blame the guy. He probably wanted to provide her a steady income and flexibility to be close to Tisha when she needed her mom.

There was one question that had been burning inside of me since I found out about this whole thing. "When did you two get married? Like... whose idea was it to actually go through with it?"

CHAPTER 13

WALKER

Dear Walker,

Well, I'm just going to pretend we're still together, because one day, by god, we'd better be.

Graduation was a shitshow. A thousand Wildes and what seems like only twelve other people in attendance. Sometimes family can be a blessing and a curse.

So here's the scary part... I've decided to join Saint in applying to the navy. I'm terrified, but I also know I can't sit around here waiting for you to change your mind anymore. I'm going to go drown my sorrows in the world's greatest oceans.

Okay, just kidding. I'm going to try and become a navy SEAL. And if that doesn't work, at least I'll get a nice dose of seamen...

Miss you, More than I can say.

Wilde

(Unsent)

I DIDN'T BLAME him for wanting to know more about my marriage. Had he been the one to leave me and marry a woman, I don't know what I would have felt like. Angry, betrayed, sad, desperate... I had no idea how he could even begin to forgive me.

"She was almost six months pregnant when Ross died. They were all set to get married that April but he died in March. Like I told you, he made me promise to marry her just to give the child his name. At first, I almost went back on that promise.

"But then I saw how sad and alone Jolie was at the funeral. She sat over on the side, not really a part of the family but not one of his friends either. I'll never forget... she was wearing this thin green dress that looked like something that came from the thrift shop, but she'd done her hair in this elaborate twist to try and dress it up as much as she could. I realized she had nothing and no one. It was going to be her and that baby living in some homeless shelter unless we helped them."

Otto's big hand lifted my face up so he could press soft kisses on my face. I closed my eyes for a minute and just soaked in the affection before continuing.

"I couldn't let her raise my brother's child alone, Otto. I couldn't." I felt like I was going to lose it. I needed him to understand. I tucked my head again and curled up even tighter against him, unwilling to have him see me cry.

"I love you."

It was all he said, but it was enough to topple the dam.

"Oh god," I sobbed into his throat. "Oh fuck, Otto. I'm so sorry. I'm so sorry." I couldn't catch my breath. The weight of what I'd done to him was too heavy a burden to bear now that I was there in his arms and he was being so fucking forgiving.

"Shh, baby, stop. It's okay. It's in the past. You did what you needed to do to give Tisha a strong start in life. How could I ever begrudge you that? I know how much Ross meant to you, and I can see now how much Tisha means to you too."

His arms held me close and his lips rested against the top of my head. I smelled the familiar scent of him and knew a comfort and love I hadn't felt in over ten years, since I was a gangly-legged teenager who didn't know the difference between a onesie and a sleeper. Part of me felt a million years old now, but part of me felt eighteen again and ready to begin my life with the man in my arms.

But there was more I needed to tell him.

"I was just going to marry her for the name at first, you know?" My voice was scratchy from the crying. "But then I realized Mom and Dad treated her and the baby differently once they were an official member of our family. Suddenly, Jolie was treated with respect if not love, and my parents treated the baby like the grandchild she is. I also knew how fucking impossible it would be for Jolie to try and raise a baby on her own, even if I could give her financial help, which I couldn't. If I dropped out of college to help her, we'd both be screwed. So as long as I kept my parents happy, they paid to support us and send me to school. One of the only ways to keep them happy was to stay married to Jolie and keep the family together."

"Do they accept Jolie now?"

I sighed. "Not really. I mean, they put up with her and act all nice, but it's mostly just bullshit because they want Tisha in their life. They respect her as my wife and as Tisha's mother. That's it."

"So you went to college and then went to work for the St. Paul PD?" Otto asked. "I can't imagine trying to do all that with a newborn. You must have been eighteen when she was born, for god's sake."

"It was exhausting, but Mom did a ton of the work. We lived with them until I'd been on the force almost a year, then we rented a little house in South St. Paul. Tisha was almost five by then, and we needed to get away from my parents, who were constantly nitpicking our parenting style."

"I can't imagine they appreciated you moving out."

I pulled back and looked at him. "They were so pissed at the neighborhood and school district we picked, they threatened to fight for custody of Tisha. There was a time I thought they might actually try it, too."

The anger in Otto's eyes didn't surprise me. He'd always tried to protect me from my parents' controlling ways. I remembered one time when my parents told me they thought I was too young for a driver's license, Otto convinced my brother Ross to teach me instead.

He was pissed my parents didn't treat me the same as they treated my brothers.

"I told them that if they pursued their claim of me as an unfit parent, it could cause me to lose my job on the force. And even if it didn't, none of my fellow officers would want to work with me again. They don't take kindly to deadbeat dads, you know," I admitted with a soft chuckle.

I felt Otto's arms tighten around me, and I laid my head back down on his chest. "But they managed to convince me to spring for private school for Tisha, and it just about broke me. It's part of the reason I agreed to move back here. That and the job would be safer and paid better since it was a promotion. You know it's an elected position, right? I was just appointed temporarily until they can elect someone permanent this fall. I'll have to run a campaign."

"I'm sure they'll re-elect you, Walker. Everyone loves you, and your family has lived in Hobie since the Middle Ages."

"Except those years in Minnesota…" I said hesitantly.

"Yeah, don't remind me. I call them the shitty years," he grumbled before taking a deep breath. "But they're over now, right?"

I nodded, and reached out to fiddle with the hem of his scrub shirt. Otto's body was warm against mine, and I couldn't help but notice how hard his muscles were underneath the fabric. I could tell his dick was soft in his pants but for every second I stared down at his crotch, it seemed to grow.

I brushed the backs of my fingers across it just to see what would happen.

A rumble vibrated through Otto's chest against my cheek.

My fingers snuck under the hem of his scrub shirt and felt body hair that hadn't been quite so thick when we were teenagers. The bumps of his abdominal muscles felt delicious under the pads of my fingers, and I heard him suck in a breath.

"Walker…"

I brought my hand back down his stomach and reached for the tie of his scrub pants, pulling one end slowly until the bow fell apart. His stiffening cock pushed the fabric out, and I couldn't resist running my knuckles lightly down it again. I leaned back to meet his eyes as if I needed to make sure he was okay with our conversation being over for now.

His eyes glittered at me in challenge, and I knew what he was going to say a split second before it came out of his mouth.

"Did you sleep with her, Seth?"

CHAPTER 14

OTTO

Otto,

I had sex with someone else today. My wife.

My wife. Those words don't even look right. They don't look real. They can't be right, can they?

Oh god, I think I might throw up. It wasn't you. All I can think is that it wasn't you, it wasn't you, it wasn't you. I can barely breathe with missing you and the wrongness I felt touching someone else. I was lonely, Otto. So very lonely for you. I just wanted to be touched. It's been so long since I felt your loving hands on me.

I'm not sure I'll ever deserve your forgiveness.

I'm so sorry. I'm so, so sorry,

Walker

(Unsent)

MAYBE IT WAS none of my business, but I needed to know anyway. I couldn't stand not knowing whose body he'd touched in the years we'd been apart.

It wasn't like I'd been a saint. I hadn't. I'd slept with a couple of guys in the navy and several more during leave times over the years.

But for some reason, the thought of him sleeping with a woman, with his damned *wife*, made me feel ten times more jealous than the idea of him having a random hookup with some guy.

Maybe it was because she'd gotten everything I'd wanted. All those years, the happy family, the rest of his youth and optimism.

I knew the answer before he opened his mouth. My heart felt like it was cut in half, and I scrambled to get up from the sofa.

"Wait, Otto. Wait," he cried. "Please let me expl—"

"It's okay," I lied. "I just need to get a drink of water and some air."

I raced out the side door and around the side of the house to the nearest spigot. After twisting it on and thanking the powers that be for the water still being connected, I took deep gulps of the lukewarm water that came out. I felt the warm May sun beating down on my back and noticed a few fat bees buzzing around the grass nearby. The house and property around it were eerily quiet compared to what I was used to. When Saint and I had left for the navy, this house had still been full of life and loud with Wilde kids.

Everyone had a roommate. Hudson and West, Saint and me, Hallie and Winnie, MJ and Sassy, and King and Cal. As soon as Hudson went to college, MJ forced West to move in with King so she could have her own room as the oldest girl. And so the musical chairs version of roommates went until long after Saint and I left.

Even when half of us were gone, there were still five kids at home. It was always crazy and always felt like home. Seeing it abandoned and hearing it so quiet were making me uneasy.

I heard footsteps on the driveway and knew Walker was coming to check on me. I stood up and turned to face him. When he rounded the corner, worry was clear on his face.

After wiping my hands on my pants, I reached out for him. "I'm sorry."

He shook his head. "Why? I'm the one who's sorry. You have every right to be pissed."

"No, I don't. We weren't together. I didn't stay faithful to you, Seth. I could hardly have expected you to stay celibate for ten fucking years."

"Yeah, but…"

"Come here."

"Why are you being so damned forgiving?"

It almost sounded like he was annoyed with me.

"Because I spent ten years mad at you! I'm sick and fucking tired of being mad at you. I love you so fucking much; all I want to do is hold you, goddammit. And touch you and kiss you and suck you off and fuck you on the goddamned grass if I have to. Now come the fuck *here*." My voice was booming by the time I got to the end, and Walker's eyes were wide with surprise.

Walker took two huge strides until he crashed into me, our mouths seeking each other out with a hungry desperation that had been brewing since the blowjob he'd given me in the barn. My hands were all over him, and I had his shirt off before he even took a breath.

My mouth didn't leave his as my muffled words barely made it over the sound of our grunts. "Outside or inside. Pick now or I'm taking you right here against the side of the house."

"Inside," he said in a shaky voice.

My hand ran down his cock and squeezed, bringing out the sexiest sounds imaginable. "Move then. Inside." I released him and smacked his ass before grabbing his hand and yanking him toward the house.

Without conscious thought, we raced to the room I'd had the last time we'd been together. It had a double bed with a twin-sized bunk over top of it and we fell together onto the double after ripping the dusty comforter and top sheet off and revealing the fitted sheet below.

I grabbed for the drawstring of his scrub pants while he did the same to mine. My shirt had disappeared at some point, and I found myself mouthing one of his nipples and pinching the other with my fingers while I dug my hip up and down his hard-on.

"I had a full health panel before taking the job in Dallas. I'm negative for everything. You?" I asked, desperate to find out whether we could have sex despite not having condoms. I knew having the conversation in the heat of the moment was a bad idea, but I also knew that this was Seth Walker. *My* Seth. And I trusted him with my body.

"Same. Haven't been with anyone in over a year."

I stopped and looked at him. "Really?"

His face, already flush with desire, turned even redder. "I… I've only ever been with Jolie and you. Well, and Carrie-Anne, but you were there. And the thing with Jolie was just… twice, I think. Weak moments where I just let the loneliness overtake—"

I cut him off with a kiss again. I didn't want to think of him lonely or naked with Jolie. The fact he'd only ever had sex without me twice in his life made me feel a crazy concoction of emotions. I leaned over him until he was flat on his back beneath me.

"I love you," I said again. "I love you more than words. I missed you so fucking much."

The emotion was threatening to cut my air off, so I swallowed around the lump in my throat and began kissing down his sternum to the happy trail below his navel.

Seth's hands rubbed across the super-short hair on my head and his legs came around my back.

"I love you too, Otto. I never thought I'd be lucky enough to be with you like this again."

I didn't dare look up at him. I was too worried I'd cry, and I didn't want to make this even more emotional than it already was. After everything we'd been through, I was ready for some damned happy times for once.

My fingers worked the waistband of his pants down, revealing his long, hard dick. My mouth watered at the sight of it, and I went straight for the tip, sucking it in and tonguing the slit to taste the salty drop there. I felt his legs squeeze tighter around me, and I nestled myself lower between his thighs.

Seth's long fingers still massaged my head lightly and caressed my face as my mouth went to town on his cock. His gasps and moans punched through the silence of the house, and I had to keep reminding myself my family wasn't there to overhear us.

"Jesus, stop or I'm gonna shoot," he gasped.

I almost laughed. "I'll bet you say that to all the perps."

His mouth opened in surprise before his face widened in a grin. "Shut up, asshole."

I took the opportunity to shove my index and middle fingers in his mouth causing his eyes to roll back. He knew exactly what I was doing as memories must have assaulted him the same way they did me.

Once my fingers were good and wet with his saliva, I brought them down to his hole and put my mouth back on his shaft.

Seth Walker was a sucker for a blowjob that included sneaky fingers.

I worked his hard cock with my mouth as I slowly pushed my middle finger inside of his tight channel. He was so fucking tight; I realized he hadn't been breached in over a decade.

"Baby, you okay?" I asked.

His eyes opened and looked right at me for a few beats until I noticed he was the one crying.

I pulled out and crawled back up to kiss him softly on the lips. "Shit, what's wrong? Did I hurt you? Do you want to stop?"

He dashed angrily at his face. "Fuck. Ignore me. Goddammit, I swear I'm not normally so fucking emotional."

I was taken aback by his reaction.

"Seth, it's just me. Don't you dare apologize to me about having feelings. I get that you have to be the big strong cop most of the time, but that doesn't mean you have a heart of stone. What kind of cop would you be if you did?"

"I don't want to be a crybaby, for god's sake. I want to fuck."

I couldn't help but smile. He sounded like the teenager I'd fallen in love with. "Oh, sweetheart. We're gonna fuck. Don't doubt that for a minute. But what made you upset?"

His chin wobbled some more when he looked at me, and fresh tears escaped.

"You always ask if I'm okay. You always look out for me, Otto. My whole life you've tried to protect me and make sure I didn't get hurt. And now this. I hurt you worst of all, and I don't know if I can live with myself now that I can't just ignore it any longer." He sniffled and blew out a breath. "When I was in Minnesota, going through college and becoming a parent and then training to be a cop, I could put this all away and pretend that it happened in a different lifetime. It wasn't easy, but I at least could do the whole out of sight, out of mind thing. But now... seeing you? I can't run away from it anymore, and it's killing me."

I lay on my side next to him and brushed my thumb across his damp cheek. "Well, you can stop that shit right now, because I'm looking at it completely differently. When you left, and again when you broke things off between us, I thought my heart wouldn't survive. I thought I'd never again be able to see you, touch you, laugh with you. And, god... it hurt so badly. *Back then.* But now? Jesus, Seth. Now I *have* you. You're here in my arms, and I never in a million years thought I'd be lucky enough to feel this way again. So, don't you see? It's the opposite of sad. It's fucking amazing. The hurt part is over, and the good shit is just beginning."

He smiled a watery smile at me and leaned in to kiss me softly on the lips. "You're the best person I've ever known. How can you possibly forgive me so easily?"

I ran a hand down his neck to his chest. "I'm only forgiving you so I can get in your pants."

He barked out a laugh and it made my heart swell to see the smile come over his blotchy face. He turned on his side to hug me. "I'll take it."

CHAPTER 15

WALKER

Dear Walker,

Well, as it turns out, SEAL school (BUD/S) is hard. Really fucking hard. So now I'm training to serve on a submarine.

I know, I know. Don't say it. I've already heard it from Saint plenty. But I haven't felt symptoms of claustrophobia since I was little. Remember that time when we were like ten and we got stuck in Mr. Parnell's doghouse? If you hadn't held my hand the whole time, I think I might have lost it.

I know what you're thinking. "Otto, you did lose it." But not as badly as I would have without you.

I was always better with you.

Wilde

(Unsent)

SEX WITH OTTO WILDE was both familiar and different. His body wasn't caught in between a teenager's and a man's any longer. It was all man.

His muscles were dense and hard under tight skin. There was no denying his time in the military. Ink covered places that had been virgin skin before, and I was tempted to map all the new images with my tongue. I'd already seen some of the more obvious ones like the American flag on his left forearm and the lariat around his right biceps. But when he'd been naked in the shower and in bed the night before, I'd been too brain dead from lust to pay much attention to anything other than the feel of him and my own skyrocketing heart rate.

Now that we were lying bare-chested together with my pants half off, I was experiencing a familiar brain-dead sensation.

"When is your divorce final?"

His question was like a bucket of cold water on my excitement.

"Ah... Next week, supposedly. Honovi said to plan on being available Thursday for the judge to sign off on it."

"And how is Jolie handling it? Is she looking forward to being able to date again?"

"Can we... can we maybe not talk about her right now?" I asked. "It's kind of doing pathetic things to my dick."

Otto's forehead creased in concern. "Seth, I didn't plan on us sleeping together until your divorce was final, so I guess I just wanted a little reassurance to help me feel like I wasn't quite the homewrecker your *wife* is making me out to be. It would make me feel better knowing she's looking forward to her chance to sleep around too, you know?"

Leave it to Jolie to cockblock me from afar. "Well, she hasn't said anything about it. In fact, all she's done is make me feel like a homewrecker too. So, see? You're not alone there."

Otto moved away from me to sit up on the edge of the bed, resting his elbows on his knees. "Fuck."

"Yes. Let's."

He turned back to look at me with a smirk on his face. "You know I want to more than anything."

"But?"

"But as fucked up as this whole situation is, she's right. I *am* part of the reason for your divorce."

"That's not true. When she and I got married, it was supposed to be just for the purpose of Tisha's legal paperwork. Then when I offered to stay married and help provide her that stability for the early years, I specifically said it was until Tish went to school. That would have been three years ago, Otto. The only reason I didn't push the divorce is because I didn't have a pressing reason to make it happen. Now I do."

"Yeah, me," he muttered. "Like I said, *I'm* the reason."

I moved over and laid my hand on his bare shoulder. "Even if you hadn't been here. Even if you were still overseas and career military, I would have needed to divorce her and move on, Wilde Man. I wasn't going to be celibate my whole life. I want a true partner. And as much as I worried I'd never find someone to love as much as I love you, I wasn't willing to go my whole life without at least trying."

Otto turned and pulled me into his arms, kissing me and scratching our unshaven cheeks together.

"I wouldn't have wanted you to spend your life without someone to love," he said. "I hope you know that."

"Of course I do. And I feel the same way. Now, can we please find our stash and fuck?"

I needed the emotional words to be over for now. I felt raw and vulnerable, too close to crying again. If I could just get Otto to shove his hard cock into me and let me lose myself in the feeling of being filled by him again... well, then, I could escape this feeling of my skin being too tight.

"Lie back." Otto's voice took on a similar command tone that always put me in just the right mood. For a brief moment, it was like I was seventeen again being bossed around by my dominant high school boyfriend.

I fucking loved every minute of it.

After sliding the scrub pants the rest of the way off, I scooted back on the mattress and waited. Otto stood up and went to the closet to find the loose baseboard panel we'd stashed all kinds of shit behind over the years. He came back and tossed the tube of lube at me before untying his own drawstring and lowering his pants to the floor.

My mouth filled with saliva. His thighs were thick with muscle. There was a large tattoo on his right hip and I realized it was his horse, Gulliver. I felt my cheeks tighten in a smile as I reached out to run my hand over it.

"Love this," I said with a chuckle. "You're so fucking gaga over that horse."

Something funny crossed his face, and I lifted an eyebrow in question.

Otto cleared his throat and turned around so I could see the ink on his back. "He's not the only thing I'm gaga over," he said softly over his shoulder.

I ran my hands up his back, noting the curved line of his siblings' initials in birth order along his side, some kind of submarine tattoo on the back of one calf, and what was probably the GPS coordinates of the ranch at the top of his spine.

Then I saw it.

If you'd shot an arrow through his heart, it would have come out in the center of the tattoo I saw last. The one of two little boys sitting side by side fishing off a dock. It wasn't just any dock. It was the crappy little dock where we always fished together growing up. And it wasn't just any two little boys. It was us. Eight-year-old us from the summer when we met.

I ran my fingers over every detail before leaning in to run my lips over it.

"Luckiest day of my life," I breathed as I tasted him.

Goose bumps came up all over his skin, and I ran my hands everywhere to soothe them. My lips moved up to the nape of his neck and sucked in a mark above the ranch GPS coordinates. He leaned his head forward as my hands slid around to his front and explored the bumps of his abdomen and the hair leading up to his chest.

His body was everything I'd never known I'd wanted. Tall, muscular, inked, plenty of hair except for the super-short buzz cut on his head... he smelled amazing and his voice had matured into an even deeper rumble than before. His eyes were the same bright green with new depths of something in them I had yet to determine. Fear, maybe... hurt... or had he seen shit while in the military that had become a part of him that way?

Otto turned and took my chin in his big hand, holding me still while he devoured my mouth. I moaned into him in relief that he was taking charge.

"Lie down, Walker," he said in a rough voice that went straight to my already pulsating dick and made it even drippier than it had been a second ago.

I scrambled back on my ass and lay with my head on the flat pillow and my legs open in invitation. My cock alternated between pointing straight up my belly to my face and standing up to point toward the top bunk above us. It knew exactly what it wanted. I couldn't remember this much precum dribbling out of me, even when I'd been a horny teenager and Otto had looked at me with that goddamned cowboy wink of his.

"Tug your balls for me." His adult voice rumbled the same words I'd heard years ago when we'd fooled around. The guy had been obsessed with watching me play with myself. My hands immediately went to my sack and pulled it gently away from my body. I couldn't help but close my eyes and groan in pleasure.

"That's it. Just like that, Seth. Spread your legs for me, baby, and bend your knees. I want to see all of you."

Oh god.

I did as he said and moved my other hand along my inner thigh to the warm skin behind my balls. One hand pulled up my sac while the other moved lower to run light fingers over my hole. My eyes were still closed, but I heard the sharp intake of breath and a rumble in his throat.

"Touch me, Otto," I begged.

The touch was light at first, and started at one ankle. He ran hands up and down the hair on my legs to my inner thighs, stopping with his thumbs pressing lightly into the crease between my upper thighs and groin. His fingers flitted featherlight across the tightly pulled skin of my shaft before beginning the trek back down my inner thighs. What the fuck was he doing? He was going the wrong way.

That was when I remembered with sudden clarity the man was a master edger.

"No!" I barked before I could stop myself. My eyes opened wide and locked with his. His own eyes looked feral and already half fucked out.

"No, what?"

"Do not edge me, motherfucker. I know what you're doing, and I will cut you. I swear to god, Otto Wilde. Don't even think about it."

His face broke into a guilty grin that was goddamned adorable.

"But I love edging you. You're so easy to tease."

"Otto." I wasn't proud of the whiny tone, but I was desperate.

He stretched his large body up over me and leaned in for a kiss. While I lost myself in the taste and feel of his mouth again, he must have searched out the tube of lube. Within seconds, I heard a *snick* sound and felt the cool gel hit my hot hole on the thick pads of two of his fingers.

It felt so fucking good, I accidentally bit down on his bottom lip.

CHAPTER 16

OTTO

Otto,

The baby turned one today, which means I only have four more years before I can come running after you like a desperate psychopath.

Just kidding.

Kinda.

Walker

PS - starting my second year of college in a few weeks. Can't stop wondering which school you chose.

(Unsent)

SETH WALKER WAS EVEN SWEETER and cuter than when we were kids. He was so responsive to me, and in much the same way as he wore his heart and his emotions on his sleeve, he wore his desire all over his skin and face.

His chest and neck were blotchy red and his cheeks were flushed a gorgeous berry color. His lips were plump and raw from kissing my stubbled face and his eyes were the same clear blue that had been visiting me in dreams since I was a child. Right now, they were pupil-blown and half-lidded, and I couldn't get enough of seeing him so desperate for me.

As I pressed my fingertips against his entrance, he squirmed so badly, he bit me.

"Ow," I said, pulling back and testing the spot with my tongue.

I could tell he hadn't meant it because his face was guilty. But instead of apologizing the way he normally would have, he surprised me.

"That's your first warning," he said, sticking his chin out defiantly. "The next bite will happen significantly farther south."

"Mmm, farther south," I mused. "That reminds me of something I meant to do."

I wiggled down until I was sucking his cock and fingering his ass at the same time, listening to the breath punch out of his lungs in one big whoosh.

"Oh fuck. Oh Jesus. *Otto!*"

I knew he wouldn't last long with that combination so I slowed my sucking down and sped up the fingering to stretch him out as quickly as I could without hurting him. He began babbling incoherently and begged me to let him come. Every time he got close, I pulled my mouth off him and concentrated on relaxing his tight channel until I felt like he could accept me without hurting too much.

"Fucking stop that shit and get on with it, dammit!" he cried out.

Bingo. That's all I needed to hear.

I grinned up at him. "Just a little more stretching?"

"Fuck you," he mumbled, knowing I was teasing him. "I hate you."

I crawled up until we were face to face again. "You love me."

"Pfft." He huffed and blushed at the same time. God, I loved him so fucking much.

"You sure about no condoms?"

He met my eyes and nodded seriously. We both knew it wasn't a decision to be taken lightly, but we both also knew that we could trust the other not to endanger us.

I reached down to grab the lube again and spread some on his cock before adding some to mine. Even that felt amazing, and I had to grit my teeth against the sensation. It was obvious both of us were going to blow as soon as I entered him.

Since the two of us had started sleeping together when we were sixteen, we were no stranger to lightning-fast fucks. We'd learned long ago that there was plenty of energy for multiple rounds when you were that horny.

I positioned myself at his entrance and looked down at him before pressing in.

"You're so beautiful. I love you," I said.

His eyes filled and became blue pools that held me completely entranced. "I love you too," he whispered. "Forever."

I tilted my hips forward and felt his tight resistance. My eyes fell closed as a groan came out of both of us. A few more pulses of my hips before I broke through the initial resistance, feeling his scorching channel clench around my cock.

"Mpfh," I cried, leaning my forehead down on his shoulder. "Fuck, you feel so good, baby. Oh god."

He hissed and squeezed my ass cheeks, pulling me in as if he wanted me to go faster or harder. "More."

"Shh, deep breath, baby. Not gonna slam you first time out," I said.

"Fuck you. More. Please."

I leaned up and took his mouth in mine, feeling the bruise from where he'd bitten me. His mewling noises came out as I thrust deeper into him slowly but firmly until I bottomed out. His legs came around my back and his arms hooked under my shoulders until we were pressed tightly chest to chest with his hard cock squeezed between us.

I felt the sticky warmth of his precum on our skin, and with every thrust of my hips, his hard dick moved across the muscles of my stomach.

After one more deep draw from Seth's lips, I pulled back onto my knees and took his cock in hand. The lube-slicked shaft pushed in and out of my fist in time with my own growing thrusts into Seth's body. His back arched and his eyes rolled back as he began crying out unintelligible words and phrases.

"Yes! Otto, god. Right there, please," was all I could make out from the babble. My own head was spinning and my entire groin was lit up with the fire of my impending climax. I wasn't going to last, so I stroked him even faster, enjoying the feel of his pleasure literally in my hands for the first time in over ten years. His strong, muscular body was laid out in front of me, splayed on the bed and writhing. He was covered in a thin sheen of sweat, enough to make the hair at his temples damp and his face red.

Suddenly, his body seemed to fold in on itself for the briefest of seconds before arching again and shooting. The move brought back years of memories of his body during sex, and the combination of his tight squeeze and those memories made me lose my shit.

"*Aghhh!*" I thrust deep inside of him and let go, pumping him full of my release and grabbing him by the side of the throat to kiss him as soon as I could take a breath.

We were both heaving with irregular breaths and trying to suck in each other as much as the air around us. The scent of sex and sweat permeated the air and the feel of our damp skin against each other was heaven on earth.

The kiss couldn't last. We were both too winded to keep at it. I stayed inside of his body and pulled him into my arms as I fell to the side to avoid squashing him.

His hand roamed up and down my chest. "That was better than I remembered."

"Same here."

"Your dick is bigger."

"Nah, your ass is tighter."

We both began laughing at the blatant lies, and I quickly slipped out of his body. I kept him close to me though and intertwined our legs together.

"I have an ass full of hot, sticky cum now," he said with a squicked-out look on his face. "I feel debauched."

I ran a hand through his damp hair, leaving it sticking up in short spikes. "You look debauched. It's fucking hot."

Worry suddenly creased Walker's forehead, and I reached out to smooth the lines. "What is it?"

"What if it doesn't work?"

"How do you mean?"

"What if we've grown apart in ways we don't know about yet? What if when you get to know me again, you don't like who I've become?"

I saw the genuine fear in his eyes. "I've had that worry too, but ultimately I guess the answer is, we'll cross that bridge when we come to it. When I saw you directing the scene last night and helping get that kid out as fast as possible, I fell back in love with you even more. When you showed up at the bunkhouse exhausted and heartsick for those families, I knew you had the same heart you've always had. And when I saw you with Tisha that day I was on Gulliver..." I blew out a breath. "Seth... you're smart, capable, sweet, and loving. You're responsible and dedicated, loyal and committed. How the hell could the crux of what I've always loved about you be so different that I wouldn't want to build a life with you anymore?"

He nodded and leaned in to tuck his face against my chest. His arm came around my back to squeeze me in a hug.

"I'm so damned lucky you're here. I never thought I'd be so lucky."

We lay in comfortable silence for a little while before he pulled back and looked at me again. "Why *are* you here, Otto?"

"What—"

He cut me off before I could ask what he meant by that.

"You know exactly what I mean. Don't play dumb. Why did you leave the navy early?"

I felt my stomach twist with familiar nerves. "It's a long story."

"We have time."

I looked around as if my old bedroom held some kind of excuse not to tell the story I wasn't quite ready to tell. I saw a framed picture of me on Gulliver and Saint on a horse named Quicksand. I looked back at Walker.

"We need to go get ready for Tisha's visit."

Seth barked out a laugh so sudden, I jumped.

"You are so fucking predictable," he said. "You seriously just used a child as an excuse?"

131

I felt my chin jut out in juvenile defiance. "It's true though. We have to go get ready. Lord only knows what time it is, and we promised her."

Seth pulled away from me, putting a palm on my chest. "Okay, Wilde Man. I'm going to let you stall on this conversation exactly *once*. But then we're going to talk about it. We're not moving forward without being totally honest with each other. Agreed?"

I nodded and tried to shoot him a look of gratitude. "Agreed."

As we made our way to the nearest bathroom to clean up, I wondered if Seth Walker would be quite so in love with me when he learned what a goddamned coward I really was.

CHAPTER 17

WALKER

Walker,
* I hate submarines.*
* No really, I fucking HATE submarines.*
* Otto*
* (Unsent)*

I WASN'T STUPID. I knew whatever had caused Otto and Saint to leave the navy was something serious. On the drive to Amarillo earlier that week, Doc and Grandpa had implied they thought Saint left because Otto was getting out. Even they didn't know the reason yet and seemed to think maybe I did.

I didn't.

And honestly, I wasn't sure if I was ready to hear it. Whatever it was seemed to be haunting him a little. Not enough to dampen his smile or make him seem like a different person, but enough to put shadows in his eyes. I wondered if, when it came down to it, I'd have to push him to get him to tell me. I didn't want things to be like that between us, but at the same time, I wasn't sure I would be okay with him holding back such an important part of himself.

I tried not to think about it as I made my way home to change and get Tisha ready for the horse ride, but it wasn't easy. The more he stalled, the more I realized it was something serious enough to be eating at him.

When I entered the house in scrubs, Jolie's jaw dropped. "What happened to you?"

"A bad auto accident last night. Spent some time at the hospital with the families." I let the implication that I'd gotten the scrubs at the hospital stand because I honestly didn't want to deal with another conversation about Otto right now.

"Did anyone die?"

"No. It was four teenagers. One lost a lot of blood but got transfusions in time. Another had their leg crushed and will require several surgeries, I think. They were lucky. Seriously lucky. When I pulled up to the car, all I could think about was what if it was Tish and her friends six or seven years from now?"

Jolie walked over to me and slid her hands around my waist to hug me. I knew she meant it as a gesture of comfort, but I also knew I probably smelled like Otto Wilde's spunk.

"Um," I said, gently extracting myself from her embrace. "I'm gonna take a shower and get ready to take Tish on that horse ride."

Her nostrils flared, and her eyes narrowed. "Where were you before you came home? Where did you sleep last night?"

Did I tell her the truth, a lie, or that it was none of her business?

"Do you really want to know the answer to that, Jolie?"

"Yes," she snapped. "I'm your wife. Of course I do."

Luckily, before we got into a fight about what it meant to be my wife, Tisha came barreling into the room. "Uncle Seth! Is it still okay for me and Cody to ride the horses?"

"Cody *and I*," Jolie mumbled.

"Yes, Tishie-poo. Just let me clean up and get dressed, okay? Then we can go pick up Cody from Uncle Johnny and Aunt Beth's. Did you eat lunch already?"

She nodded and continued jumping around with excitement while I disappeared into the bathroom.

When I was finally dressed and ready to go, I asked Jolie if she wanted to join us. Obviously, I hoped like hell she'd say no, but I extended the invitation anyway as a gesture of goodwill. If I was still going to be in Tisha's life, then Jolie was going to have to get used to seeing Otto Wilde. I just hoped Otto would be okay with it.

"Is *he* going to be there?" she asked, looking down at her fingernails.

"Yes. *He's* the one who issued the invitation. And *he's* the one whose horse it is," I replied. "And *he* has a name. It's Otto."

"Don't you think I know that?"

"I wasn't sure. The way you were talking..."

"I'm pretty sure he wouldn't want me there," she said. I could tell it was a test.

"Not true, actually. He's a kind person, Jolie. He would want you there because he would want you to see your daughter ride a horse for the first time. He would never want you to miss that experience." And I knew as soon as I said it, it was the truth.

Jolie's face seemed to soften. "Well... when you put it like that..."

I smiled at her and reached for her hand. "Come with us. It'll be fun. I promise. Haven't you ever wanted to ride a horse?"

Her cheeks turned pink and she looked like a teenager again the way she was when I met her. "Yeah. Actually, I have. Do you think he'd let me ride one too?"

I tugged her out the door where Tisha was hopping around like crazy waiting for me to unlock the vehicle.

"I'm sure he will if I ask him nicely."

Otto, please forgive me for doing this to you, I thought before getting in the car and starting the engine.

When we pulled up to my brother John's little rental house, Cody was already outside chomping at the bit. I got out to make sure John and Beth knew we were there, and I made my way into the house through the front door.

"Anyone home?" I called out.

"In here," Beth said from the direction of the kitchen.

I made my way through the tiny space they used as a dining area, stepping over some of the kids' toys and narrowly escaping knocking over a stack of mail hanging halfway off the table.

Beth was just taking something out of the oven when I came in, and John was grabbing a beer out of the fridge.

"Just wanted to let you know we were here. We'll probably bring Cody back before dinnertime unless you think he wants to stay over at our place tonight?"

"Can I stay over too?" Their daughter Eliza came racing into the kitchen from the family room with eyes as big as saucers. She was always trying to be a part of Cody and Tisha's friendship, and I felt sorry for her every time she got left out. I'd already tried begging my brother to let Eliza come ride the horses with us, but he and Beth thought she was too young. Inviting Hal had been pointless. He was way too cool to hang with his uncle and cousin, not to mention he was a stereotypical moody teenager.

"That's up to your mom and dad, sweetheart," I said, looking at John and Beth. John just rolled his eyes and Beth looked at me with a new strangeness in her eyes I hadn't noticed before.

"Is Jolie going to be there?" she asked.

I was taken aback by her question. "I... assume so?"

"Then that's fine."

"Wait." I glanced down at my niece. "Liza, honey, why don't you go upstairs and pack up your pajamas okay? Your mom or dad can drop you off at Tisha's place before dinner."

As soon as she wheeled back on out of the room, I shot a look at my sister-in-law. "What the hell are you implying?"

John held up a hand. "Wait just a second, Seth."

"No. I won't wait just a second, John. Are you saying that from now on if Jolie isn't around, I'm not allowed to host my freaking niece and nephew for a spend the night? Please tell me that's not what you're saying here."

Beth's eyes flicked over to her husband's, and I saw the answer clear as day. My stomach rolled with the implication. "What? Seriously? Like Jolie was the only thing keeping your kids safe in my house all these years?"

I could hear the panic in my own voice, but I couldn't help it. This couldn't be happening.

My brother clasped my forearm and squeezed to get my attention. "Seth, calm down. Beth just feels like maybe we should keep the overnights on nights when Tisha is at Jolie's house. If the two of you aren't going to be living together anymore, we're concerned about what people are going to think. I mean, you have to admit a single uncle having little kids over for—"

I put my hands over my ears. "Don't. Jesus, John. Please. Please stop and listen to yourself." I could feel the anger rising up inside and part of me knew I needed to leave before it reached the surface. "I have been a parent to a little girl for nine years. Do you think I have once done anything inappropriate to that child?"

Just saying the words made me feel like I was going to vomit.

Beth looked at me with a strange kind of sympathy in her eyes. "No, of course not. We're not saying that at all. We just think it's in everyone's best interests to keep your reputation intact, Seth. What would it look like if the Hobie sheriff was accused of hosting groups of young children overnight at his house?"

I looked at John, sure my eyes were pleading with him not to be the man he was showing himself to be. "I'm your *brother*." I turned to Beth. "It would look like Sheriff Walker was allowing his little girl to have a freaking sleepover, Beth. That's what it would look like!"

"Uncle Seth!" I turned to see Tisha's bright face as she ran into the kitchen to fetch me. My nephew Hal hung back in the doorway, looking for all the world like he'd heard every word we'd said. "Come on! We don't want to be late. Gulliver is waiting for us."

"Be right there, Tishie-poo," I stammered. Once she was gone and Hal seemed to have disappeared too, I turned back to John and Beth. "Just tell me one thing. Is this about the divorce or is this about me being gay?"

Beth looked away, but my brother wasn't quite so chickenshit.

"We just think it would be better for everyone if the two of you stayed together. It's worked for all these years. I don't see why you can't keep up appearances with Jolie and then go have your fun in secret down in Dallas every once in a while the way you probably did in Minnesota. Can't you see what this bullshit is doing to Mom and Dad? You move back down to our tiny southern town and then throw divorce and gay into the mix? Jesus, Seth. Stop and think what you're doing to the rest of us. To that little girl!"

I couldn't believe what I was hearing out of my own brother's mouth.

"From the day I left here until we moved back, I never once hooked up with someone outside of my marriage. I have slept with a sum total of one man. The same man I'm going to spend the rest of my goddamned life with. And if you think that makes me trash, or if you think I don't deserve to share my life with someone I love the way you and Beth do, then fuck you, John."

I turned to leave before doing something I'd regret. All I wanted to do was find Otto. I needed to get to Otto.

Jolie's eyes widened when I jumped in the SUV and slammed the door. "Everyone buckled up?" I asked, trying to calm down for the sake of the kids.

"What happened?" she asked as I pulled out of the driveway.

I noticed my hands shaking on the steering wheel. "John and Beth, ah… are upset about the, ah… split."

Jolie turned around to glance at the kids in the backseat before turning back to me. We had talked to Tisha several times about the divorce. She was very aware of what was going on and why, but I still didn't want to use the "D" word too often around her.

"What did they say?" she asked softly.

I cleared my throat. "They wanted to make sure you were going to be around tonight to chaperone the sleepover."

"I don't understand."

I glanced at her again before looking back at the road. "They wanted to make sure it wasn't going to be… a one-*man* show." Again, speaking in code to try and outwit a couple of nine-year-olds wasn't always easy, but it seemed like the two of them were pretty chatty in the backseat. Hopefully they weren't paying attention.

"Why would they... Oh." She seemed to think about it for a minute. "Well, I can see where they're coming fr—"

"Don't," I growled. "Please don't, or I swear I'm going to lose it, Jolie."

She didn't say a word for the next few minutes, and when we pulled down the long stretch of drive to the Wilde ranch, I asked her for a favor because I knew if I didn't, I was going to burst wide open in front of the kids.

"Can you give me a few minutes to talk to Otto in private before you bring the kids in the barn?"

CHAPTER 18

OTTO

Otto,

There's a blizzard going on right now and we're under at least eighteen inches of snow. It's all I can do not to daydream of riding the trails with you on a hot summer day.

I can picture your smoking hot butt in tight jeans and the T-shirt damp with sweat and sticking to your back. You'd be wearing the green ball cap that day so I would know what was in store for me at the end of the ride.

Wherever you are, Otto Wilde, I hope you're happy and getting plenty of saddle time on a good horse.

Love always,
Walker
(Unsent)

I WALKED out of the barn when I heard the vehicle approach, but the minute I saw Walker hop out, I knew something was wrong.

Before I even had a chance to say hello, he strode past me toward the barn door. "Come with me for a minute?"

I turned back to Jolie and was surprised to see her give me a slight nod of approval. Her eyes looked concerned, and I wondered if maybe

I'd misjudged her before. I turned to follow Walker into the barn. The minute I rounded the corner out of sight of Jolie and the kids, Seth was on me.

His entire body trembled as he clung to me in a tight hug.

"Whoa, whoa," I said, bringing one hand around his back and one to cradle the back of his head as he buried his face in my neck. "You okay? What happened?"

He didn't say anything, just held on.

"Shh, it's okay. You don't need to say anything," I assured him. "Whatever it is, I'm sorry. I'm here for you. You're not alone."

His trembling didn't stop, and I had a hard time trying to determine if it was sadness, fear, or anger causing it. I heard the kids outside squealing with happiness. They probably ran over to the fence closest to the car to look at the horses I'd saddled who were tied to the rail at the side of the barn.

"If this is about bringing Jolie, you know I don't mind. Right?" I asked softly. Sure, it had been a surprise, but I'd never keep her from seeing Tisha have a new experience.

"No, it's not that."

I rubbed Walker's back and murmured reassurances into his ear as he steadied his breathing and calmed down.

"Sorry," he mumbled after another minute. "I didn't mean to ambush you."

"Ambush me anytime, Sheriff," I teased softly. "Do you want to tell me what happened?"

He pulled back from the tight hug and looked at me. I ran a hand along his jaw.

"My brother and his wife don't think it's 'appropriate' for me to be alone with the kids overnight anymore." He used finger quotes for the word *appropriate*.

I felt acid begin to bubble in my gut. "What? Are they serious?"

He rolled his eyes, but I could see the shame in them. I wanted to kill his bastard of a brother.

"They're serious. And they had the audacity to claim it was for my own good, the good of my reputation as sheriff."

"What did Jolie say?"

"We haven't really had time to talk about it. The kids were in the car."

I smoothed my hands down his chest and rested them on his hips. Sunlight streamed in through the open windows of the barn, and I knew we couldn't keep the kids waiting much longer.

"Well, if you want to talk about it some more. I'm here. You're not alone. And, hell, if they have a problem with the single-parent thing, maybe you won't be single for long," I said with a wink. Walker's face flushed and his eyes widened. "But if it's the gay thing... ain't nothing we can do about that now, can we?"

I leaned in for a quick kiss and then patted his ass before pulling away to gather the bucket of little apples I'd brought.

"Thank you," he blurted.

I turned around to look at him and was surprised to see a wide grin on his face. "For what?"

"For talking me down. You're always so cool under pressure, Otto. Always have been. It's like nothing rattles you."

"You're wrong about that, Sheriff. But that's a conversation for another time. Now let's go show these guys how to ride a horse."

As soon as we came around the corner to where the kids were chatting happily at the horses and Jolie was wringing her hands nervously, the kids squealed and jumped up and down, throwing their arms around each other. I couldn't help but smile at how close they clearly were. It reminded me of my relationships with my own siblings and cousins.

"Hey guys. Who wants to ride a horse today?" I called.

Jolie's worry seemed to dissipate and Walker's stress faded as I introduced myself to everyone and began talking to the horses.

"DemonShanks, did you want to eat, I mean give a ride to, a nice young lady today?" I asked the black mare with the white blaze on her face.

"*DemonShanks?*" the kids screeched.

"Oh, wait. Is this the one with the all-black hooves? I can't see because I'm too tall. Can someone shorter than I am look and see?

They look alike. DemonShanks has all black hooves and Patty Cake has two white socks. Other than that, they're identical."

They squatted down to investigate before jumping up with smiles. "It's Patty Cake!"

I clutched my chest and took two steps back before resting my hands on my knees. "Oh thank goodness. I didn't want to say anything, but I was worried. That DemonShanks... well, let's just say his last rider never came back. But Patty Cake is a sweetheart. She likes long walks in the sun and eating clover. Oh, and apples."

I saw Jolie smile out of the corner of my eye and come a little closer to the black mare. After taking a few apples out of the bucket, I reached out to hand the rest to Walker.

"You want to show Jolie how to give them an apple while I show the kids? You can start with that dappled gray on the end. That's Angie. She's Doc's horse."

He took the bucket from me and gestured for Jolie to follow him. I handed each of the kids an apple. "Okay, first I'm going to show you how to properly greet the horse and let it get to know you. Never, ever approach an animal without your parent's permission or another adult, okay? You never know what their temperament is like ahead of time. Now, in this case, I've picked the sweetest horses we have for today's visit. This chestnut gelding's name is Lego. He's my brother Cal's favorite. I thought maybe you'd like to ride him, Cody."

The little boy nodded his head vigorously. I showed him how to greet the horse and then hold the apple out flat-handed for the horse to take. When those giant lips nibbled the tiny apple off Cody's palm, both kids giggled.

"Now it's your turn, Tisha. This is Patty Cake and she's the horse my Aunt Gina and my sister MJ always fight over. She's a total sweetheart and will take good care of you today."

We repeated the process of meeting the horse and feeding her an apple before I reached over to give one to poor Gulliver who was leaning his neck toward me so much the other horses snorted at him. I overheard Tisha tell Cody about Gulliver.

"That's Mr. Wilde's horse. He's painted."

I chuckled to myself. "He's a paint horse and his coloring is called pinto, which is sort of like patches of brown and white. So Gulliver is a Paint like Patty Cake is a mustang and Lego is a quarter horse."

Jolie and Walker came back over to us and listened while I explained the bridle, reins, saddle, stirrups, and anything else I could think of that was important.

Once I'd covered it all, I handed the kids helmets that Doc and Grandpa had picked up when I originally mentioned inviting Tisha over for a ride. I'd had a classmate in school who got thrown into a tree on a trail ride once and ended up with a head injury. Ever since then, Doc and Grandpa had been sticklers for minors wearing protection on our horses. We had plenty of helmets for adults too, but it was their choice to wear one.

Walker helped me show everyone how to mount up and helped me adjust all the stirrups. I'd tried my hardest not to look as he held onto Jolie's ankle while adjusting hers, but I couldn't help but see it anyway. Stupid tendrils of jealousy wound their way through me, and I tried desperately to remember I was the one who'd been naked in bed with him that morning, not her.

But it was almost impossible to ignore the fact she'd had almost ten years of his life I hadn't had.

Once instructing the kids on how to hold the reins and do some basic maneuvering, I mounted Gulliver and nudged him with my boot heel to start toward the nearest path between two paddocks. I looked back to make sure Walker was bringing up the rear and he tipped his head at me before sending me a wink and smile.

God, I loved that man.

"Okay, everyone. You asked for the trail with the crocodiles, right?" I called down the line, causing the kids to call back to me asking for the one with bunnies and deer instead. Before turning back forward, I saw Jolie flash me a grin.

Progress.

THE FOLLOWING DAY, Grandpa, Doc and I drove the truck to Dallas to gather my things and stop in at my old firehouse to tell the guys good-bye. I'd only worked there a few months, but I at least owed an apology to my friend Tanner who'd helped me get the job. He turned out to be very understanding and told Doc and Grandpa he wasn't surprised at all I was taking the opportunity to work for Evan Paige.

"That guy's hot as hell, isn't he?" Tanner joked.

My jaw dropped.

"What? You don't agree? Total silver fox."

"You're gay? How the hell did I not know that?"

He shrugged and grinned. "I think you weren't looking, Wilde. I tried making a play when we were on the boat together, but you just seemed oblivious."

I shook my head. "What about here? These past few months? We could have gone out, visited the clubs."

He laughed. "Otto. Your head has been in the clouds the entire time you've been back stateside. When you first got here I asked if you wanted to get a drink with me and you told me you weren't thirsty."

Doc and Grandpa laughed and looked at me with knowing glances. I felt my face heat up.

Tanner's eyes softened. "I just figured you had someone already."

"I did. I just didn't realize it at the time," I admitted.

Tanner squeezed my shoulder. "I'm glad. But now I've heard through the grapevine that gay runs in your family, so I'm expecting an invitation to the next Wilde family gathering so I can meet more hunky Wildes. How 'bout it?"

"I'll see what I can do," I said with a grin. "Sounds like a plan. My brother Saint is gay and lives in Dallas, but he's never in town. Too bad the other Dallas brother is the straight one."

"I don't mind the drive up to Hobie and the lake, Otto. After you telling me about the ranch... hell, I'd love a chance to just come and wander around a little. Enjoy the quiet."

Doc reached out a hand to shake. "Tanner, you're welcome at the Wilde ranch anytime. We have plenty of room and don't need any notice you're coming. We'd love to have you."

We had lunch with Hallie and Winnie downtown before packing up my stuff at the apartment and heading back to Hobie. My cousin Felix had offered me his little cabin on the ranch since he'd moved to Monaco to live with his boyfriend. It felt a little silly referring to the king of an entire country as a boyfriend, but that's what he was. Felix had snagged himself a royal without realizing it. I was happy for him. He deserved to be adored, and the man he'd found to spend his life with was crazy in love with him.

When we finished unloading my things into the cabin, I called Chief Paige to let him know I was ready to start as soon as he needed me. He told me to come by the station the following morning to get started.

Once off the phone with the chief, I texted Walker to let him know I was back. Within thirty minutes, he was knocking at my door and tumbling into bed with me.

That night I fell asleep with a smile on my face and feeling like my life was truly beginning. I had a nice place to live, a good job, my beloved grandparents just across the yard, and the love of my life wrapped securely in my arms.

Things were going to be amazing.

And they were. *They totally were.*

Until they weren't anymore.

PART II

BURNING IT DOWN

CHAPTER 19

WALKER

Walker,

I had a dream last night that we were in a secluded cabin somewhere in a snowstorm. No doubt that was my desire to get somewhere cold and fresh for once and away from these sweaty, stinky fuckers I live with, but there was a huge bed with clean sheets, and I sank into your hot body over and over and over again while the storm raged on outside the cabin windows.

When I woke up, I felt the loss of you much worse than I have in a long time. My body remembered yours, Seth, and it missed you with every fiber of its being.

Just like I do.

Wilde

(Unsent)

MAY TURNED into June and life seemed to be perfect. The divorce was final, I'd begun furnishing the house on the lake, and most nights found me naked and pressed up against Otto Wilde's hard body.

During the day I spent most of my hours at the sheriff's office preparing for our big summer festival, the Hobie Hootenanny, over July Fourth weekend. It was a huge event that pulled in people from all over the state for the long weekend. Lake house rentals were booked solid, the water was full of speedboats and pontoons, and every local farmer and craftsman was present to sell their prized creations. Music groups performed round the clock for four days straight and it was known all around as an event not to miss.

In addition to the usual Fourth of July antics like driving and boating while intoxicated, there would undoubtedly be damage to public property, violations of noise ordinances, illegal firework usage, and all kinds of other law enforcement challenges. This required us to bring in extra help, which meant lots of training and coordinating for the sheriff's office.

Thank god for Luanne. She's been doing her job for ages and knew exactly what we needed to do. I pretty much just followed along and did what she said. That particular afternoon I was busy going over the credentials of a few of the temporary security personnel we'd hired to assist us.

It wasn't the first time I'd heard Otto's voice over the emergency band, but it was the first time I heard his voice tight with fear.

"Responding to suspected arson inside tornado shelter at seventy-eight nineteen Abernathy."

I immediately pictured Mr. Jones's rusty old underground shelter. It was one of those ancient prefabricated cement boxes in the ground and probably had canned goods from the 1970s in it as well as highly flammable items like old polyester bedding and kerosene for lamps.

Otto was claustrophobic. *Highly* claustrophobic.

"Lu, I'm going to see what's going on at Mr. Jones's," I said, quickly grabbing what I needed from my desk before bolting out the front door to my vehicle. "Call me if you need me," I said over my shoulder.

When I pulled up, the largest of the two Hobie trucks was parked out front and the crew was gathered in the backyard by the shelter. I hustled out of my vehicle and approached the backyard. The smell of smoke was apparent so it obviously wasn't a false alarm, but I heard two of the crew members laughing and ribbing Otto.

"Dude, it was your call, remember. That means you do it, Wilde

Man." I recognized the voice as a guy named Daevon we'd played soccer with in high school.

"Fuck," Otto muttered, coming up from the last two steps of the shelter and into the summer sun. When he removed his SCBA mask, I noticed his face had black smudges on it, and I could see the remains of some burned-up items on the ground near the shelter's entrance.

"What happened?" I asked.

The four firefighters turned to me, and I saw Otto's face flush even redder than it already was from the heat of the day and the fire.

"Probably some kids pulling a prank," Otto said. "Accelerant on a pile of blankets and paper. Luckily since most of the shelter is cement, it was mostly just smoke and easy to contain. Why are you here?"

"I..." I looked around, realizing he probably didn't want me to call out his claustrophobia in front of his station mates. "I was just passing by and heard the call. Thought I'd lend a hand if needed."

Otto knew I was full of shit. He'd always been able to see right through me.

One of the other firefighters placed a meaty palm down on Otto's shoulder and grinned at me. "Stick around, Sheriff. You'll get to see Wilde here climb a tree."

I raised an eyebrow at Otto. "Is that right?"

"I'm making them lift me up on the ladder. I ain't climbing shit in this gear," he scoffed. His face had a grin on it so I knew it was nothing bad, but I still wondered what they needed to get in the air for when the fire had been underground.

The guys made their way back to the ladder truck and removed their turnout gear until they were back in the simple dark uniforms of the HFD. Otto's shirt stuck to his body with sweat and his pants were gloriously tight on his narrow waist and full ass. His biceps pulled the fabric of his short sleeve cuff tight, and I could just barely see a peek of his lariat tattoo poking out. Miles of tanned Otto skin lay hidden underneath that uniform, and I imagined running my tongue along it later that night.

I fucking loved drooling over that man in his uniform.

"Sheriff?"

"Huh?" I turned to see who'd called me and found all four fire-fighters staring at me with cocky grins.

Daevon laughed. "Uh, we asked you if you wanted to ride in the bucket with your boy. What do you say?"

As much as I would have loved to play fire truck with my boyfriend, I shook my head. "Oh, ah… no, thanks. What are you guys doing, anyway? What's with the bucket ladder?"

And since when is our relationship totally cool with the Hobie firehouse?

"Mr. Jones's cat didn't take kindly to our efforts this afternoon and took his leave up the old oak tree," another guy said, gesturing up at a tiny little fur ball in the huge tree. "Lieutenant Wilde is gonna fetch it."

"That ain't my cat," Mr. Jones said from his front porch. "I don't have a cat."

I turned to face the little old man. "Hi, Mr. Jones. Sorry about all this," I called.

"You gonna catch those fuckers that torched my place?" he spat.

Otto spoke too low for Mr. Jones to hear on the porch. "Yeah, Sheriff. You gonna catch those fuckers?"

"Shut up."

"What did you say?" Mr. Jones shouted from the porch. "You tell me to shut up, son?"

"No, sir! I said they're going *up* to get the cat."

"It's not my cat, goddammit. It's just a stray."

"I understand," I assured him. "But I believe they'd like to rescue it all the same."

Otto and his buddies were cracking up at this point, and I was wishing I'd never decided to come help the asshole.

"I gotta go," I mumbled, turning to my car.

"Stay," Otto said with a chuckle. "Please stay. Don't you want to see how exciting it is on the Hobie fire force?"

"Riveting," I cracked. "I'm starting to wonder if this whole thing wasn't a prank call at my expense."

"Load up, Wilde," one of the men called. "Poor little fire kitten needs your big strong manly self to rescue it. When I tell you to smile, pose pretty with the kitty so I can Instagram it."

Otto rolled his eyes and shot the guy the bird before climbing up onto the vehicle and making his way to the bucket.

Just then my radio squawked with a call from Luanne to report to another scene.

"Gotta go. Be careful up there," I called. "Wouldn't want you to get taken down at a scene by a four-pound feline."

"Smart-ass," Otto said, turning his middle finger to me. "If I end up mauled to death by this hell cat, you're the one who's going to have to tend to my wounds."

Wolf whistles split the air as his crew went wild with the teasing. I felt my face heat up as I headed to my car. I heard the guys telling Otto he was the official new cat daddy.

"Like hell I am," he said. "I'm not a cat person. I'm a horse person."

"Maybe your horse needs a new barn cat," someone suggested.

"I am not taking this cat home. You can forget about it right now. One of you is taking it to the animal shelter after work," Otto said.

I smiled as I realized he was happy at his job and worked with a great bunch of guys. I already knew everyone at the firehouse from having worked with them for more than six months already, but it was still reassuring to see them all giving each other hell in the way men did when they enjoyed each other's company.

It didn't surprise me at all when I let myself into Otto's cabin that night, to find him asleep on the sofa with a tiny flame-orange kitten curled up on his chest.

"Don't say a word," he mumbled in his half-sleep.

I couldn't help but laugh. "Hello, Fire Kitten. Or shall we call you Scaredy Cat?"

"No, something more manly. Blaze maybe. Or Spike." His eyes were half open and he looked edible.

"Mm," I said, thinking. I sat on the edge of the sofa near his hip and ran my hand along his stubbled cheek before petting the soft puffball on his chest. "How about Princess or Puffy?"

"Tiger. Hellcat maybe," he said with a pout. "Ooh! I know... DemonShanks."

I laughed. "No DemonShanks. First of all," I said, scooping up the tiny little thing, "it's a girl cat. Secondly, it's the sweetest-looking baby ever. I'm thinking Gidget."

"Fang."

"Gatito. Means *little cat* in Spanish."

"Asesino. Means *killer* in Spanish."

The kitten's wide eyes blinked sleepily at me, and its whiskers were about ten times the size of the little thing's face.

"Otto. This is the cutest little baby ever."

"Then you keep it," he grumbled, turning his back to me. "They made me bring it home."

"You are so fucking adorable; I can't stand it. They didn't make you do shit."

"Mmpfh."

I kissed the kitten's tiny head and placed her down on the floor so I could take her place on top of Otto.

"Missed you," I murmured. He shifted under me, and I lay down on top of him, leaning in to press my lips to his and take the kiss I'd been craving all day. Other than the fire call earlier, I hadn't seen him in three days because of our schedules and my time spent working on building a birdhouse with Tisha now that she was out of school for the summer.

I felt his hands come around me and immediately squeeze my ass, pulling our cocks together in a slow grind. Otto smelled like the shower he must have taken when he got home, but when I heard his stomach growl, I knew he'd waited for me to get here before eating dinner.

"You hungry?" I asked between kisses.

"Starving."

"Want me to cook?"

"No food, just you in my mouth," he groaned against the skin of my jaw.

I reached between us and did my best to unfasten my uniform shirt and pull it off before chucking it away. I sensed Otto's hands undoing the Kevlar vest next and felt the cool relief of it being removed from the damp undershirt below. After peeling that one off too, I was finally bare chested and able to appreciate Otto's air conditioning on my skin.

"Ahh. God, so much better."

His hands came up to rub through my damp chest hair, and his grin was self-satisfied. "Agreed. *So* much better."

I tugged off his T-shirt and ran my hands across the rounded curves of his broad shoulders and biceps before moving to unfasten his fly. "Pants off. Naked time."

His grin got wider, all teeth and promise. "I love naked time with you, Sheriff."

I continued unfastening his pants until I had to stand to remove my own and yank down his.

My eyes bugged out.

"No underwear? Naughty, naughty Wilde Man."

I rewarded his commando decision with a few licks to his hard length while reaching down to cup his balls and tug on them a little. His gasp and subsequent moans jacked me up even more. My cock was dripping all over his leg.

I pulled off his dick and looked up at him. "I want to fuck you over the back of this couch."

Otto's pupils blew and his breathing sped up. "Hell, yes." He scrambled up and turned around to hug the back of the couch, presenting me with the most fuckable ass in Texas. "Lube in coffee table drawer," he grunted.

I squeezed an ass cheek with one hand while reaching for the drawer with my other. I knew full well where the lube was. This wasn't our first living room rodeo. We'd had so much sex in the past month, it was a wonder we hadn't burned our dicks clean off from overuse.

Once I had a finger full of slick, I ran it down his crease to his hole and popped it right in. I'd been spending so much time with my fingers in his ass lately, there wasn't much need for prep. Most of the time it was a combination of fingers and mouth since he was usually the one fucking me when we had anal sex, but every now and again, something seemed to come over him and he wanted me inside him.

I wasn't complaining.

I loved having sex with Otto any way and every way imaginable. There was nothing the two of us could do together naked that wouldn't excite me. I still felt unusually lucky every time he chose to be with me, and part of me worried it was all going to come to a horrible end one day.

It didn't take long before I lubed myself up and knelt behind him, aiming my dick toward his hole and grabbing onto his hips as I pushed in.

One of Otto's hands came back to clutch mine, and I intertwined our fingers before squeezing him in reassurance. "I love you," I whispered behind his ear before dropping kisses there and tilting my hips more.

He gasped at the invasion and pushed back slightly to take more.

"Seth," he breathed.

"Mm." I licked the salty skin of his neck and nibbled along one of the tendons down the back of his neck. "God, you taste so good and feel so tight around my cock, Otto."

"*Seth*." His hand gripped mine as his other steadied him against the back of the couch as I picked up the pace of my thrusts. "Fuck, yes."

I ran my free hand down the muscular, inked plane of his back and finished with a squeeze to a rounded cheek. I pulled the cheek to the side so I could see my cock sliding in and out of his stretched entrance.

"Jesusfuckingchrist, Otto," I murmured. "God, that's hot."

I rubbed a thumb at the top of his crease, a spot I knew he loved to have me tease.

"Mm-hm, like that. Just like that, baby," he said, almost to himself. He seemed to be in the zone and feeling nothing but pleasure. I reached around to grab his erection, pressing my entire front against his back before stroking him off.

His hand was shaking as it fluttered near mine, almost as if he didn't know whether to help me stroke him off.

"Shh, I have you. Just let go, sweetheart," I cooed in his ear.

The sensations in my own groin were reaching critical mass, and I needed him to get off before I blew. His cock was swelling and pulsing in my hand until suddenly he was coming with a shouted curse.

I stroked him through his climax as I continued to thrust in and out of him. It wasn't until he took a swipe of his cum off my hand and reached back to offer it to me that I lost it. I pressed in deep and cried out, trying my hardest to muffle my scream into his skin instead of deafening him.

The blast of pleasure shooting through me made my legs feel weak and tingly and my balls and ass feel amazing. Otto's body was still squeezing periodically as he had aftershocks, and it seemed to milk every last bit of energy out of me.

We finished in a sweaty heap on the sofa, panting and clinging to each other before one of us started us both off laughing. I opened my eyes to see his happy face when I noticed an angry feline perched on the back of the sofa staring down at us with all the judgment in the world.

"Oh shit," I said with a laugh. "Your cat doesn't like us having sex. Maybe we should name her Prudy."

"Phoenix. Medusa. Thor."

"Chastity. Lady Bug. Babette."

Otto stood up and winced, reaching a hand back to cup his ass. "Ouch. You pounded the hell out of me."

"Hell yeah, I did," I said proudly, puffing up my chest a little.

That earned me a laugh. "Shower time, Sheriff. I'm hungry, and it's a 10-39 situation."

Ten-code radio speak for *Urgent, Use Lights and Siren.*

"Ten-four, Lieutenant."

Once we were cleaned up and had on shorts and T-shirts, Otto suggested grilling some steaks while I fixed a green salad.

"Want me to text Doc and Grandpa to join us?" Otto asked from the open door of the fridge.

"Sounds good." I noticed a couple of bottles of Patron sitting out on the counter. "You planning on getting us all shitfaced or something?"

He looked to where I was pointing and grinned. "Nah, those are left over from Cal's twenty-first birthday party months ago. I noticed them in the bunkhouse and asked Doc and Grandpa about them. They said I should grab them so any minors coming to visit couldn't get their hands on them. You want a shot?"

"I think I'll stick with beer. Last time I had tequila I ended up..." I thought about one of the times I'd slept with Jolie. There was no way Otto wanted to hear about that. "I ended up regretting it."

When Grandpa and Doc arrived, they brought a tin of homemade oatmeal cookies for dessert. The four of us sat down to dinner outside with beer and some soft jazz music Otto had piped through a wireless speaker somewhere. It was a nice summer night and a couple of large pots of flowers were dotted around the wide deck off the back of the cabin making a nice spot for an impromptu summer gathering.

We'd shared several casual meals like this already with Doc and Grandpa over the past couple of weeks and it was nice to see them so happy together and invested in their grown grandchildren's lives.

"I haven't seen your brother King around yet. Where is he living these days?" I asked Otto between bites of food.

"He travels internationally for work. That's all I know. It's all kind of hush-hush, so we tease him about being a spy. When he's around, he stays with Sassy in the apartment over West's medical practice or in Dallas with Hudson."

"What about Cal? Is he still in college?"

Doc answered this time. "He graduated from A&M last month but didn't walk in the ceremony. He got a job on a boat in the Virgin Islands for the summer, and they needed him to start as soon as he could."

"Wow. That's incredible. I remember he used to swim like a fish. He was always in the lake come summertime."

Otto nodded. "We went down there to see him in March and spent a weekend with him. That's when I was still living in Dallas."

Translation: *that's when we weren't speaking to each other.*

"Ah. I see. Good for him. Does he want to pursue sailing as a career?"

160

The three of them nodded and then Grandpa asked me about John. "How's your brother been? We've talked about Ross but not John."

I shrugged. "He hasn't been the same since Ross died. He was an absolute basket case until he found Beth. She's been a godsend, honestly. She and the kids helped give him something positive to focus on. Beth's kind of become John's security blanket of sorts."

"And he works at the insurance company with your dad, right?" Doc asked.

"Yes. He's an agent. Sells policies. I'm surprised you haven't heard from him yet trying to sell you guys something." I'd said it as a joke, but I noticed the two older men share a quick glance. "Oh, maybe he has?"

Doc shrugged and looked down at his plate. "Well, we told him the truth. Weston's been working with a friend of his in Dallas for years on the ranch's policies."

I reached out and squeezed Doc's arm. "Doc, you don't have to justify your decisions to anyone, least of all me. It's none of my concern. John and I aren't that close anyway. Hell, I think he's closer to Jolie and Tisha than anyone since Cody and Tisha spend so much time together."

We moved on to other topics and away from the subject of family. They talked about traveling to Monaco soon to visit with Felix and Lior, and discussed the likelihood of Otto's parents, Bill and Shelby, returning to the States for a visit anytime soon. Apparently the chances were slim to none. It seemed they were happy there.

"That reminds me, Otto, they were talking about selling off the house, but wanted me to ask you if you'd rather have it," Doc said.

"Why are they thinking about it now?" he asked.

"Apparently, someone's interested in it."

Otto looked at me with furrowed brows before looking back at his grandfathers. The house Otto had grown up in bordered my parents' ranch. "Isn't is part of the Wilde ranch?"

"No. We separated it out and signed it away to them when the house was built. And now that we're no longer ranching cattle, we don't much need all the land we once had. It's more a question of whether or not one of you kids wants to live there."

Otto looked at me again with a raised brow this time. "Do we want to live there?"

I felt a warmth flood my chest and placed a hand there before realizing what I was doing.

"Can... can we think about it?"

"Sure. I'll tell the Realtor to tell the interested party to simmer down a little," Doc said with a smile.

Within forty-eight hours, it was a moot point.

The house was torched and burned straight to the ground, taking decades of Otto's family memories with it.

CHAPTER 20

OTTO

Otto,

I drew my firearm in the line of duty for the first time today. Scared the piss out of me. A teenager was whaling on his mother in a domestic disturbance. She had allegedly bought his younger brother the wrong kind of basketball shoes which led to an argument which led to a screaming match which led to him smacking her. When she smacked him right back, he went to town on her with his fists.

Thank god the drawn weapon was enough to make him stop. But the whole thing was such a reminder of how quickly one small thing sets off a series of escalating events, you know?

Wherever you are, Otto, please be safe,

Walker

(Unsent)

THE DAY before I got the call that my childhood home was on fire, I had a simple plan. I wanted to buy Tisha a pair of cowgirl boots for her birthday. She was turning nine in two days, and I knew she would flip out if Walker gave her a nice pair of boots for riding.

He already had several gifts for her. A new pair of sunglasses she'd wanted and a gift card for games on her iPad among other things. But he wanted to give her something that would really make her lose her shit. There was a western wear shop on the edge of town that would have ropers in her size, but the problem was, he couldn't remember what her size was. So he'd sent me to Jolie's house to check. He'd texted Jolie first to ask her, but she couldn't remember offhand either. Then he asked his mom, who was looking after Tisha for the day while her parents were at work. But she said Tish only had a pair of cheap rubber flip-flops on that didn't have the size listed.

Jolie had agreed to let me go over to the house to check the closet. Things between us weren't good necessarily, but ever since I'd let Jolie come over with Tisha a few times to ride the horses, we'd found a mutual neutrality that worked for us. We didn't talk overmuch or spend any time alone, but she'd smile nervously at me and I'd nod my head back politely. It wasn't much, but it was ten times better than it could have been.

In the meantime, Tisha went back and forth between Jolie's house and Seth's lake house. The issue of him being alone with her wasn't brought up again except when Cody or Eliza wanted to stay over, and then everyone so far had just tried to keep sleepovers to the nights Tish was at Jolie's. I knew it was killing Walker, but he told me he wanted to keep the family strife down as much as possible right now by not making waves.

It killed me watching him take it on the chin, but I had to respect his decision.

When I pulled up out front of Jolie's house, I used the numeric keypad code to let myself in. I'd noticed John's car out front of their parents' house on my way down the ranch drive and wondered if the Walkers were watching John and Beth's kids too.

When I entered the house, I made my way back to the room Walker had indicated and found the pair of shoes he said were most current. After taking a quick snap with my phone to make sure I got the size right and didn't forget it, I quickly let myself back out of the house and keyed in the code again to lock the door behind me.

Just as I was hopping into my vehicle and smiling to myself about how cute Tisha's collection of toy horses spread out all over the family room was, I could have sworn I smelled smoke. I made my way around the outside perimeter of the house trying to follow the smell to the origin before calling it in. Sure enough, there was a pile of dry debris smoldering up next to the foundation of the home. It was almost like someone had deliberately raked a pile of dry leaves and branches from the nearby stand of trees over to the side of the house and then dropped a live flame on it.

It was small enough that I was able to quickly douse it with a nearby garden hose before it spread, but I really did wonder how the hell it had started.

I dialed in to work and got Chief Paige on the line. "Hey, Chief. I was running a personal errand and put out a little brushfire in someone's back yard. I'm not sure, but my gut says someone deliberately started it… Is this something I should worry about or…"

"Whose backyard?"

"Jolie Walker. She lives in the smaller house at the Walker ranch."

"I'm not doing anything right now, so I'll come take a look. It's pretty dry these days. I mean, it's not out of the realm of possibility it could have started the way brushfires always do."

"It's in the shade, sir. I agree it's unlikely it would be arson, but I'd feel better if I wasn't the only pair of eyes on it."

"Be there in ten."

I hung up and dialed Walker.

"Sheriff Walker," he said in the voice that could make me come six ways from Sunday.

"Hey, it's me."

"Well, hello there, hot stuff. Did you find what you needed at the house?"

"Yeah, I did. She's a size four. But I also found a little brushfire out back."

"What?"

"Evan's on his way over to take a look. It's a little strange."

"Is it still burning?" His voice went from flirty to serious in a nanosecond.

"No, no. I put it out easily with the hose. It's fine. It's just… I don't know, Seth. Something's off about it. It's like someone deliberately piled up dry tinder right up next to the house and then set fire to it."

"I'm on my way," he said in a rush.

"Baby, stop. It's fine. There's no rush. Please don't kill yourself on your way here, okay?"

"You gonna stay there and wait for me?"

"Yeah. I'll be here."

I heard a car crunch across gravel out front and went to greet the chief. But when I got around the side of the house, it was John's car that had pulled up.

"What's going on?" he asked. The man I'd known since I was a little boy eyed me like I was a bank robber.

"I came to check on something and noticed a little brushfire out back," I said, pissed at myself for sounding so defensive. "I put it out. It's fine."

More tires on gravel. We both turned to see Chief Paige's big HFD vehicle picking its way down the driveway.

"If it's fine, why's the damned fire chief here?" he accused.

"Just protocol," I lied. The man was being an asshole. If Jolie didn't have a problem with me stopping by the house when she wasn't there, I didn't see why John should.

Evan got out of his vehicle and greeted John with a big smile. "Hey, John. How's it going? I heard the insurance business booms in the summer when the lake house rentals and sales pick up. Are the tourists keeping you busy?"

Chief Paige was known for being a big personality around town, someone who knew everyone and always made a point to say hello. John fell under his spell the same as everyone else.

"Hey, Chief. Sure, things are fine. How about you?"

"Just making sure Lieutenant Wilde here is following procedure by making sure a brushfire is completely doused before leaving the scene. I'm sure it's fine."

John looked from me to the chief before making his way back to his vehicle. "Well, I'll see you two later. I'll let Jolie know what's going on when I get back to the office." That last part was clearly aimed at me.

As soon as he was gone, Evan rolled his eyes at me and nodded toward the backyard. "Show me what you got." We began walking, and he couldn't help but mumble under his breath, "Guy's a prick."

I snorted. "You said it, not me."

"He was looking at you like you were robbing the place, for god's sake. Does he think you're that desperate for a bunch of women's clothes and plastic toy horses?"

I froze where I stood before swiveling to face him. "Repeat that, please?" I asked with a knowing grin.

He must have realized what he let slip about the toy horses because his face turned engine red.

"Fuck."

I barked out a laugh and let out an enormous whoop, pumping my fist in the air like an idiot. I felt bubbles of relief fizz inside my whole body, and a weight I didn't even realize was still on me suddenly lifted.

"What the hell's your problem, jackass?" he grumbled. "I didn't even get lucky. Just came over for dinner one night."

"Oh my god. You have no idea how good it is to hear Jolie is dating. Jesus fuck, Walker and I have been waiting for this. No more feeling like we're the bad guys."

"Glad to be of service. Now shut the hell up and show me where the fire was."

Familiar footsteps rounded the corner, and I looked up to see my angry boyfriend's long, lean legs eating up the yard.

"What happened?" he snapped.

"Chief Strange-Love had dinner with your wife," I blurted. The grin on my face was probably maniacal, but I couldn't help it.

"Say what now?" Walker turned to Evan with a glare.

Suddenly, my excitement fizzled. "Oh. That's... that's unexpected," I muttered. "Dammit. Here and I thought it was good news. 'Yay, Otto, now we don't have to feel so guilty. Now you aren't the only home-wrecker in the bunch...'"

Walker blew out a breath and turned to me with forced patience. "Baby, seriously? First you tell me that someone may have set fire to my daughter's house and then you tell me someone's dating my ex-wife? What the fuck is next?"

"I ran into your brother and confirmed he still hates me. Bad things come in threes?"

He blinked at me before yanking me to him for a quick kiss. His lips were gentle despite his stress, and I tasted the remnants of coffee on his mouth. "I'm sorry. How are you? I should have asked that first of all. Did you get hurt putting out the fire? Let me see your hands."

Evan stood there staring at us with a goofy grin on his face. "Holy shit, that's the sweetest thing I've ever seen. You two are sickening."

I had little dancing hearts in my vision and couldn't see much other than Seth Walker at the moment. "I'm fine. Not hurt."

"Good. Now tell me what happened."

I tried to shake myself out of the little mini love stupor and focus on what I'd found. I pointed out the burned area even though it was obvious and then described what I found before I put it out with the hose.

Evan took some photographs before squatting down and raking through the debris after putting on a pair of gloves. He pulled out one of the half-burned sticks and peered at it more carefully. "This is from a cherry tree." He looked around at the obvious lack of cherry trees in the backyard.

"There's one at my parents' house up the drive," Walker said. "Maybe Tisha brought it home with her one day and was playing with it in the backyard."

"You have a dog? Some reason she'd be playing fetch?"

"No."

"Hm."

He rifled through some more and met my eye, holding up a recognizable lump of wet cardboard tubing. I sighed.

"What?" Walker asked. "What's that?"

I pulled a rubber glove from where I knew Walker kept a pair in his uniform pants pocket and put it on before reaching for the item from Evan. "It's what's left of a toilet-paper-roll fire starter. You put lint or other flammables inside of this, shove a match into it, and then stick it under the pile of leaves and sticks. Usually it burns so quickly it's never detected. But in this case we got lucky. I must have doused it before it finished burning."

"Wait... wait. Doesn't that mean that whoever started this fire did it within *minutes* of you discovering it?" Walker asked.

Evan's eyes met mine again before he answered for both of us.

"Yep."

CHAPTER 21

WALKER

Seth,

I know we're not speaking anymore, but I can't stop thinking about you... can't stop loving you. Just because you're being a selfish ass, doesn't mean my heart has suddenly learned how to beat on its own, without yours.

It's particularly bad right now because I'm home on leave in Hobie. Hobie without you is just the worst.

I did something ridiculous today. You'd totally laugh and make fun of me for it, but I don't care. Mom showed me two antique wedding bands from the Canadian side of her family and wondered if any of us kids would ever want to use them one day or if she should just get rid of them. One was her grandfather's Celtic band and the other was her own father's wedding band with the inscription Maintiens le droit inside it. It means "Maintain the law" in French. My grandfather on that side of the family was a Mountie, remember? It reminded me of you, so before I could think about it, I asked if I could have it. You always said you wanted to be a cop, Seth. And you're going to make an amazing one. If we ever see each other again, I want you to have this ring.

I hope wherever you are and whatever you're doing, that you're happy and fulfilled. I think I can survive being apart if I can think of you happy somewhere in the world.

. . .

My love forever,
   Otto
   (Unsent)

IT WAS the middle of the night when I got the call about the house fire at Bill and Shelby's old place. I was dead asleep at the lake house, and Otto was at his little cabin on the ranch. It was a rare night the two of us had ended up sleeping apart. The dispatcher's tone pealed through my quiet house, and I was up dressing within seconds.

"Walker," I grumbled into the phone, expecting an auto accident or domestic disturbance that needed extra hands. But what I hadn't expected was to be told about a massive inferno between the Wilde ranch and my parents' place.

"Where? Say again?" I barked.

The overnight dispatcher repeated the address, and I felt a momentary relief it was an abandoned house on fire rather than one with people sleeping in it. But then I realized it was only separated by some woods from the house where my girl lay sleeping in her bed.

"I'm on my way," I told the woman before clicking off and dialing Jolie. The phone rang and rang while I finished dressing and grabbed my things before racing to my vehicle. No answer.

I hung up and tried again. Still no answer. Next I tried my parents' house phone and heard my father's voice pick up on the fourth ring. He sounded surprisingly awake for the middle of the night.

"Hello?"

"Dad, it's me. Bill and Shelby's old house is on fire and it's serious. I can't get a hold of Jolie, so I need you to go over there and move them to your place please in case the fire spreads through the trees."

"Oh, wait... hold on a minute, Seth."

I heard muffled noises before my father came back on, and I assumed he was getting dressed. "Got it. I'm headed there now. I'll get them. Don't you worry."

On the way to Bill and Shelby's I thought about how selfishly thankful I was Otto wasn't on duty, but I realized he needed to know what was going on. I dialed his number but got no answer. I tried again with the same result. It wasn't like him to mute his phone. The Hobie Fire Department was small enough that if extra hands were needed, they'd call him in on his days off. For that reason alone, both of us slept near our phones at night.

I tried one more time.

When I got to the scene, I realized he'd already learned of the fire and responded to join his crew in fighting the blaze. I spotted him pulling on turnout gear as fast as he could before grabbing an SCBA with a tank from the truck. What the fuck was he doing with breathing gear when he wasn't going into the dwelling?

As soon as the mask was on his face, he raced toward the house.

"No!" I shouted, running for him at top speed as soon as I figured out what he was up to. "Otto, stop!"

Either he didn't hear me or he ignored me on purpose. His single-minded purpose was apparent in the way his legs ate up the ground. Several of his crew tried to stop him, but he entered the side door by the kitchen before anyone could get to him.

"Otto!" I screamed again. I got almost to the door before someone practically tackled me to keep me from entering the place. "Stop. We need to stop him," I said in complete panic mode. The house was already partially engulfed and walking into it was a suicide mission.

My heart hammered with fear, and my lungs were quickly filling with smoke. I realized the person holding me back was Daevon. "You have to go in there and get him," I said. "You have gear on, Dae, you can get him."

He shook his head. "Chief is on the radio chewing his ass out but said no one goes in after him. It's too dangerous."

I scrambled out of his arms and raced for the truck. I knew where they kept the extra sets of gear. I'd fucking go in there myself and get him if I had to. What if he got hurt? What if a beam fell and brought him down again like the branch had during the Amarillo fire?

Chief Paige grabbed my arm. "Sheriff, I can't let you do that."

"Someone has to go get him. If you won't, I will." My voice was hoarse and begging, my throat scorched raw from the thick smoke on the scene and my screaming at Otto to stop. "Why did he do that? There's no one in there."

Suddenly, Otto's figure appeared in the doorway again and he stumbled out onto the driveway. I raced for him and noticed he was carrying something in one of his hands. A photo album maybe.

Smoke and heat came off his gear in stifling waves as I approached.

"You motherfucker!" I screamed. "How could you do that?"

His head popped up and he noticed me for the first time, eyes going wide and mouth dropping open. He pulled his SCBA off and dropped it and the photo album to the ground before holding both hands up to me in defense.

"Seth, I..." he began.

"Fuck you. I fucking hate you, you selfish prick. *Fuck. You.*" I'd never been so angry and terrified and heartbroken as the moment I'd seen the love of my life walk into a burning building. I turned around and raced for my vehicle, not even bothering to man up and be the goddamned sheriff on the scene of an emergency.

One of my deputies was assisting Chief Paige who was the incident commander, but I still acted unprofessionally by lighting out of there as if the house wasn't the only thing on fire.

I got as far as the end of the long ranch drive before I realized my face was wet and my chest was heaving. By the time I pulled back up at my lake house, I was practically hyperventilating.

I didn't even notice the headlights behind me the whole way.

"Seth, wait!" Otto called, jumping down from his vehicle and racing toward me. He'd removed the turnout gear and most likely left it on scene with the truck, and he was only in an old T-shirt and athletic pants. The T-shirt stuck to his sweat-slick skin and there were soot marks here and there across his face where the mask hadn't covered him. It had been a while since he'd buzzed his hair and the short locks were sticking up half damp and every which way from his helmet.

"Baby, please," he called. "Please don't be mad at me. I had to go in there."

That was when I realized he was crying too. He never cried. The man was stoic as hell. I was the crybaby of the two of us. The sight of the tear tracks on his face and the sadness in his eyes gutted me.

I raced toward him and grabbed him in my arms in a tight hug.

"You fucking jerk," I cried into his neck. "No you didn't. How could you do that? What was so important?"

He pulled back with a sniff and shrugged.

"I grabbed my mother's favorite photo album. It's like the family Bible, Seth. I couldn't tell her it was gone. Those are her babies in there."

I pulled him in tight again, caught between wanting to kill him and kiss him.

"Don't you understand that this is her baby right here?"

CHAPTER 22

OTTO

Otto,

Tisha woke up in the middle of the night last night with croup which means she was struggling to catch her breath. I thought I was going to lose my shit. My fingers couldn't dial 9-1-1 fast enough. Even though my mind knew the breathing sounded worse than it was, thinking your loved one is in danger.., god, it's terrifying.

I hope you never know what it's like to fear for your child's life. But then again, it comes with the territory of being a parent, and I've always wanted you to be a parent. You'll make an incredible father, Otto. You are smart, kind, loving, and fun as hell. If only I could be there when you meet your first child. Wilde Man, I'd give anything in the world to share that with you.

Love always,

Walker

(Unsent)

I DIDN'T TELL him the truth. Well, not the whole truth anyway. I hadn't just wanted to save my mother's photo album. I'd wanted to save some of the letters I wrote to him and never sent. And more than that, I'd wanted to grab the wedding band that had been in my mother's family for generations. Originally, there were two of them. One was her grandfather's and one was her father's. When she'd showed them to us, she'd handed the rings to Hudson first, but he'd passed one of them to me without even saying a word.

It was our maternal grandfather's ring, and I wished with my whole heart I could give it to Seth Walker one day.

I wanted to tell him the truth—that the idea of putting that ring on his finger was one of the only things that gave me a sliver of hope during some of my darkest times. I'd stashed it in my secret spot in my closet, but thanks to the make-out session we'd had previously, the little velvet bag it was in had been left sitting on my dresser. Had it still been in the wall, there was no way I'd have been able to get it before the fire overtook me.

Things really did happen for a reason.

After we made our way into the lake house and showered off the smoke and sweat, we fell asleep wrapped around each other's naked bodies under only a thin cotton sheet. I was still burning up from going into the house on a hot June night, and the only thing keeping me pressed up against Walker's warm body was my desperation to reassure him I was here and I was safe.

He seemed to drift off to sleep pretty quickly, but I couldn't shut my brain down. I'd texted the chief to ask if there'd been any thought as to the origin of the fire, but he'd insisted I get some rest and we could talk it through later the following day.

I'd already known he'd call in an arson investigator simply because of the coincidence of the little blaze behind Jolie's house. The investigator we used was a woman named Teresa who worked out of a neighboring county. Luckily, we didn't have enough arson in our county to justify having a specialist on staff full-time. I knew the chief was well trained in arson investigation, but for something like this, he'd be sure and cover all his bases with an expert.

I closed my eyes and retraced my steps as I'd entered the house, begging my subconscious to present some kind of explanation for my parents' house burning down. It had been hot, yes, and dry too. But my parents' house was surrounded by nice, old hardwoods that gave plenty of shade to the house on and off throughout the day. It wasn't like any part of the house burned in the sun all day. Not only that, but it had withstood the Texas summer sun for over thirty-five years and never caught fire before, so what could have possibly changed?

The only thing I'd learned from my quick trek through the house was that the fire seemed more pronounced in the back bedroom on the main level and all along that corner of the house. As I raced up the stairs, the blaze seemed to be moving outward and upward from there. Had there been accelerant? Had there been lines or flames in unusual formations? I racked my brain to remember what I'd seen, but I couldn't make out anything of note.

I must have finally fallen asleep because when I awoke, the light in the room was completely different. I looked at the clock on Walker's bedside table and saw it was quarter past noon. The sheriff himself was clinging onto me like a baby koala, and I took the opportunity to run my fingers up and down his muscular back to the rounded top of his ass.

He had a gorgeous body. I thanked my lucky stars he hadn't spent the past ten years in clubs being fondled and fucked by any man who found him attractive. If I pictured him with other men, it made me feel stupidly protective and snarly, which wasn't exactly fair. I hadn't been celibate during those same years. Maybe he felt that way about guys I'd hooked up with.

"Why are you frowning?" His sleep-muffled voice blew warm puffs of air across my chest.

"Hm? Oh, just picturing you fucking random strangers in a club," I confessed.

His eyes opened wider. "Why? That make you hot?"

I chuckled and dropped a kiss on his head. "No. Not so much. Quite the opposite, in fact. More like it makes me homicidal."

"We could always go into Dallas one night and test it out. See if the reality makes you hot or homicidal. I've never been."

I turned to look at him more fully. "You've never been to a dance club?"

"Not a gay club, no. I went to a country music dancing place once because Jolie made me go. That hardly counts."

"I'd love to take you to a club in Dallas. I'll bet we could get Saint and some of my other siblings to go with us. Hallie loves to go dancing. Cal's legal now too, come to think of it. Too bad he's not around. Hudson won't go. He doesn't like to dance or stay out late for that matter. We made him go one time and he got hit on the whole time."

Walker's face turned serious. "You heading into the station today?"

I nodded. "Evan was calling in Teresa what's-her-name, the arson lady from Valley Cross. I want to see what she has to say."

Walker sat up and turned to put his feet on the floor, revealing all of that satiny-smooth skin I'd been fondling on his back. I wanted to taste him again and felt my mouth begin to water at the thought.

"Hop in the shower, Wilde Man. If you're a good boy, I'll let you suck me off before you go."

He looked back over his shoulder and winked at me.

God, I loved him. The man was a fucking mind reader.

And I was prepared to be a *very good boy*.

By the time I got to the firehouse, it seemed an investigation was in full swing. I met the woman from Valley Cross, who'd asked me to call her Teri.

"Lieutenant Wilde, may I ask you a few questions about the nearby incident a few days ago and your recollection of events last night?" she asked.

"Yes, ma'am."

I wondered if I was going to be reprimanded for defying the chief and entering the premises or if he'd give me a little leeway since it had been my childhood home.

We sat down in a small meeting room with a table and four chairs in it. There was a window that looked out on the main engine parked in its bay, but Teri immediately closed the blinds to give us privacy.

"Let's start with the incident at Mrs. Walker's house the other day. Can you tell me what you found?"

I described arriving at the house and making a quick trip inside to find the shoes in Tisha's closet before locking the house back up and noticing the smoke smell.

"And how did you know from what direction the smoke was coming?" she asked, pen poised over her notebook page.

"I could smell what direction it was coming from, and when I turned my head that way, I saw a thin plume of smoke coming from around the back of the house."

"When you approached the property that day, did you notice anything out of ordinary? Any vehicles or people you weren't expecting?"

I opened my mouth to tell her no when I remembered wondering why John's car was at his parents' house.

"I don't think it's important, but I did notice that John Walker's vehicle was at the main ranch house. I assumed he'd stopped by to see his parents. But, no, I didn't see any vehicles or people near Jolie's place."

"Do you know this John Walker?"

"Yes, ma'am. He's the brother-in-law of the woman who lives in the house where the fire happened. He's Sheriff Walker's younger brother."

She was all business as she asked the questions, and I realized she was probably the closest thing to unbiased as we could get on this. That was a good thing.

Wasn't it?

"And what kind of relationship does John Walker have with Jolie Walker? Do you know?"

"I… I… Surely, John didn't set a small fire behind his sister-in-law's house," I said. "Why would he do something like that? It doesn't make any sense."

She stopped writing and looked at me with that smile that said, *I'm the one asking questions here.*

"I don't know their relationship besides being in-laws. That day was the first I've seen John in over ten years," I explained.

"And what is your relationship with the homeowner, Jolie Walker?"

I blinked at her.

Well, that was complicated, wasn't it?

"I'm... I'm dating her ex-husband?"

Again with the smile. "Is that a question, Lieutenant?"

"No. Sheriff Walker and I are in a committed relationship," I said more firmly.

"And Jolie?" she asked.

"Um... we're... we get along fine. We see each other about once a week when she brings her daughter to my family's ranch and rides horses with Sheriff Walker and me."

"Would you say you're friends?"

"Not really. More like acquaintances, I guess."

Teri made several notes in her book before looking back up at me. "According to witnesses, you appeared on scene within seconds of the first responders last night. How did you discover that your parents' house was on fire?"

That was an easy one.

"I couldn't sleep so I got up to check on one of the horses in the barn. She'd been acting a little off earlier when I'd fed and watered her, and I wanted to make sure she wasn't showing signs of colic. I smelled smoke in the air and worried there was an incident the chief might need my help with."

"How did you determine where it was coming from?"

"I went back to my cabin and turned on the emergency band."

"And still got there that quickly?"

"I live on the same property. Well, I mean... my parents' house is... *was* on the edge of Wilde ranch property, and I live in a cabin on the ranch."

"Who was the last person to enter your parents' home?"

"I don't know. Presumably the arsonist," I said, getting annoyed. Why did I feel like a suspect suddenly?

Teri's head popped up. "What makes you say this blaze was set on purpose Lieutenant Wilde?"

Fuck.

"Ah, because I'm being questioned by an arson investigator, for one," I said with a little too much sarcasm. "Because I can't, for the life of me, think of any other reason a fire started on that property. The power wasn't on. The gas was cut off. The sun doesn't reach any part of the house long enough to heat things up. You tell me, Teri. Was it arson?"

She ignored my question. Not rudely, really, just professionally.

"According to the after-incident reports, you put on turnout gear and went into the dwelling."

Uh-oh.

"Yes, ma'am."

"Can you tell me why you broke protocol and entered an unsafe situation in which there was no human rescue or recovery needed?"

I swallowed. "It... it was my childhood home, ma'am. I wanted to grab a couple of items of significant sentimental importance."

"Such as?" She was still taking notes.

I cleared my throat. "My mother's favorite photo album and her grandfather's wedding ring," I said, looking down at my clasped hands on the table.

At that, Teri stopped writing and reached across to squeeze my wrist. I looked up to see sympathy on her face.

"I'm truly sorry about the loss of your childhood home, Lieutenant. I can't imagine how hard that is for your family. I've been told your parents live in Singapore currently. Do you have brothers and sisters?"

I snorted but at the same time felt my eyes begin to smart. "Yeah. There are ten of us."

"Ten?" Her eyes widened. "Wow. I'll bet there were heaps of good memories made in that house."

I thought of the time Hudson and West tried piercing MJ's ears for her in the downstairs bathroom and created a bloodstain in the tile grout the shape of Florida, the time my dad tried to surprise my mom with her very own space after secretly renovating a storage closet so it could fit a recliner and white noise machine, the time Saint and I put five tiny frogs in Hallie and Winnie's underwear drawer, and the countless times I snuck Seth Walker up the backstairs and into my room for a sleepover in elementary school and then later a hot-and-heavy make-out session when we were in high school.

"Yes, ma'am," I whispered. "Lots of good memories."

When the interview was finally over, I learned I was on paid leave for a few days.

"Why?" I asked the chief.

"Give you and your family a chance to process things, Wilde. Don't worry about it."

"Is this about me breaking protocol? Because—"

"That too. I'm going to take some time to think about it. I'm of two minds about it, Wilde, and I don't want to rush into anything here. Let's let Teri do her thing while you take a few days off, okay?"

"Yes, sir."

On the way back to the ranch, I finally got up the nerve to call Grandpa and Doc. They'd been calling and calling, but I'd texted I had to go into work and couldn't talk.

"Otto, that you?" Grandpa asked. "You okay, son?"

"No," I admitted. "Can I come over?"

Silence for a beat before an angry Grandpa snapped over the line. "Goddammit, Otto. Since when do you need to ask to come to our house? What the hell?"

I was taken aback by his tone. "Sorry. I'll be there in ten."

I hung up before he had a chance to respond and called Walker.

"Sheriff Walker."

When I spoke, I could hear myself losing it. "Seth?"

"Baby, what's wrong?"

I felt my throat sting and my jaw ache. Maybe it was just because I hadn't slept well.

Yeah, right.

"They put me on paid leave."

"What? Why?"

"I don't know. But, Seth... I felt like they were questioning me. Like... like they thought maybe I'd set the fires."

"That's fucking ridiculous," he said angrily. "Evan Paige knows you didn't set those fires."

"Well, whatever. I'm headed to Doc and Grandpa's. We're going to have to call Mom and Dad to tell them about the house."

"I'll meet you there," he said quickly, like he was going to disconnect the call.

"Wait," I blurted.

"Yeah?"

I thought about what I wanted to tell him. What I wanted him to know. That his support, his belief in me was something I would never take for granted. I wanted to tell him how much I loved him to the very marrow of my bones.

But instead, I croaked, "Thanks."

OF COURSE it was another goddamned love posse, Wilde style.

When I pulled up to the ranch, I recognized my aunt Carmen's Subaru, Uncle Hollis's Lexus sedan, Hudson's SUV, West's truck, and MJ's Mini Cooper. Before I even had a chance to turn off the engine, the dogs were flying off the porch and Doc was wringing his hands in the doorway. I saw Nico walk out behind him to hand him Pippa. That guy knew exactly how to bring down Doc's blood pressure. Give him a baby to hold. Worked every time.

I saw his face soften into a smile as he dropped a kiss on her messy hair and cuddled her close to his chest. Her chubby thighs stuck out from some kind of shirt thing that snapped together in the crotch. The fat rolls were impressive and her bare feet kicking in Doc's grasp were cute as hell. Seeing her was enough to put a smile on even my face, which was saying a lot.

"Hey," I called to Doc as I approached. I leaned in and kissed his cheek before dropping a smooch on Pippa's head. "How the hell did everyone get here so quickly?"

Nico stepped forward and gave me a completely unexpected hug. I stood there in shock for a minute before returning it. The guy was pierced and inked to within an inch of his life but was still one of the sweetest men I knew. My brother was lucky as hell to have found him.

"I'm so sorry, Otto," he said into my shirt.

"Thanks," I mumbled. "It was just a house and some stuff. At least no one was hurt, you know?"

He pulled back and gazed at me. "Sometimes 'stuff' is where the memories live. Don't discount your feelings. Losing your childhood home sucks, plain and simple."

I thought about everything he'd gone through as a teen runaway and knew he, of all people, understood one's attachment to a place, a *home*.

"Yeah. It sucks," I agreed.

Doc dumped Pippa into my arms. "Here, if that ain't a cure for what ails you, don't know what is. Come inside and cool off." He and Nico turned to enter the house.

I pulled my niece in for a snuggle and inhaled her baby scent for a moment to center myself before going inside. She smelled like a combination of some kind of baby lotion or shampoo and crackers. Her tiny hand immediately went for my sunglasses, and I took them off to hand them to her.

Gravel crunched, and I turned to see the Hobie sheriff pull up.

Walker.

He got out of the car looking like every slow motion scene of a hot cop stepping out of a vehicle. It was almost like a porn clip. Thick, muscled thighs in tight uniform pants, a full weapons belt riding on his hips, arm muscles popping out of his uniform sleeves, and aviator sunglasses on his tanned face.

I whistled low in my throat, and Pippa giggled.

Just when I was preparing to walk into his arms for the hug I'd been wanting all afternoon, he took off his glasses and met my eyes.

Shit.

Something was wrong.

CHAPTER 23

WALKER

Walker,

I've been back at Pearl Harbor for several weeks... I met a man. It's weird... I've slept with other people since joining the navy, but this was the first time I actually considered more than just a quick fuck with someone. We went out to dinner, and the date went so well, I stayed over at his place instead of ducking out of there after the sex. We spent the entire next day at the beach together talking and laughing.

How is it that four years after seeing you for the last time, I still feel like I'm cheating on you?! Nick is a good guy, Seth. But he isn't you. And he won't ever BE you. How the fuck am I supposed to go forward into a relationship knowing I'm always going to be settling for second best?

God, that pisses me off. I hope you sleep with some asshole who gives you crabs.

Wilde

(Unsent)

AFTER I'D GOTTEN off the phone with Otto, I'd gotten a call from the arson investigator.

"Sheriff, the fire at the Wilde home last night was definitely arson,"

Teri said, right off the bat. "And as of right now, we can't rule out Lieutenant Wilde as a person of interest."

Even though Otto had kind of warned me they were thinking along those lines, hearing it spoken by an authority on the matter was extremely disconcerting. "What? That's ridiculous. Give me one reason Otto Wilde would torch his family's home."

"We don't know that he did, Sheriff, I'm only informing you that because he's a person of interest at this time, I'd like to suggest you tread lightly around him while we look into the matter."

"Tread lightly? What the hell does that mean?"

"It means, Sheriff, you are not at liberty to share information about the investigation with him, including the fact he's a person of interest, and it would be in your best interest to limit communications with him altogether while we get to the bottom of this," she said. "I'm sorry, Seth. This is standard advice I'd give anyone else in your position. I believe you know that."

I'd always known Teri to have a sterling reputation. A no-nonsense investigator who was both thorough and fair. Deep down, I knew she was only looking out for Otto's and my best interests as well as the best interest of the departments involved.

"I understand," I told her. "I appreciate you keeping me in the loop."

"Of course. And I promise I'll try to get this cleared away as quickly as possible. You have to know I don't want to find out Otto was involved in this any more than you do. But until his name is cleared, we need to keep this investigation aboveboard. Agreed?"

"Agreed."

When I pulled up at the Wilde ranch, my stomach was twisted in knots. How the hell was I supposed to tell Otto I had to stay away from him?

"Walker, what's wrong?" he asked. The man looked so vulnerable holding Pippa to him like he needed every bit of comfort he could get.

"Can we talk in private for a minute?"

I saw the worry in his eyes right away. "Sure, let me just take Pippa in, and I'll be right back. You want something cold to drink?"

I shook my head.

When he came back out to the porch, I was sitting on the swing trying to think of what to say to him.

He sat next to me on the swing but didn't touch me. I reached for his hand and threaded our fingers together, which seemed to relax him a smudge. He looked over at me with a quirked eyebrow.

"What is it?"

I blew out a breath. "I... I have to take some time apart... from you."

His face fell. "I understand."

I reached for his chin and held it so he couldn't avoid meeting my eyes. "Do you?"

Otto swallowed but then steeled himself. "Yes, I do. And I completely respect that. I hope you know I understand you're in a tough spot."

"If by tough spot, you mean not being able to make love to my boyfriend whenever the hell I want to, then yes. I'm in a tough spot," I growled.

His face softened into a grin. "Your loss, Sheriff."

"No shit." I leaned forward and sipped from his lips for a few minutes. "I love you so much, Ottowa Wilde. You know that, right?"

His eyes sparkled. "I do."

"And you know I will do anything, *anything*, to support you, right?"

"I know that too. But don't be stupid. Promise me. Just stay out of it and do what Teri says. This will be over soon since I didn't actually do anything."

"Agreed. In the meantime I want you to promise me you won't try and investigate this shit on your own."

Otto just looked at me. I knew him almost as well as I knew myself, and there was no way he was going to heed my warning. But I also knew he wouldn't lie to me or make false promises

"Otto... promise me."

"We're not going to talk about it, Walker," he said.

"Fuck," I muttered. "Don't be an idiot. Nobody wants an idiot for a life partner."

189

Otto's face broke into a smile like the damned sun. It was blinding. "Who said anything about a life partner?" he teased.

I leaned forward and kissed him again, hard and fast and full of tongue. When I pulled back, we were both hard and panting.

"I did."

⁓

After pulling away from the Wilde ranch, I went straight to Jolie's place. I'd talked to her briefly on the phone earlier in the day, but hadn't had a chance to really explain what was going on. It was a Saturday, so she was at home with Tisha. They were outside in the driveway washing the car. Tisha had on a blue-and-white-striped bathing suit, and Jolie was in an old T-shirt and running shorts. They looked like they were having a ball.

"My two favorite ladies," I called out as I stepped out of the vehicle.

"Uncle Seth!" Tisha yelled, racing for me. I grabbed her up and held her to me even though she was soaking wet from the hose. Her skinny arms and legs were all gangly angles and her hair was in wet strands stuck to her face.

"You helping Mama wash the car, Tishie-poo?"

"She said we could have ice cream after."

When I set her down, she went back to the bucket of suds and picked out the huge sponge before going to work again on the car.

I met Jolie's eye and nodded toward the front porch.

We sat on the steps leading to the front door before I turned to her. "Otto's parents' house is completely burned to the ground. They think the fire was set deliberately."

Her forehead creased with concern. "Is he okay? The poor guy. He grew up in that house, didn't he?"

I nodded. "After what happened here at the house and then over there... well, I'm just wondering if you've seen anyone or anything strange around here lately."

She seemed to hesitate for a minute before looking away and tightening her jaw.

"Were you going to say something?" I asked. "Anything at all would be helpful, even if you think it's irrelevant."

"Tisha said she saw Otto over there last night after dinner, Seth."

I felt my heart rate pick up. "What? When? How?"

She shrugged and picked at the edge of her shorts. "She, Cody, Hal, and Eliza were playing outside after dinner and asked if they could stay out there when the sun started going down so they could catch lightning bugs. They had a jar with holes poked in it. Well, I guess she went as far back in the trees as she could to find them. Later, she said 'daddy's friend Otto' went into his mama and daddy's house while they were all catching bugs."

That couldn't be right. He would have mentioned it to me last night.

"What time was it, do you think?" I asked, rubbing a hand over my mouth.

"Late. I think the sun didn't go down until around nine and then it took a while for it to get dark enough to see the bugs. Beth was here for a couple glasses of wine so we just sat in the kitchen and let the kids play... I think by the time we put the kids to bed it was after ten. Beth didn't want to drive home, so she crashed in the loft and Hal slept on the sofa. I asked Hal about it the next morning, but he said he didn't go back far enough in the trees to see anything."

I needed to ask Otto about it, but Teri had specifically told me not to discuss it with him. Did this mean I needed to tell Teri what Jolie had just told me?

My lungs felt constricted. Of course I had to tell her. Otherwise I was breaking the law. Obstructing justice and withholding a witness statement.

Fuck.

"Dammit, Jolie," I said, standing up. "I'm going to have to report this. Don't talk to her anymore about it, okay? There's a nice woman named Teri who's going to want to ask her some questions. We'll both be there with her when she does. But until then, try not to discuss it."

"You don't think Otto set the fire, do you?"

"Of course not," I snapped. I scraped my top lip with my teeth.

"Sorry, Jolie. I'm just... this is just a strange situation. I didn't mean to snap at you."

Jolie reached out to take my hand in hers, twining our fingers together as if we were a couple. I'd held her hand like that a million times over the years, but this was the first time I noticed how small and delicate it was. I almost felt like I could crush it by accident.

"Your parents came over this morning to check on Tisha, and your dad was talking about an article he'd read that said sometimes firefighters start fires so they can be the big strong hero who saves people. It's called firefighter arson. You don't think Otto—"

"Don't be ridiculous," I said. "He would never do such a thing."

But the following day, I learned he'd been accused of doing it once before.

On a submarine of all places.

We were in my office to allow Teri to question Tisha, when Chief Paige pulled me aside. It seemed like his intention was to reassure me, but the result was the complete opposite.

"You're not worried about what happened on his last deployment, are you?"

"What?" I asked, surprised as hell Otto would have talked to Evan Paige about something he still hadn't talked to me about.

"The fire on board the *Poseyville*. That doesn't necessarily have any bearing on what happened here. You shouldn't worry."

"What fire? What's the *Poseyville*?" I felt like I was in some kind of movie where I was the stupid character always a step behind everyone else.

"The reason Otto left the navy, or at least I assume it was the reason. There was a fire on board the submarine he was on, the *Poseyville*, and he was the sailor originally blamed for it."

"You're kidding?"

Evan shook his head. "No. He hasn't told you about this?"

"No. When did he tell you?"

"He didn't. He gave me the name of a commanding officer he served under as a reference, and that guy told me the whole story."

"What was the story?"

"Someone used Otto's personal belongings to start a fire in Otto's rack. When Otto's shipmates were able to put out the fire, they discovered Otto practically catatonic in a small space behind the blaze. He'd been trapped, and the suspicion was immediately on him for setting the fire. He was unable to answer questions or defend himself when they questioned him, so the suspicion remained on him for setting it or at least letting it start through some kind of negligence since it was in his rack with his personal belongings."

Picturing Otto stuck on a submarine was bad enough, but stuck in a small space during a *fire* on a sub? God, what that must have done to him.

"How did they determine he didn't do it?" I asked.

"They didn't, at first. They sent him to a nearby ship that had medical facilities to evaluate him. And while he was off the boat, another fire was started, similar to the first. They determined it was another sailor who was deliberately trying to find a way to get off the boat even though the kid maintained it was Otto who set the first fire. The point is, Otto was exonerated and given the option to return to his duty station or get an honorable discharge. He chose the discharge."

"Jesus," I said, rubbing the back of my neck. It felt like I was carrying the weight of the world on my shoulders. Despite what Evan had said about this not having any bearing on Otto's guilt for the Hobie fires, I knew if anyone found evidence to support actual charges of arson, the suspected arson on the boat would come back up. "Does Teri know all this?"

"I don't know, but if she doesn't yet, she will. At least, I'm sure she'll discover it if she finds any evidence linking him to the fire at his parents' place."

"There can't be any. He didn't do it," I said for what felt like the millionth time.

But if he hadn't done it, who had? And what the hell had he been doing there earlier that evening?

CHAPTER 24

OTTO

Wilde,

Oh my god. My brother John is living back in Hobie now and heard you're in the navy serving on a SUBMARINE? Are you fucking crazy?

Do you not even remember the doghouse? Or the bathroom cabinet? Or the drain pipe under the bridge at the lake? Or the goddamned mega slide at that stupid street fair thing we went to during spring break? God, you're an idiot.

My hands are fucking shaking right now. You are such an imbecile. I hope you're okay and not scared to death.

Smh,

Walker

(Unsent)

IT WAS like *Poseyville* all over again. Being suspected of starting a fire when I was a goddamned firefighter was beyond insulting, offensive and frustrating. I felt like a caged animal. One silver lining in the cloud was the youth soccer camp I was helping put on that week with my sister Sassy.

West had recently made a very large donation to the Hobie Youth

Center in Nico's name, and as a result of the influx in cash, participation in the center's programs by local disadvantaged youth was way up. One of their missions this summer was helping kids stay safe and active while their parents were at work, so Sassy and I had scheduled some week-long mini camps to offer the kids some variety in the center's day camp options. The group we had this week was a mix of kids from all over Hobie, but they were all third through fifth graders at Hobie Elementary School which meant many of them knew each other.

The day after seeing Walker at the ranch, I arrived at the youth center early to set up a skills drill and was just running through it myself when Sassy showed up.

"What're you doing here so early? I thought you had a shift at the firehouse?" she asked, jogging the last bit from the parking lot to the field. She had on her old Hobie High soccer shorts with a high-tech tank top, shin guards, and cleats. Her wild hair was pulled back in a ponytail.

"I'm on paid leave," I grunted. "You sure you're up for this? If you're upset about Mom and Dad's..."

She shook her head. "Screw that. It was just a bunch of stuff. Yeah, it's sad, but so's life, you know?"

I stared at her. "Since when are you so pragmatic?"

She shrugged. "When I heard you ran into the fire, it very quickly put things in perspective for me. Human beings versus possessions. No comparison. *Asshole.*"

"I'm sorry."

"Why'd you do it?"

"Look, can we not do this right now? I'm already feeling like a total ass because I can't even be around my boyfriend anymore. I know I fucked up, but can you save the lecture for another time?"

Sassy dropped the net bag of soccer balls she was carrying and walked up to wrap her arms around my waist. She was a tiny thing, the one we affectionately called Runt sometimes, so she only came up to my collarbones. But her hug was strong and true, and feeling the familiar comfort of a sibling offering me support was soothing.

"Thanks," I said, squeezing her tight before pulling back. "Now, let me show you what I've set up here for the kids."

I picked up the bag of balls and began unloading them into a pile on the grass. Sassy reached out and put a hand on my arm.

"Wait."

I straightened up and looked at her, taking a quick glance at the door to the center to make sure none of the kids had started making their way to the field yet. "What is it?"

"I know you don't want to talk about it, but... why were you at Mom and Dad's house the night of the fire?"

"Um... to help the crew fight the blaze? What do you mean? I'm a firefighter. It's my job."

"No, no. I mean... earlier. Someone said you were spotted a few hours before the fire started. Why were you there? Did you see anything at that time that seemed odd?"

Her question didn't make any sense. "I wasn't at the house before the fire. Only after. Where did you hear that?"

She seemed to stop and think for a minute while I noticed the kids filing out of the building and coming toward us.

"Stevie. I met him at the shop for a coffee this morning, and he said he'd overheard Mrs. Parnell tell someone in line at the bakery that they had an eyewitness that put you at the scene of the crime."

"Who is it?"

She winced. "Nobody seems to know for sure, but someone saw the investigator interviewing Jolie Walker."

Fuck me.

Maybe things weren't as amicable between us as I'd thought.

AFTER THE SOCCER CAMP ENDED, I made my way to the town square to pick up some takeout from the Pinecone to take back to the ranch. My brain was spinning a mile a minute, trying to determine whether Jolie really would deliberately lie about seeing me at my parents' house or whether she truly thought she saw me. Or was it possible my speculation had gone too far? Maybe Jolie was just being asked if she saw anything and she wasn't the supposed eyewitness. But who else would be in a position to see someone at my parents' place? You either had to be on the Wilde ranch or the Walker ranch to see my parents' house.

I tossed a halfhearted smile at a couple of ladies I knew from growing up and noticed both of them shooting me sympathetic glances. I wondered how long it would take for the townspeople of Hobie to look at me like a damned criminal?

How could anyone think I'd set my parents' house on fire? The idea was simply ridiculous.

I was building up a pretty decent head of steam when I practically bulldozed into my brother upon entering the restaurant.

"West!" I cried, grabbing for him to keep him from running into the woman in line in front of him.

"Otto, jeez. What the heck?"

"Sorry. I wasn't paying attention. Why aren't you at the clinic? Just taking a lunch break?"

"Nah. I had a case at the hospital that didn't take as long as I expected, and Goldie is handling the patient appointments for the rest of the day. My plan was to pick up lunch and then kidnap Nico to take him to the lake for the afternoon before we have to pick up Pippa from the ranch." He seemed to notice the haggard look on my face because he quickly called me out on it. "You look like shit, brother."

"Gee, thanks."

"I heard the rumors. I assume you have too?"

"The one in which I'm the leading role in the movie *When Good Boys Do Bad Things?*"

He smiled and clapped me on the shoulder. "If it's any consolation, we all know you didn't do it."

Memories of the *Poseyville* fire reared up in my mind again. If word got out about why I'd left the navy, public opinion would change in a snap. Being the principal suspect in one fire is defensible, but two fires? Not so much.

"Who could have done it, West? You've been here for several years.

Any guesses? Bad teenagers? Drifters? Who? Shit like this doesn't happen in Hobie."

He eyed me for a moment while he seemed to think it through. "Who stands to gain?"

Who stood to gain by burning down my family home? Presumably, my parents stood to gain insurance money, but their alibis of being in Singapore pretty much ruled them out. It could possibly be a revenge thing or act of aggression on our family by an angry individual... but who? And why now?

What about the little brushfire at Jolie's house? Was it a practice run? Or was it intended to just be a warning of some kind? Did the arsonist believe it would actually catch and involve Jolie's house? Or was the hope it would spread from hers to ours?

In both cases, no one was supposed to be there. So maybe one saving grace was an arsonist who didn't mean anyone physical harm. But as a firefighter I knew all fires had the potential to result in harm to first responders. Whether or not personal harm is intended, it often occurred.

West and I made our way to the bar and ordered our meals to go. The bartender gave each of us a glass of ice water while we waited, and I went back to ruminating on the problem.

"Means, motive, and opportunity," I muttered. "Who had all three?"

West spun the sweating water glass between his hands on the bar. "Well, it doesn't sound like the perp needed much means, so let's move on to motive and opportunity. Of the people related to us and Jolie, family, friends, etcetera, who lacked an alibi for both fires?"

"Wait," I said, a niggling thought at the edge of my mind. "Wait."

I turned to face him as the memory came in loud and clear. "Someone was trying to buy Mom and Dad's house. What if that had something to do with this?"

"Do we know who it was?"

"No, but surely Doc can ask the real estate agent, right?"

"That would definitely be motive. Once the house is gone, the assumption would be the owners might be way more willing to get rid of the property and take the cash from the insurance payout rather than tackle the hassle of rebuilding."

"That has to be it. The only other person I could think of was John," I admitted. "Or Jolie, but I really don't think she would do that. At first I think she was jealous of me with Walker, but now we get along better, and I know she's been on at least one date with someone."

"John? Why would John want to set those fires?"

I shrugged. "No idea. Unless his idea was to implicate me. I know Walker's family hates that he's with me. They wanted him to stay married to Jolie."

West's eyes bugged out. "Even though he's gay? That's cruel."

I lifted an eyebrow at him.

"Damn," he muttered. "This is one of those million moments I have to thank god we were raised by a bunch of gays and allies. I forget how lucky we are sometimes."

"Incredibly lucky," I said.

"No kidding," West agreed. "But would John really do that to his niece and sister-in-law?"

"No one was supposed to be at either place. And the fire at Jolie's wasn't likely to turn into a big blaze like the one at Mom and Dad's. It probably would have burned out before catching the house on fire."

"Would an amateur know that, though?"

"No. Probably not… God, West. Walker would die if he thought his brother had done this. I can't imagine what he'd think."

"Are you going to tell him?" my brother asked.

"What? No. It's pure speculation based on practically nothing," I countered.

"Not nothing. He was at the scene of the first crime and home alone during the second one. What if he was angry when Jolie got the little house on the Walker ranch instead of him and Beth?"

I thought about that for a minute.

"I could see him being upset about that. According to Walker, the family never really saw Jolie as a true Walker. The idea of her ending up with one of the two Walker homes would most likely burn his gut."

"Motive," West murmured before taking a final sip of his water and reaching to take a large paper bag from the bartender. "Talk to Seth, Otto. At least tell him you didn't do this."

I sighed. "He knows that, West."

"Tell him anyway. And then tell him about the *Poseyville*."

My jaw dropped open. "Who told you?"

His hand clamped down on my shoulder, strong and warm. "Doesn't matter. You know I love you no matter what. Which is why I'm telling you to get your ass to the sheriff and tell him your story before he hears it through the dreaded Hobie grapevine. He deserves to hear it from you, Otto."

I closed my eyes. He was right. But what happened when he heard about what a fucking nutcase I'd been and how when it came down to it I'd failed at the very thing I'd entered the navy for—putting out fires.

"He's going to think I'm a loser," I confessed in a low voice.

West's face softened. "He already knows you're a loser, but he loves you anyway."

Leave it to a brother to be a jackass even when he's loving you.

CHAPTER 25

WALKER

Walker,

We had a training exercise in which we were supposed to start an actual fire on the boat. I thought it was a joke at first, but I never found out because we were called to rescue a stranded SEAL team. Thank god. (I still think maybe my commanding officer is fucked in the head, but whatever.) The point is, if I'm ever in this damned metal tube when a legit emergency happens, I hope the sea takes me quickly. What irony to be highly trained in fighting fire while literally surrounded by the world's largest body of water.

Wilde

(Unsent)

THREE DAYS AFTER THE FIRE, I was called in to a meeting with the arson investigator and the fire chief. We met in the small conference room at the firehouse to discuss the progress of the case.

That was where I found out that Otto had gone from a person of interest to the sole focus of the investigation.

"You've got to be kidding?" I asked Chief Paige before turning to the investigator. "No disrespect, Teri, but Otto Wilde did not start this fire. There's just no way he would do that. If he wanted to burn down his parents' house, why didn't he save his parents' important papers first or remove the photo album before the blaze?"

Even as I said those things, I realized how pathetic they sounded. If it had been any other random suspect, I could have easily explained away those things.

Teri's voice was calm and steady. "Sheriff Walker, I appreciate what a tough position this puts you in, but right now the only suspect we have is Lieutenant Wilde."

I appreciated her still using his rank when referring to him, and it was a reminder that she was a professional who wouldn't want to take a wrong step in charging an innocent person with a crime. She continued speaking.

"I didn't say he was guilty of the arsons, Sheriff, only that so far he is the sole person we know for sure had motive, means, and opportunity."

"Do you have any actual evidence?" I asked.

"As you know, we have a witness statement that puts him at the scene of both fires. We also have a personal connection between him and both locations. He is a trained firefighter, which means he is very familiar with how to set fires."

I threw up my hands. "Exactly. Which is why if he wanted to burn something down, he'd know how to do it without implicating himself."

Was I the only person who could see how stupid this was?

"Why would he have started that fire at Jolie's house? Give me one potential motive," I demanded.

Teri exchanged a look with the chief before the chief answered. "Maybe he was trying to prove to you that he could protect your family."

I wondered if punching the guy would cause me to lose my job.

Probably.

"He doesn't need to set a fire to prove that to me, Chief," I snarled. "And he doesn't need to actually put out a fire to prove to me he knows how to do it. He's a trained firefighter. He's responded to any number of fires before. Why would he think a tiny garden brushfire would impress me?"

Teri held out her hand. "Let's all calm down and stop speculating for a moment. What we need right now are some new leads. We were finally able to process some of the evidence from the big fire and discovered it was started with a crude incendiary device similar to a Molotov cocktail or bottle bomb. It was made with a bottle of Patron tequila. The problem is anyone can get Patron at any liquor store."

I felt my stomach roll and my vision went pitchy around the edges as I remembered the two bottles of Patron on Otto's kitchen counter. *Fuck.* "Patron? Are you sure?"

"It's a very distinctive bottle shape, and it was found in a back guest bathroom by a broken window. We're sure. My crime lab has it right now."

My mind sifted through thoughts a mile a minute. Anyone could have lifted one of the Patron bottles out of the bunkhouse before Otto grabbed the last two. Maybe there had been more? Most friends and family of the Wildes knew the bunkhouse was always left unlocked and available for someone who needed a place to crash. They didn't worry about security because you couldn't drive onto the ranch that far without Doc and Grandpa hearing from the main house.

I needed to talk to Otto.

But I wasn't allowed to discuss the case with Otto.

Fuck. *Fuck.*

"Have you asked him about it?" I asked.

"Not yet. He's headed in right now for another interview."

"Does he know he's an actual suspect at this point?" I asked. "He might want a lawyer present or a union rep."

"No, and we're just having a chat with him at this point. He's not an official suspect yet," Chief Paige said.

I tilted my head and stared at him. "Explain the difference between an unofficial suspect and an official one," I said. I'd been challenged the same way on many occasions in my job.

Teri cut in. "The difference is we have absolutely no evidence with which to charge him. So right now we're still focused on gathering evidence."

Chief Paige locked eyes with me. "You know as well as we do, Sheriff, that it's not an interrogation requiring a Miranda warning unless he's in custody or being detained. As this is a voluntary information-gathering inquiry, there is no need for legal or union representation."

It wasn't often that I sympathized this much with suspects, but boy did the tables turn when it was the person you loved on the receiving end of any law enforcement "inquiry." I hoped like hell Otto wasn't stupid and that he recognized quickly he'd be better off with representation of some kind before answering too many questions.

But knowing my man, he'd be one of those guys who claimed, "Why do I need representation when I've got nothing to hide?" I could just hear him saying it right now.

Damn it all to hell.

I needed to find a way to warn him without actually contacting him.

After a few more minutes of going over the preliminary results of the evidence collection, there was a knock on the conference room door.

Evan stood to open it, revealing Stevie on the other side with an arm full of pastry boxes and a drinks carrier with several cups of coffee in it.

"Oh bless you, Steven," Evan said dramatically. "I shall be forever in your debt."

Stevie preened under the attention from our resident silver fox while he flitted into the small room to deposit the spoils on the round table.

"An assortment of baked goods and coffees. Nico said when you stopped by this morning the line was so long you left. He wanted to make sure you knew how sorry he was," Stevie explained. "He loves taking care of Hobie's heroes."

Evan looked surprised. "Wow. Talk about service with a smile. Tell him he didn't have to do that. How incredibly generous of him."

Stevie laughed and shrugged. "I think he's hoping if the bakery ovens ever catch fire, you'll bust your ass double time because you'll feel indebted to him. I'm not sure he much cares about the bakery itself, but his precious ink emporium is upstairs. God forbid something happen to his tattoo gun."

Evan's deep laugh filled the room. "Tell him it's a deal."

After we all gushed over the treat, I offered to walk Stevie out. We passed several of the firefighters hauling equipment through the engine bay, and I had to grab Stevie's arm to remind him how to walk.

"Eyes forward, kitten," I said with a laugh.

"Ngh," he groaned. "They're so fucking beautiful. I've always wanted to play with a fireman's hose."

My face must have looked some kind of smug because Stevie took one look at me and rolled his eyes. "I don't want to hear about it. Never mind. No need to brag."

"What? I didn't say anything."

"You didn't have to. I can tell by your face your man has an impressive pipe. Now, what did you want to talk to me about?"

"Who says—"

He held up his hand. "Save it, Walker. What's up?"

"Get a hold of Otto and tell him…" My conscience tangled up my stomach. It was unethical for me to do what I was getting ready to do. "Tell him…"

"Tell him what?" Stevie's eyes searched mine, clearly trying to read between the lines.

"Tell him I miss him and I love him," I said softly. "Okay? Will you do that, please?"

Stevie surprised me by pulling me into a tight hug. His slender frame felt almost fragile against me, and I thought, not for the first time, that he deserved someone to love him like he was the only person on earth.

"I will," he promised with a sniff. "He's a lucky bastard, Sheriff."

I shook my head. "You've got it the wrong way around Stevie. I'm the lucky bastard."

When I returned to the meeting room, I could tell something had changed. Teri and Chief Paige both looked disturbed, and Teri was finishing up a phone call. Once she was done, she looked at me with a sigh of resignation.

"Sheriff Walker, I'm afraid I'm going to have to ask you to recuse yourself from any involvement in this case and let my office handle it from here."

"Why? What happened? Who was on the phone?"

"That was the crime lab with some test results. I'm afraid Otto Wilde has officially become our prime suspect in this case."

CHAPTER 26

OTTO

Otto,

Why won't perps get it through their thick skulls to keep their mouths shut and LISTEN to the Miranda Rights? I can't even begin to tell you how many idiots go away because they say shit they shouldn't or because they think they can handle an interrogation without an attorney.

Promise me, if you're ever brought in for questioning on anything, you'll say nothing except the word attorney. Promise me.

Love always,
Walker
(Unsent)

THE TEXT from Stevie was strange.

Something's up with the sheriff. It's like he wanted me to warn you but wouldn't say what about. Said to tell you he misses you and loves you.

What the hell? Since when did Walker send me love messages through Stevie?

I tried calling Stevie but got no answer. He was most likely busy with the lunch rush at the bakery since they'd started offering savory pastries and premade salads. After he didn't answer, I tried Walker. Also a no-go.

When I pulled up to the firehouse, I saw why. His vehicle was parked out front.

I texted him.

I just pulled up at the firehouse.

Hopefully he'd come out and see me before I went inside. I wanted to touch him and hold him so desperately, I was afraid if I walked in and saw him while everyone was watching, I wouldn't be able to avoid making a lovesick fool out of myself.

Within seconds, the door to the firehouse flew open and the sheriff came striding out.

Thank god.

I hopped out of my vehicle and waited for him. It took him about two seconds to reach me and I grabbed for him, fisting the front placket of his uniform shirt and yanking him toward me in a brutal kiss.

He let out a sound between a grunt and a squeak as he landed against my chest. His hands reached for my arms to keep from tripping me back into the SUV, and his mouth opened immediately.

"Love you," he said quickly into my mouth. "Get a lawyer. Now."

We both froze and pulled back to stare at each other.

"Shit. Fuck. I'm sorry," Walker blurted. "Fuck."

"It's okay," I said. My voice was too shocked to sound reassuring. "Thank you. But I didn't do anything wrong—"

His eyes narrowed and bore into me until I realized he was chastising me without saying a word. I simply nodded and gently pushed him away from me.

"I, ah... I need to talk to you later about something," I said.

Worry creased his forehead, so I quickly moved to reassure him. "It's not about the case, I swear. It's just something else I need to tell you about before you hear it from someone else."

His face softened. "Yeah. Okay. Do you want to come by the lake house tonight?"

"No, I was actually wondering if maybe you wanted to go fishing,"

I suggested. "We could meet in our usual spot an hour before sundown. Catch them coming up as the water cools."

He smiled. We both knew neither of us gave a damn about actually catching fish. Never had. "Yeah. Yeah, I'd like that. Do you have gear for me?"

I returned his smile with a sigh of relief. "Of course. See you then."

We didn't touch again because I knew I'd grab on to him like a fucking limpet if he came near me. I wanted to steal him away just the two of us and go hide out somewhere until the mystery of the fires had been solved. But I was a responsible adult and so was he. No running away for either of us.

I entered the firehouse with my head held high. Teri and Chief Paige were waiting for me in the meeting room. They offered me something to drink as well as something sweet from a bakery box, but I declined. It galled me being treated like a guest in my own damned station.

"Lieutenant Wilde, thanks for coming," Teri said with a welcoming smile. "Thank you for agreeing to talk with us again."

I nodded.

"First things first. We need to clear up a few things you answered before. Where were you when the Walker fire started?"

"I've already answered that question," I said calmly. "Several times."

"We'd like you to answer it again," Chief Paige said. He wasn't gruff or anything, just conversational.

"Am I a suspect in these arson cases?" I asked.

The hesitation from both of them was too long for my comfort, and when it came, Teri's answer wasn't reassuring.

She sighed. "We just want to ask you some clarifying questions, Lieutenant Wilde. That's all."

I nodded again. "And I just want to be sure that if these questions are geared toward the implication I may have been involved in setting these fires, that I have adequate representation from counsel. Are you asking these questions today with the intent to connect me to this crime?"

"We're trying to determine who committed this crime, Otto. We're not trying to pin something on you that you didn't do," Evan interjected.

I turned to face him. "So are your questions about who may have committed this crime or are they about me and my actions, specifically?"

"Well, you, of course," Teri explained. "Your experience is the only one you can testify to."

"Then I would like to request union representation, please."

Teri spoke first. "Several years ago, in Round Rock versus Rodriguez, the Texas Supreme Court—"

I held up a hand. "I'm familiar with the case. Are you denying me my right to union representation? Because that case was about internal investigations and discipline action. This case is about a very public arson. Two of them, in fact."

Chief Paige butted in. "I'll call for a rep. Sit tight."

The process took a while, and when the union rep finally arrived, I was pleased to learn he was well versed in this type of situation. Under his advisement, I ended up explaining again that I was at Jolie's house getting the shoe size when the first fire was presumably set outside, and I was in my cabin on the ranch when the fire was presumably set at my parents' house.

"Do you or have you recently owned a bottle of Patron tequila?" Teri asked, scratching notes in her ever-present notebook.

The question came out of nowhere and took me aback. "Excuse me?"

She repeated the question while my mind raced.

"I do own a bottle of Patron currently. I also recently gifted a bottle to John Walker."

Teri and Chief Paige's heads raised in a type of double take.

"I also happen to know you can probably find a bottle of it in a quarter of the personal residences in this county, so if you think that's evidence of a crime, you're mistaken."

Teri met my eyes and I knew by her look things were getting ready to get exponentially more complicated.

"No, but a bottle of Patron with your fingerprints on it *is*."

The union rep shut things down very quickly after that, asking if I was being charged with a crime. When both Teri and the fire chief shook their heads, the rep escorted me out and advised me to stay cool while he looked into things further.

My hands shook with anger the entire way home. I wanted to scream and shout that the arsonist had to be John Walker, but at the same time, I didn't want to believe it. How could Seth's brother do such a thing? And why?

When I pulled past the main ranch house, Doc came out on the porch waving his arms for me to stop. I parked and joined him and Grandpa in the kitchen.

"It was John," Grandpa said while Doc poured us some iced tea from a pitcher in the fridge.

"What?" I spluttered. "How do you know? You think he set the fires?"

They both stood there and stared at me. "Well, no. I don't know," Grandpa said. "I was just telling you who was trying to buy Bill and Shelby's house. It was John Walker."

I smacked my hand down on the kitchen table. I was pissed as hell. "Dammit, I knew it. I need to call Chief Paige."

"Hold your horses, hotshot," Doc warned. "Tell us what you know first. What's going on?"

So I told them everything I knew about both fires, including Beth's sleepover with the kids that night, which left John alone at home with no alibi.

"I think you should tell this to your rep rather than calling Chief Paige directly," Grandpa suggested. "Or better yet... wait. No, never mind."

"What were you going to say?"

He rolled his eyes. "I was going to suggest telling the sheriff until I realized you'd be implicating his own brother. That's a nonstarter."

"He's going to hate me regardless," I said, knowing the truth of it.

"No, he won't. More than anything, he's a believer in the law, Otto. He'd want the guilty party held responsible for the crimes," Doc said gently. "If John did this, it's not your fault. Seth can't blame you for someone else's actions."

"No, but none of this would have happened if I'd just stayed in the navy instead of taking the coward's way out."

Silence descended over the room until Grandpa lost his ever-loving shit and his voice boomed throughout the house.

"Bullshit!"

Doc and I jumped and turned to stare at him. Grandpa was red-faced and fuming. Doc reached out a hand carefully to place on Grandpa's shoulder. "Sweetheart?"

"No, Liam. This is bullshit and you know it. Nothing angers me more than hearing one of our children insult themselves. Otto, you are the farthest thing from a coward there is. When you didn't make it through SEAL training, you accepted a posting on a damned submarine despite having experienced claustrophobia as a little boy."

"I thought I was over it. That wasn't brave," I interjected. "It was stupid. I still can't believe I passed the test."

"Not only did you serve on a sub for years, Otto, but you also stayed in way longer than you intended in order to look out for people like your brother."

I opened my mouth to argue when Grandpa lifted a hand to shut me up.

"I know that's why you did it, Otto. Saint told us after your crew rescued that SEAL team, things changed between the two of you. You seemed more concerned about his missions and his safety. That's when you re-enlisted for the next tour too. You chose service over personal comfort, Otto. And when a fire fucked up your naval career, you still chose to serve your community as a firefighter."

"I stayed in to avoid facing real life," I mumbled, second-guessing every decision I'd ever made. "And because it's all I'm trained for."

"That's not true and you know it," Doc said with a kind smile. "You're highly trained as a medic and could have easily chosen to be an EMT instead."

Exhaustion washed over me as the full implications of what was happening in my life hit me all at once.

"Can we talk about how brave I am later? Right now I just want to go hide under my covers," I admitted with a thin smile.

"Fine. Call your rep. Tell them about the real estate thing and then grab a nap. We can go for a ride after dinner if you're up for it."

I stood up and stretched. "Can't. Walker said he'd meet me at the dock for some fishing. I need to tell him about what happened on the *Poseyville.*"

They both stared at me with worried expressions, but it was Doc who spoke. "Shit, Otto. He still doesn't know? Why'd you keep that from him all this time?"

I blew out a breath.

"Like I tried to tell you… I'm a goddamned coward."

I MADE my way to the cabin and climbed into bed without calling my union rep. The last thing I needed to do was make a rash decision, and implicating John Walker in these fires wasn't something I would take lightly.

It wasn't like me at all to nap in the middle of the day unless I'd been fucked into a nice stupor, but I was feeling emotionally wiped out and more than a little stunned at the day's revelations. Sleep claimed me right away, and I barely woke up in time to change clothes, gather up supplies, and get to the fishing dock to meet Walker.

When I walked through the trees toward the clearing at the edge of the lake, I spotted the familiar green ball cap Seth had stolen from me before sucking me off in the men's room one summer after a pickup basketball game in the park. We were sixteen and had been officially dating for about four months. After that, every time I asked for my hat back, he'd get a knowing grin on his face and ask, "You mean the BJ hat? It only changes heads when someone *gives* head."

And so it had gone. If he was wearing it when I went down on him, I stole it back and vice versa. Seeing it on his head reminded me of the last time we'd swapped it. I hadn't been wearing it at the time, but he'd taken it anyway. The night before his family moved to Minnesota, we'd snuck out and met in the bunkhouse at Grandpa and Doc's place. We'd spent the entire night memorizing each other's bodies and making each other come as many times as humanly possible until finally passing out from exhaustion in the wee hours of the morning.

When I'd woken up, he'd already been gone long enough to make it home and on the road without an official goodbye. I'd agreed it was for the best. Teenage boys weren't known for their loving moments, and I was sure it would have been a whole bunch of kicking dirt around with our shoes and mumbling bullshit.

But as I'd lay there in the bed alone, I'd cried my motherfucking eyes out for that kid. For ten years we'd been joined at the hip. Where Otto Wilde went, so went Seth Walker. Even our teachers at school got so used to the two of us together, when they said "Walker and Wilde" everyone knew it meant Otto and Seth. Not John, not Ross, not any one of my million siblings. If one of us showed up somewhere without the other, it was always, "Where's your other half?" Even when we were ten years old.

So that morning when I'd awoken without Seth Walker's slender, teenaged frame next to mine in bed... I'd thought my life was over. And when he'd sent me the letter claiming to want to break things off with me, I'd known it for sure. All that had been left for me after that was to run as far away from Hobie and my heart as I could get. Distract myself with something so grueling, so challenging, that I didn't have a spare moment or molecule of energy to spend missing my other half.

And now here he was again. Right in front of me and mine for the taking.

A branch cracked under my shoe, and he turned to face me. The faded green hat looked like it had been beat all to hell, as if maybe he'd worn it every single moment we'd been apart.

"Hey," I said across the remaining few feet between us.

He paused just a beat before flinging himself at me, crashing against me the way he always did when he was upset and tightening his arms around my neck to bring the two of us as close as possible.

I breathed him in. His hair was damp from a recent shower, and I could smell the Irish Spring on his skin. He smelled amazing. Familiar and sexy, clean but ready to get dirty again. I reached my tongue out to swipe against his neck, tasting the slightest hint of salt, most likely from the heat of the afternoon as he made his way through the trees to wait for me under the setting sun. His muscles felt firm under my hands as I ran them up under his shirt and enjoyed the bare skin of his back. The shorts he was wearing were loose enough on his hips for me to sneak my fingers down under the waistband and feel the smooth, rounded cheeks of his ass.

He moaned into my neck and thrust his pelvis into mine. "You gonna start that right off, Wilde Man?" he asked in a muffled voice. "Not that I'm complaining..."

I knew the mature thing to do would be to sit down and talk. But fuck mature.

After grabbing the hat off his head and sticking it on my own head backwards, I sank to my knees in the scrubby grass leading up to the little dock. My hands fumbled with his shorts until I managed to get them open and shove them down, revealing a sexy as hell pair of tiny black briefs underneath. I glanced up at him in surprise.

"These your fishin' pants?" I teased, pulling out one leg band before letting it snap back in place on his gorgeous ass.

His face bloomed pink, and I thought I might have just fallen even more in love with him if that was at all possible.

"Just because I wore scrubby clothes on the outside, doesn't mean I can't put a little something special on underneath for a certain someone," he said. The corner of his mouth turned up in a little smirk that was cute as hell. My heart couldn't take how much I loved him.

"Well... I apologize in advance for this then," I said before stripping them off him so fast, there was a tiny plume of fictional smoke left in their wake.

Walker's face lit up in a grin as he pulled his T-shirt off just as quickly. "You'll notice I'm not complaining."

I nuzzled my nose in his groin and wrapped my arms around his ass for a moment just to feel him and smell him and know he was mine. His fingers came up to skate across my head, no doubt feeling the pokey stubble of my buzz cut. After inhaling his scent one last time, I pulled away and ran my tongue around his balls before swiping up his shaft and taking the head of his cock into my mouth.

Seth's fingers tightened on my scalp as I began to bathe his cock in saliva and suck on the head with increasing pressure.

"God, Otto, just like that," he groaned. "Just like that, baby. Feels so fucking good."

I opened my eyes and looked up at him to find him gazing down at me with adoration. My fingers went to town fondling his ass with one hand and his balls with the other. I wanted to touch him everywhere, feel every inch of his delectable skin.

"Shit, gonna come," he gasped as I felt his length stiffen in my mouth and his balls tighten in my hand before the hot rush of his ejaculate hit the back of my tongue. Walker's hands held me tightly to him as he cried out and shot into me. I watched him throw his head back in relief and took the opportunity to appreciate his naked torso. After releasing his balls, I ran my hand up his stomach, over the bumps of his muscles and the wiry hair of his happy trail to his pecs to flick a nipple. He winced and pulled away with a grunt.

"Stop, asshole," he grumbled. "Let me have my moment."

"Your orgasm celebration moment?"

His grin was smug. "Yes. Let me wallow in it for a minute. You're damned good at sucking dick."

I moved to stand up, grabbing his underwear from the ground nearby and handing it to him. I had half a mind to sniff it first, but nerves about our upcoming conversation stopped me.

He put his clothes back on and reached out his hand for me. When I moved to grab up the fishing supplies I'd brought, he spoke in a quiet, serious voice.

"Leave it."

CHAPTER 27

WALKER

Walker,

I have to decide whether or not to re-up for another four years. This is one of those times I wish I could just call you and have my best friend back for five fucking minutes. Why did it have to be all or nothing? If you didn't want to be my lover, couldn't we still have been best friends? Even though I have a thousand siblings, no one knows me as well as you do.

I think in the end it comes down to this: if I can't have you, then what the fuck does it matter? Might as well stay in and serve my country. But if I re-up this time, I'm probably looking at the whole twenty.

Wilde

(Unsent)

I COULD TELL RIGHT AWAY something was eating at him. It was in the way he touched me, the way he'd met my eyes while he was going down on me. I wanted to tell him that there was pretty much nothing in the world he could tell me that would cause me to stop loving him, but I stayed quiet and let Otto be the one to speak.

We kicked off our shoes and sat side by side on the end of the dock the way we had a thousand times before. I reached for his hand and brought it to my lips before threading our fingers together and placing our joined hands in my lap.

"I want to tell you what happened on the boat," he said.

"Okay." Even though I'd heard some of it, I wanted to hear his version. There was no telling if what I'd heard was accurate.

"First of all, I joined up because Saint was doing it. You know he always wanted to be a navy SEAL. So, stupid me decided I'd go be one too."

He took a breath and looked out over the lake toward the setting sun before continuing.

"But that shit was hard," he said with a chuckle. "And I washed out pretty quickly. Saint made it, of course. He wanted it way more than I did anyway. But when I was faced with what to choose instead, I tried to make up for my failure in BUD/S by choosing something else challenging and specialized. Submariner. Which, again, was stupid."

He ran his free hand over his short hair and turned to me with a sheepish grin. "I was fucking nineteen years old, you know? I was an idiot."

"Why subs? You were claustrophobic, for god's sake," I reminded him.

"I thought by then I was over it. All that stuff about me being terrified of small spaces happened when I was little. Plus, I was able to pass the psych evals and figured that meant I was fine."

"And were you? Fine, I mean?"

I watched Otto closely to read the truth on his face and in his body language. He shook his head.

"No. I wasn't fine. I mean... I was fine at first. It was a challenge, but I got used to the confined spaces. That part didn't bother me as much as things you don't realize like not being able to get away from jerks you serve with or not being able to feel the sun on your skin or a breeze of fresh air. But I enjoyed the work. I appreciated being well trained and cross-trained the way submariners are. And after this one experience we had where we had to rescue a SEAL team on a botched mission, I realized how critical our service was. By the time we extracted this SEAL team, they were in rough shape. We'd been the closest US military personnel to them and when we brought them on board, you'd have thought we were the ones who were the heroes. I really think they figured they were dead out there."

"So you re-upped," I said. "After your first four years."

"Yeah. I kept picturing Saint needing that kind of support and I thought, why not? What's waiting for me back home anyway? At that point, I truly thought I'd be a lifer."

"So, what happened?"

"I liked my shipmates for the most part, but there was this guy named Ken who was a total ass. He and I split a rack space, which meant when I was on duty, it was his to sleep in and vice versa. It's called hot racking, and it's pretty common on a sub. But it meant I couldn't avoid him. He was a major complainer. Hated serving on a boat, hated the food, hated his assignments, hated his shipmates. You name it, he hated it, and he let everyone around him hear about it. There were rumors that he was the kid of someone important, which is why he never got disciplined for his big mouth, but I'm not sure I believe that. He was just smart about when he smack-talked and when he chose to shut up.

"One night when I was coming off a shitty shift where a bunch of stuff went wrong, I lost my patience. The minute he bitched at me about something—I think that time it was the way the sheets were on the rack wrong—I lost my cool."

I interrupted him. "That's not like you. You usually get quieter when you're truly pissed."

"I know. It was just a bad day, and I was so tired, I'd lost my filter. So I told him to shut his fucking mouth before I shut it for him, and then I proceeded to tell him that he needed to learn when to keep it shut in general. That's it; that's all I did. The next thing I knew, I was waking up stuffed in this tiny closet cubby thing next to our rack, and there was smoke everywhere. When I finally managed to kick the closet door open, I saw the rack was on fire. I was so out of it, I didn't know what the hell had happened at first. It wasn't till later that I remembered fighting with Ken and then falling asleep. I had a vague sense that he was the one who trapped me in the cubby. He must have gotten me up and over to the closet while I was still half asleep. Who knows? I wasn't even sure at first the fire had been deliberately set."

I reached my arms around him and pulled him in for a hug, pressing my lips to his cheek before laying his head on my shoulder. "I'm sorry. You must have been terrified."

"That doesn't even begin to describe it. When I thought I was trapped in the cubby space, I completely panicked, but then when I finally busted the door open and learned I was trapped behind a fire? Fuck, Seth. I thought that was it. There's damned fire extinguishers everywhere on a sub, but I just happened to be in this tiny space where there was literally nothing to help me put out the fire. And I was a damage controlman, which meant putting out fires was my *whole job* on that boat. I'd never felt so useless in my life."

"So what happened? How'd you get out? What'd you do?"

"I completely gave up. Like total panic, gone, see ya later. I curled up into a ball like a pill bug and just waited for it to be over. I remember hoping that if there was an afterlife, it at least had fresh air and a nice cold shower. I was hot and suffocating from the smoke. I had a balled-up T-shirt over my face, but it wasn't going to help for long. Then suddenly I heard shouting—other shipmates trying to get the flames out so they could get to me. I don't remember much after that until I was on board the bigger ship in their medical bay. Apparently the corpsman on my boat kept me pretty well sedated. I was lucky we were running close to a fleet, otherwise I would have been stuck on that fucking boat for god knows how long."

I ran my hands over his back and arms in an attempt to soothe him while he spoke. "What happened after that? Did you tell them you'd fought with Ken? Did they know if it was deliberate?"

He straightened up and faced me. "When they put out the fire and found me, I was holding a lighter, Seth."

"What? How? Why? That's incredible. Did the guy plant it on you like some kind of bad fucking movie or something?" The idea of someone trying to pin a crime on Otto made me see red.

He shrugged. "I guess. But the first thing Ken did was make it very clear to everyone that I'd threatened several times previously to burn the rack. He told everyone he'd thought I was joking around so he didn't report it."

"That conniving bastard. You could have died, Otto. Christ."

He pulled his knees up to his chest and dropped his chin onto them. "But the thing is… I was so confused and my memory was so spotty. I didn't know for sure I *hadn't* done it. I mean… I knew I wouldn't have, but at the same time, why would he? There's a difference between being an ass and being a criminal. It was hard to believe someone would set fire in a working sub *on purpose*. It's suicide. And what if I'd somehow done it in my sleep? I was so doped up with antianxiety meds at that point, I couldn't even think straight. And I was so afraid of accidentally incriminating myself, I just didn't speak."

"What happened after that?"

"I guess the guy was so desperate to get off the boat, he did it again. Only this time, I wasn't there to blame, and he got caught. That's when they offered to send me back, but by then I couldn't stomach the idea of being trapped on a submarine again. I managed to get in touch with Saint and asked his advice. He'd heard through the grapevine about what happened—a fire on a sub is a big fucking deal—and he knew how upset I must have been. He said since both of our eight years were up, we could just separate from the navy instead of re-upping."

"Wouldn't that take time? To… I don't know… give them your notice? How does that work in the navy?"

Otto looked away, off into the distance where the sun was just a sliver over the far side of the still lake. "I wound up getting offered a medical discharge for stress and PTSD, but I was afraid if I accepted it, it would prevent me from being able to get other jobs in the future. So Saint hooked me up with a buddy of his who told me how to negotiate to stay in the final six weeks without having to go back on a submarine. I was able to get a temporary transfer to dry land to work out the rest of my time. I stayed in Pearl Harbor until Saint was done; then we came home together."

"How are you feeling about it now?" I asked carefully. I didn't want him to feel like I was psychoanalyzing him, but I did want to know where his head was.

"Guilty for Saint leaving the navy. That's my biggest regret."

"Do you think he wanted to stay in? Has he told you that?"

He shrugged. "No. He said he was ready to get out. Said half the time he was stuck pushing paper and when he was actually on missions, the general consensus was bitterness that they didn't get paid more for the amount of shit they went through. The private sector is pretty hard core about trying to recruit SEALs away from the navy, and I guess it gets pretty tempting."

"He's a big boy. I think he would have stayed in if he wanted to stay in. What about you? Do you wish you could have stayed in the navy?" I asked him. "I mean, if the fire hadn't happened?"

Otto turned to look at me, and every shred of worry and fear he'd expressed went away in an instant. His smile was wide and bright before he answered.

"Hell no, Sheriff. Then I wouldn't be sitting here with you. And I will never, ever regret that."

We sat in silence for a while, listening to the frogs croak and the crickets chirrup in the long grass. Night bugs flew around but didn't bother us much over the water. There was a slight breeze across the glassy surface that seemed to help cool off the warm night a bit and the two of us just enjoyed the peaceful moment together.

Otto's words seemed to come out of nowhere. "It was hard enough thinking about naming Ken in that arson aboard the boat, Seth. I can't imagine implicating someone I know in these Hobie fires. What if I was wrong? What if something I said implied an innocent person committed these crimes? I don't think I could live with myself."

I looked at him closely. Did he know something he was holding back from the investigation?

"But Otto, you can tell them facts. Facts are facts. They're not implications."

He shook his head. "Sometimes a bag full of facts can make a pretty damning implication. Look at my situation on the *Poseyville*. I was found at the scene with a fucking lighter, Seth. It was my rack, my personal belongings. Those are facts, and the implication was pretty clear at the time."

I reached for his hand again and held it tightly. "If you couldn't be a firefighter, what would you want to do?"

"I've always wanted to be a firefighter," he argued.

"I know that. I'm asking what you'd want to do if you couldn't do it anymore for some reason. Let's say your lungs were fucked up or something."

He thought for a moment. "I guess I wouldn't mind coaching kids sports or even teaching physical education. I've been loving the soccer stuff Sassy and I have been doing. But you'd need a college degree for that, I think. The teaching anyway."

"Otto, if you have the honorable discharge, you qualify for the GI bill and tuition assistance. You could get your degree if you wanted to. It's not too late."

He met my eyes before speaking. "Maybe I can work on my degree if I end up in prison."

CHAPTER 28

OTTO

Otto,

I did it. Tisha turned five last week, and I flew to Hobie to find out where you were with the intention of begging you for another chance. I stopped at the ranch and visited with Doc and Grandpa who told me you'd just re-upped for another four years in the navy. Apparently, you're based in Pearl Harbor, but you're deployed god-knows-where.

Fuck, Otto. Fuck. They suggested I write you a letter, but I can't do that to you. How can I tell you I'm ready to be with you when you're stuck on a fucking submarine for the next four years? And it's not like I can move to Hawaii and leave Tisha...

Fuck. Did I miss my shot with you? What the hell do I do now?
Walker
(Unsent)

WALKER WAS PISSED by what I'd said. I'd only been half joking. On the one hand, they weren't close to having enough hard evidence to charge me with a crime, much less convict me of one. On the other, I'd decided I couldn't try to pin this on John Walker either. If I was asked a direct question, I wouldn't lie, but I wasn't going to go out of my way to provide motive to the investigator to help pin this on someone else either—especially Seth's brother.

"You're not going to prison, asshole," he barked. "Stop saying that shit. You didn't do anything wrong."

I reached for his face and pulled him in for a soft kiss. "I know. I'm sorry. But you have to admit it's scary to even be considered a suspect in a crime you have no alibi for."

"Do you have any suspicions of your own? Who you think might have done it?"

The earnest look of hope on his face crushed me. What if it was John who'd set the fires? That would crush Seth.

"No, baby. I'm sorry," I said.

Walker looked at me funny. "You're lying. Why are you lying to me?"

I blew out a frustrated breath. "Because I don't want to speculate when the truth is, I have no idea who did it. Can we change the subject? Besides, I thought you weren't supposed to be talking to me about the case?"

It was his turn to look squirrelly. "I had to recuse myself."

That hit me by surprise more than it maybe should have. "What? Are you serious? Shit, Walker. That means they really must think I did it." I scrubbed my face with my palms and tried to stay calm. "What did they say? Wait. Don't tell me. I don't want to get you in trouble."

He shifted on the dock until he was straddling my lap. I wrapped my arms around his waist to stay upright. His solid presence against me and in my arms was a balm on my worried spirits. I pressed my face into his soft T-shirt and exhaled, feeling my shoulders drop along with my blood pressure.

"I love you, Otto," he said before leaning down to kiss my forehead. "More than anything. Well, except maybe Tisha. But that's fair, right?"

I leaned back to look at him with a grin. "Yeah, that's fair. She's pretty lovable. You and Jolie have done an amazing job raising her, Seth. You should both be proud of the young lady she's becoming."

He beamed. "I am. We are. I'm lucky to have her, you know? She's been worth all the other shit." His smile dropped. "I can't wish it hadn't happened, Otto. I wouldn't give her back for anything."

I tried to give him a reassuring smile. "Sweetheart, I wouldn't ask you to. I truly believe everything happens for a reason. Maybe Jolie and Tisha needed you more than I did. In fact, I'm sure they did. And if going without you for a sum total of only eighteen years of my life is the price I have to pay to have you with me all the other years? That's no different than most couples, right?"

"I'm not sure you can count the first eight years," Walker said with a wink.

I tightened my arms around him and felt his cock brush my stomach through his shorts and my shirt. "Think of all the frogs I didn't get to catch with you. All the baseballs I didn't get to pitch to you, and the playgrounds I didn't get to chase you on. Think of all the sleepovers we didn't get to have and the games of toy soldiers—"

His mouth landed on mine and shut me up quickly, stealing my breath for a few passionate moments. The evening scruff was prickly on his chin but the warmth of the air had finally brought out some of that delicious sweat on his lower back. I snuck my fingers under his shirt to smooth my hands over the slick skin there.

"Barbies," he gasped, pulling back from the kiss with a laugh. "Not toy soldiers. MJ's Barbies."

I felt my face heat with embarrassment. "It's not my fault she abandoned those poor things to an old shoebox. They needed someone to play with them."

Walker's laugh was like honey I wanted to sip straight from his gorgeous pink lips. "Lesbian abandons Barbie collection foisted on her by unsuspecting Auntie Brenda. Gay boy swoops them up and proceeds to match tiny shoes to ball gowns. It's the same old story since time began…"

"Shut up," I cried, spinning him to his back and climbing on top of him to hold him down. "You're so cruel. What about you and your stuffed lizard?"

"You shut your whore mouth about Purple Pansy," he warned.

"Best damned dragon of all time. A *war* dragon, if you want to know the truth. Specialized in kung fu and… other war stuff."

I couldn't stop laughing. "It had a sequined purse," I said through tears. "And a matching hair bow."

"She was incognito!" He tried to escape my hold but was laughing so hard it was easy to keep him still.

We wrestled around on the deck until both of us were panting and hard, arching our dicks into each other with desperation.

"Otto," he gasped. "Otto, I want you to take me home and fuck me hard. Please."

I stopped my incessant dry-humping and smoothed damp hair off his forehead. "I will never say no to that, Walker. Now get your ass up and double time it to the lake house. First one there gets sucked off."

His pupils widened. "I'll suck you off regardless, but not until after you fuck me. I need you to fuck me."

Something in the way he begged me made my heart hurt for him. I realized how unsure of things he was, maybe about the future of the two of us if I really was going to get accused of these fires, or maybe just plain old insecurity despite all my attempts to reassure him.

I stood up and pulled him up by the hand, yanking him into a full-body hug before he could bolt for his SUV.

"Do you have any idea how much I love you, Seth Walker? I will do whatever you say, whenever you say it. Do not ever question my devotion to you. Do you understand? I would do anything for you. *Anything.*"

He nodded against my shoulder and mumbled a yes.

In the following days, as the truth of who set the fires finally came to be, that promise would be put to the test more than I ever imagined.

CHAPTER 29

WALKER

Seth,

Something terrible happened. There was a fire on the boat, and I was caught behind it. I thought my life was over and all I could think about was your beautiful face. If I ever get out of the fucking navy, I'm coming to find you, Even if you tell me to fuck off, at least I'll get to see your face one more time.

Otto

(Unsent)

THE FOLLOWING couple of days were so normal, they gave me a false sense of security. I spent the workday busting my ass in preparation for the Hootenanny, which was only a week away. Locals came streaming into the office to double-check traffic plans, security protocols, scheduling of events, and the layout of the stalls and booths. Had it not been for Luanne, I would have lost my ever-loving mind.

At night, I fell into Otto's or my bed with naked abandon, seemingly trying my hardest to make up for the ten missed years of making love to the other half of me. We spent hours mapping each other's grown bodies, learning stories behind new scars, and daydreaming of plans for the future.

When I had Tisha over one night, Otto surprised us by giving her a giant flamingo raft and convincing us to go swimming in the lake behind the house before grilling hamburgers for dinner and making ice cream sundaes for dessert. Tisha loved Otto, and the feeling was obviously mutual. He had a million dumb jokes in his arsenal, and for some reason, they hit the perfect mark with Tisha's own corny humor. When Tish fell asleep at the end of watching a movie that night, Otto untangled himself from me and carried her to her bed while I continued watching the movie.

It was a life I could see clear as day—Otto and me with regular visits from Tisha—but maybe I'd started wanting it too much. Because suddenly I began to obsess about losing it all. It started with a visit to the sheriff's office on Thursday morning from Mattie McCutcheon, a busybody of the highest order and the head of the PTA at Hobie Middle School.

The doors burst open, and the four of us working at the time all snapped our heads up to see what the hell was happening.

"Praise Jesus and pass the potatoes, you're here," she gasped, seeking me out among my dispatcher, deputy, and clerk.

"Mrs. McCutcheon, nice to see you," I said, standing and making my way to the front counter. "What can we help you with today?"

"It's that firefighter. You know, the *gay* one." She whispered the word *gay* in case it was contagious or in case God overheard and smote her right where she stood.

At least that was what I guessed.

But how she didn't know that the *gay* firefighter was sleeping with the *gay* sheriff in this tiny, nosy town was beyond me.

"What about him?" I asked, trying not to snarl. Out of the corner of my eye, I saw Luanne reach for her Minnie Mouse letter opener. As if she'd cut a bitch should Mrs. McCutcheon go a smidge too far.

"He did it. He set those fires. I heard it from a witness."

Of course my mind immediately shot to Tisha since she was the only official eyewitness to anything as far as I knew.

"Who's the witness?" I asked. "And what did they say?"

I knew it was improper of me to ask. I should have shuttled her off immediately to Chief Paige instead. But I couldn't help myself. I needed to know.

"Well, as you know, my son is best friends with your nephew, Hal. I overheard them talking about it last night by the swimming pool when they didn't realize I was there."

Which meant she was spying on them from the shadows, no doubt.

"Go on," I encouraged.

"Hal said that he didn't want to get anyone in trouble or anything but that he'd seen that firefighter set the brushfire at his aunt Jolie's house that day." She finished her big announcement with wide eyes and an expectant gaze. "So what do you have to say about *that*?"

My stomach rolled even though it sounded like typical teenage bullshit bragging to me. "Did he say why he was there that day?"

"Something about being at his grandparents with his brother and sister. Said he could see clear as day from his grandparents' house."

I swallowed down the sigh trying to escape. There was no way you could see the back of Jolie's house from my parents' house. Clearly Hal had been making shit up. The fact he was implicating Otto made me see red, though.

"Mrs. McCutcheon, Otto Wilde is the one who put *out* the fire. Even if Hal saw him, how would he have been able to tell whether he was setting a fire or putting one out? And you can't see the fire from my parents' house anyway."

Her jaw stuck out. "Aren't you going to write this up in a report? I know what I heard."

"That's another thing, ma'am. You hearing a couple of boys gossiping is just hearsay. It's not evidence."

"Then are you going to interview the witness?"

Oh boy, someone sure liked her *Law and Order* episodes.

"I'm not, since he's my family, but I'll make sure to let Chief Paige know what you told me so he can look into it as part of the investigation."

I could just picture Hal pissing his pants when big, strong Evan Paige stared down at him in an interview.

The woman in front of me sniffed and glanced at the other people in the office. "See that you do. I'll check in with him myself just in case."

You do that, lady.

"Yes, ma'am. Have a nice day."

Once she was gone, I turned to Luanne with a sigh. "Let Chief Paige know I'm on my way, will you please?"

She rolled her eyes and I could have sworn I heard her mumble, *Nosy bitch.*

When I arrived at the firehouse, Chief Paige was out front overseeing the washing of one of the engines. Several firefighters were displayed in tight, wet undershirts or none at all while their muscles bunched and shifted as they dragged large sponges across the shiny red surface of the truck. Wet spray caught the sun and shot rainbows across the driveway as the men laughed and teased each other, clearly enjoying some cool water on the hot June day.

Hnngh.

"Sheriff Walker," Evan called. "See something you like?"

"Huh?"

His knowing grin totally busted me, and I blinked to get all that eye candy unstuck from my retinas. I had my own hot firefighter, after all. I didn't need to drool over these other ones.

"Need to talk to you," I said. "You got a minute?"

"Sure, come on in and we'll find a private place to talk."

We made our way to the same meeting room and shut the door.

"What's up?" he asked, clasping his large hands in front of him.

"Mattie McCutcheon claims she overheard my nephew Hal say something about seeing Otto set the fire at Jolie's house," I said. The tension was knotted all through my shoulders and jaw, and I knew I'd have a raging headache before the day was over.

"Shit," Evan said before leaning back and running a hand through his hair. "Do you think it's true?"

"No. But I'm ethically obligated to tell you about it, and I know it means you'll have to interview him."

"I'm sorry, Walker. I really am. This can't be easy for you." I could tell he meant it. There was sympathy in his eyes.

"Easier on me than poor Otto. It's killing him feeling so helpless about everything," I admitted. "The sooner you get this thing figured out, the better."

"Then I'll get on the horn with Teri and see if we can get the ball rolling with Hal."

"You need John and Beth's numbers?" I asked.

"Nah. John and I go back. I'll give him a ring and set it up. Thanks for letting me know. Hopefully nothing comes of it."

Once I was back at my desk, I couldn't stop running through possibilities in my head. I remembered Otto implying he had a suspect in mind. Was it something concrete or just supposition? And why wouldn't he be straight up with me about it?

I left the office early so I could spend some time with Tisha. She was at my brother's house that afternoon because Beth had taken all the kids to the community swimming pool earlier. When I pulled up at their house, Tisha, Eliza, and Cody were running through a little plastic baby pool in the yard, aiming squirt guns at each other and generally having a great time while Hal sat on the front porch with his nose in his phone. I'd already made myself swear not to ask him about anything having to do with the fire, so I concentrated on collecting Tish.

"Uncle Seth!" Tisha cried when she saw me. She made a beeline for me, and I had only a split second to decide whether or not to allow her soaking wet body to crash into my dry uniform.

What the hell? Who cares?

"Hey Tishie-poo, how was your day? Did you guys bring the water fun home from the swimming pool?" I asked, as I squatted and gave her a full-on hug.

"Uh-huh. And Aunt Beth let us have corn dogs for lunch at the pool too. Can we make corn dogs for dinner? I really liked them."

I thought about the fish I'd been planning on grilling and the produce I'd bought at the local farmer's market.

"No way, chickie. Healthy dinner tonight, I'm afraid." I tried to ignore her falling face, knowing full well she'd forget her disappointment when she had a face full of fresh corn on the cob and strawberries later. "Is Uncle Johnny home yet?"

"Yeah. He's inside with Aunt Beth," she said. "Please can I play some more?"

"Five more minutes then I need you to dry off so we can go home, okay?" I said, dropping a kiss on her wet head and letting her go back to the kiddie pool fun.

After making my way into the house, I heard voices coming from the kitchen.

"The Realtor said they might be more open to selling now that the house is gone," John said. "Fingers crossed."

"Do you think it'll be cheaper to build now that the house is gone, or will it cost a bunch to haul away the debris from the fire?" Beth asked. I heard the clanking of dishes as if someone was emptying or loading the dishwasher.

I froze in place as I realized they were talking about Bill and Shelby's house.

"I'm not sure, but I'm meeting with Danny Steiner tomorrow to ask him a bunch of questions. And I already heard from my dad about Hobie First National helping us with the financing."

"I'm trying really hard not to get my hopes up, John," Beth said. I could hear a smile in her voice. "But can you imagine if we're able to do this? And Cody and Eliza can just walk out the backdoor to play with Tisha any old time? I'm sure Jolie will sleep better at night knowing we're right there too. And your parents are thrilled to death. I just wish they'd given us the little house from the get-go. Yeah, it would have been small as heck, but we could have added on. But no, they gave it to the one person in this family who's not even really a Walker. God, what were they thinking?"

"They were thinking Seth was going to live there, Beth. How the hell were any of us to know he was gonna bail like that and let Jolie have the damned house?"

I felt my hands begin to shake as the conversation sank in and I realized they were planning on buying Bill and Shelby's property and building a house on it. Not only that, they were pissed Jolie and I had gotten the little house on the ranch instead of them. But they would have been sardines in that tiny house with three kids. Surely, they didn't resent not living in what was basically a guesthouse?

Beth sighed. "Well, at least now it ought to be affordable for us. I hate to say it, but I'm kinda glad it burned down."

There was a pause before John spoke. "I'm glad you're happy. You've put up with a lot in this family. You deserve something nice finally. You know I'd do anything for you, right?" The sound of a quick kiss could be heard over the beginning rumble of the dishwasher. I took the opportunity to turn around and sneak back out of the house, grabbing Tisha's shoes and backpack on the way to the door.

There was no doubt in my mind that had I gone into the kitchen, all hell would have broken loose and I would have said any number of things I couldn't take back. My brain was going a million miles a minute and jumping to all kinds of outrageous conclusions.

When John told Beth he'd do anything for her, did that include setting fire to Bill and Shelby's house?

And when Otto used almost the same exact words to me only a few nights before, did that mean he'd cover up his suspicions of my brother to protect me?

When Tisha saw me, her face fell. "It's already been five minutes?" Eliza and Cody started complaining, and I noticed Hal was nowhere to be seen.

"Come on, baby girl. We have to go. I have to get home and make a phone call to the fire chief."

CHAPTER 30

OTTO

Otto,

My parents are moving back to Hobie.

I can't decide whether I'm angry or heartbroken. We got into a fight about them moving back and they ended up admitting to me that the only reason we moved to Minnesota in the first place was to get me away from you.

I'm in shock. I had no idea they were trying to get me away from you. We tried so hard to keep our relationship from them... I guess we weren't as stealthy as we always thought. So they must have been pleased as fucking punch when I married Jolie. They got to pretend they had a het son instead of a gay one. I'm learning that the older I get, the more jaded I become. Now I can see why old people are such curmudgeons. They're just over it. They have no more energy to put up with assholes.

There isn't a night that goes by when I don't soothe myself to sleep with thoughts of you.

Stay safe at sea and come back home one day, sailor, Maybe I'll be there waiting for you when you do.

Walker

(Unsent)

. . .

I threw myself into soccer camp to try and get my mind off the arson cases. I was still on paid leave from the station, and all I had was time on my hands. When I wasn't at the soccer field, I was at the barn, pampering the horses and taking time to exercise each one. It got to the point Doc and Grandpa were probably sick of seeing my face.

So when Thursday afternoon came around and Sassy begged me to go to a party at the lake with her, I leaped at the chance. Anything to get my mind off my own damned boredom.

It was one of those parties where tons of different people all showed up at the lakeside park and formed little groupings of their own. Some were families with picnics and swimsuits, some were teenagers with cell phones and attitude, and some, like my group, were adults who just wanted to drink a few beers and shoot the shit.

Someone had beach music playing from a stereo speaker and Sassy's good friend Stevie couldn't help but complain about "the oldies station." When West and Nico walked up without Pippa, I quirked an eyebrow.

"Where's the girl?" I asked.

West was the first to answer. "We left her with a stack of cash and a bowl of kibble. She'll be fine."

Nico slugged him in the belly. "Your grandfathers have her for a sleepover. Doc was unusually needy this time when it came to the begging."

"You sure it wasn't West who was begging for some baby-free time with his boo?" Stevie asked with a leer.

West made a comically exaggerated nod, which made everyone laugh. When he sat down on the giant blanket we'd spread out, Nico immediately settled half on his lap. I always got a kick out of seeing Nico be so affectionate with West. I remembered him as a surly teen years and years ago, so seeing him with a gorgeous smile on his face and hearts in his eyes when he looked at my brother was the best thing ever.

And West was no different. The way he looked at Nico was like he'd been given the most precious gift and had no plans whatsoever of squandering it.

"You two are disgusting," I muttered into my beer.

Okay, so maybe I was a little jealous. My boo wasn't there to shoot me heart eyes because he was busy fighting crime and hoping his boyfriend wasn't a serial arsonist.

I needed another beer.

Or four.

Six beers later, I noticed Hal Walker with a group of teens by one of the fire pits in the park. The kids were trying to figure out how to start a fire, and it was turning into quite the comical scene. I wondered if I should give the fire chief a heads-up that there were unaccompanied minors fucking around with the fire pits.

"Not on active duty," I mumbled. "Not my job. None of my business."

Stevie spoke up from right beside me, and I startled. "You and your boyfriend both talk to yourselves out loud. It's kind of adorable."

"Who? Seth?" I asked, like an idiot.

"No, Jimbo Callahan," he said with a straight face.

It wasn't until I racked my brain to place the name that I realized I'd had too many beers. "Don't know the guy."

"Really? Because he said you're fantastic in the sack. Shame."

"Huh?" The guy was confusing as hell. "I never dated a guy named Jimbo Callahan. I've never dated any guy whose name wasn't Seth Walker. And I don't plan to either."

Suddenly, there was a hush around us, and I realized I'd said that louder than I'd intended. Sure enough, a big chorus of *awww*s came next. I rolled my eyes. "It's not a secret," I huffed. "I'd post it on a billboard if it wasn't already so damned obvious."

Nico's arm came around my shoulders. "Aww, a lovey-dovey drunk. Those are my favorite kind."

"He's very handsome, don't you think?" I asked him. "Seth, I mean. Not Jimbo."

Nico's lips tightened, and I got the feeling he was trying to hold back a laugh. "Oh, I don't know. Don't knock Jimbo till you've tried him. But yes, Sheriff Walker is mighty fine."

Something about that rubbed me the wrong way. "Shut the fuck up with your mouth. He's mine. Hands and eyes off."

My siblings and friends began laughing. Sassy's eyes lit with merriment. "Big brother, no one's trying to horn in on your man. Nico has his own Wilde child."

"*I'd* like to horn in on my man," I grumbled.

"That makes two of us," Stevie said with an exaggerated sigh. He dropped his chin into his hand and batted his eyelashes. The fucker was messing with me.

Sassy's laugh got louder. "Careful, Stevie, that growling sound can't be a good sign."

"Someone get him another beer," West said.

"Where is Walker tonight?" someone asked.

I shrugged since I hadn't heard from the man all day, but Stevie was apparently privy to information I didn't have.

"He has Tisha tonight."

I swung my head around and regretted it. "Who says? How do you know?"

"It's Thursday. Doesn't he have her every Thursday night?"

"Oh, right. I've lost track of the days of the week."

Sassy scooted closer and linked her arm through mine, resting her head on my shoulder and offering me some love. "Do you want me to drop you off at the lake house on the way home?"

I thought about slipping into cool sheets in Walker's dark bedroom and feeling his bare skin against mine. I swallowed and nodded, feeling a lump in my throat and an overwhelming sense of longing.

"*Please.*"

And that's what would have happened, if I hadn't stood up right then to go to the facilities building and passed by the group of teenagers right as Hal Walker showed all of his friends how to make a toilet-paper-roll fire starter.

WHEN I WOKE up the next morning alone in my own bed with no one but Fire Kitten for company, the events of the previous day washed over me and reminded me that I'd accidentally stumbled upon a clue the night before. Either Hal had learned the toilet roll trick from his father, or Hal was the one who'd started the fires.

Either way, if one of them was responsible for the fires, Seth would be devastated.

He'd already lost one brother; I couldn't imagine him watching the other one go to jail, even if only for a couple of years. Plus, knowing Seth, he'd try to take responsibility for supporting Beth and the kids while John was gone.

But if it was Hal? That would gut him even more. Working in law enforcement had put him up close and personal with the reality of what starting your life with a criminal record can do to a kid. Even if the record is sealed, being in the system at a young age can seriously limit opportunities from there on out.

I couldn't... *wouldn't* be responsible for pointing the finger at either of the Walkers for the arsons, even if that meant allowing the suspicion to remain on me.

The bigger problem was keeping my suspicions from Seth. He always knew when I was lying, and he also knew I didn't commit these crimes. So it stood to reason he was going to get antsy if the focus of the investigation remained on me. I wondered if maybe I needed to lay low.

I fumbled on my bedside table and dialed the chief.

"Evan Paige," he answered.

"Hey, Chief. It's Otto."

"Hey, Lieutenant. How's it going? You hanging in there?"

His voice sounded sincere and concerned.

"Yes, sir. But I'm bored and restless as you can imagine. I was wondering if it would be okay if I went down to Dallas to visit my sisters this weekend or if you thought I needed to stick around here for any reason," I began. I didn't want to ask straight up if I was allowed to leave the county, but that was sort of my intention.

"I don't see why not. You wouldn't have been on the rotation this weekend anyway. Go and have a good time."

"Thank you. Ah... any developments on the case?" I had to ask since being in limbo was killing me.

"I'll be honest, Otto. We got a tip that John Walker may have had something to do with the fires, but it turns out he had an alibi for the big one at your parents' house. So, unfortunately, that was a nonstarter."

"What? What kind of alibi? I thought he was home alone." My surprise popped out before I could stop myself.

"That's what we assumed when Beth told us about being at Jolie's house with the kids. But it turns out he was called out that evening to be at a meeting first thing the next morning in San Antonio. Left Hobie around dinnertime and checked into the hotel outside of San Antonio around eleven. Was at the meeting at seven thirty the following morning and drove back right after. Since the fire was at two in the morning, he couldn't have done it."

My stomach dropped. That meant the arsonist was most likely Seth's thirteen-year-old nephew.

"Oh," I said. "Well, I'm glad John didn't do it."

"Don't worry, Otto. We haven't stopped looking at other options. Hang in there."

"Yes, sir."

When I ended the call, I noticed a couple of missed texts and calls from the night before from Walker. I dialed him back.

"Thank god, baby. Why weren't you answering my calls? I would have come over there if I hadn't had Tish," he said in a rush when he answered. Just the sound of his voice made me want to cry or scream or beat my fists against the mattress. Why couldn't things be easy for us for goddamned once in our lives?

"Sorry. I was at the lake with West and Sassy and them," I explained. "I must not have heard the phone or accidentally had it on silent. I drank too much."

His chuckle came over the line like a soothing balm. "Aww, you have a sick head this morning? Poor baby."

"I'll drive through for some grease and knock it right out. I'm, ah…" He was going to flip when I told him I was going to Dallas. "I'm going to run down to spend the weekend with the girls."

He knew I meant my sisters MJ, Hallie, and Winnie. Hallie and Winnie shared an apartment next door to MJ. They didn't live too far away from Hudson and Saint's places, so it would be a weekend of gathering my sisters and brothers around me to take my mind off the shit here.

"Oh. You are? You're... wait." I heard the muffled sounds of him talking in the background, probably to Tisha. When he came back on the line he seemed rushed. "Otto. Can we talk first? Before you leave, I mean?"

I ran my free hand up over my head while the two sides of myself warred with each other.

"You want to come over?" I asked when the horny, lovesick side came out ahead.

"Yeah. Let me drop Tish off at Jolie's and I'll be there in twenty minutes."

"Okay. See you then."

Before I had a chance to hang up, his voice boomed over the line at me. "Do *not* leave before I get there."

My face split into a wide grin at his bossy tone. "Yes, Sheriff."

I got up and showered, cleaning everything thoroughly in case he was in the mood to play. I had no idea what his mindset was, but I knew I was craving his naked skin on mine and his tongue in my mouth, if not in other places.

By the time he got there, I was revved up and ready to go. I had half a mind to take him in the damned driveway before he even had a chance to get in the house, but I forced myself to stay in the doorway and wait for him to come inside.

It turned out I didn't have to guess at his mindset. The minute he walked through the door, he slammed it behind him and shoved my back against the wall.

"Oof," I grunted, grabbing for him. He was all over me, hands and mouth, a knee pushing between my legs and then a thigh shoving up underneath my balls. His hip rode across my hard length and horny shit started spewing from my mouth. "Yes, fuck. God, Walker, what's gotten into you? Do it. Whatever you want, it's yours."

"Mmpfh," he muffled into my mouth as his hands ripped the shirt up over my chest and arms. He pulled away just long enough to get it over my head before his mouth was invading mine again. "Want you naked."

I fumbled for my fly and shoved my shorts down as quickly as I could. I hadn't put on any underwear in hopes something like this would happen.

"Free ballin', Wilde? Really? Naughty boy. Naughty, naughty boy," he murmured, moving his kisses under my jaw and down my throat.

While I stood there naked, he was in full uniform.

"Cuff me, Sheriff," I teased. "I've been very bad."

"Shut up or I'll have to pull out my nightstick," he said with a laugh. His teeth nipped at my collarbone and I hissed in pleasure.

"Please, officer… please show me your nightstick."

He laughed some more. "Oh god, don't. I'm losing my boner."

I reached out and cupped his package to discover he was very definitely not losing his boner. "Liar," I crooned before dropping to my knees. He didn't have his gun belt on, so it only took me a couple of seconds to undo his pants and pull his cock out.

The fact he was still wearing his uniform was making me hotter than ever and the feel of the cool air-conditioning on my skin reminded me I was completely naked at his feet while he was fully dressed standing over me.

"Fuck," I groaned. "Gonna come before I even get your dick in my mouth."

"Nuh-uh. Suck me first. No coming yet for you." The adoration in his eyes belied his words while his fingers trailed a soft line down the side of my face.

That sweet man couldn't boss me around if he tried. Even when he thought he was being commanding in bed, he was tender and loving.

I mouthed his cock while I worked on getting his shoes and socks off. His own fingers went to the buttons on his shirt and began fiddling each of them open.

"Why, Walker?" he mumbled to himself. "Why didn't you just leave the shirt and vest off when you knew this was gonna happen?"

I smiled around his fat dick as I remembered Stevie's words from the night before about talking to ourselves. He was right. We both did it.

"Get naked," I said before deep-throating him and shoving his pants to the floor along with his boxer-briefs.

"Holy fuck, Otto," he cried out. He curled over my head and panted while I swallowed around him and hummed. "Oh god, just like that, baby. Shit."

I gave him a few more wet sucks before pulling off and standing up. "What do you want, Seth?"

His pupils were blown and his cheeks ruddy.

"Huh?"

"You want me to fuck you over the back of the sofa? Up against the wall? You want me to ride you? What do you want?"

He looked dazed but at least he was finally, gloriously naked.

"I want you to rim me and then fuck me," he said, nearly blowing the top off my skull and the cum out of my balls. "Is that okay?"

I snorted and howled before grabbing him and yanking him toward the bedroom. "Seriously? *Is that okay...* he wants to know if I have any interest in rimming his gorgeous ass and then fucking him silly. Idiot sheriff."

When I tossed him on the bed, I saw his sheepish grin. "Otto, I've been having these fantasies lately about your tongue in my ass. I was thinking about it at work the other day when Old Man Parnell came in to make his weekly complaint about dog shit in the square."

"Gross. We do not mention shit when we're rimming. Got it?"

"And all I could think about was thank god he's not gay so no one had to rim the old bastard. But then I wondered if Mrs. Parnell is into—"

"No!" I barked the word and let go of him long enough to clap my hands over my ears. "Jesus, stop. Seth, god... my dick. It's turning into a wet noodle."

"Then I'm gonna have to slurp it," Walker said before doing exactly that. Within seconds it was hard as steel again.

"Hands and knees, beautiful," I said, leaning in for a deep kiss before smacking his hip and allowing him to roll over.

He presented his ass to me in a giant cat stretch and then looked back with a feline grin.

"You remind me of Axe," I said.

"Who's Axe?"

"You know, my cat."

"You mean, Kiki? Muffin? Daisy?"

"How 'bout Harley or Jett? Scorch, maybe," I said as I ran light fingers up and down his crease. He sucked in a breath.

"Poppy or Skittles perhaps," he said before groaning as my lips came down on the sensitive ring around his hole. "Oh my *fuck*."

"Mm-hmm."

I teased and mouthed and sucked the hell out of him until he was whimpering and begging me to fuck him. My hands held his cheeks open and my eyes stayed open to watch his back muscles shift as he arched and cursed under my touch.

"Otto, Otto!" he cried. "Please. Don't..."

"Don't? Do you want me to stop, sweetheart?" I asked, knowing there was no way in hell the answer was yes.

"Fuck you. Don't stop," he gasped. "More."

I pulled back and looked at his spit-slicked hole, stretched from my mouth and tongue. "You are so fucking hot like this, baby," I told him. "Stay right there."

"As if I'm moving from this spot. I don't think my limbs work," he muttered into the pillow.

I returned with the lube and slicked up my fingers. When they slid inside of him, we both groaned in relieved pleasure. "Fuck, Seth. God, you feel good. You ready?"

"Ungh."

I chuckled as I leaned up and across his back to whisper into his ear. "I'm going to fuck you into this mattress until you can't even grunt anymore."

"Ngh."

I loved it when he got like this—when he was so turned on he couldn't make words—all he could do was lie there and take it. My lubed cock pushed against his entrance and was engulfed by his heat.

"Fuck," I breathed. "Fuck, Seth." I ran my hands along the skin of his back, noticing a few familiar constellations of freckles that had been there for twenty years. As my hips rocked into him, I leaned down and ran my tongue over the well-known patterns.

His hot channel sucked me in and held me tight, ratcheting up my lust to stratospheric levels. His body felt amazing around mine and I thrust farther in with each snap of my hips to get even closer to him. Seth screamed out his approval and reached a hand back to grab at my hip and pull me even closer. His knees gave out at one point and he collapsed onto the bed flat, but I kept going. My hips pistoned my cock in and out of him until my head felt like it was buzzing with twenty tequila shots.

"Baby, fuck," I choked. "Lift up so I can stroke you off."

My fingers threaded through his and our arms were outstretched above him on the bed. He was moaning and mewling incoherently and didn't move to give me access to his cock. Suddenly, he cried out and jerked, and I realized he was coming from friction with the mattress. The thought of him coming like that without us touching him was hot as fuck.

"That's it, god Walker, so hot," I breathed before my own climax finally hit. I shoved as deeply into him as I could as I felt the cum shoot out of me, emptying my balls as well as my mind and leaving me boneless and relaxed for the first time in days.

I lay fully pressed against the length of Seth's back. Our skin was slick with sweat, and he was no doubt in an unpleasant puddle. I shifted off his back and noticed my release leak out of him onto his inner thigh. The sight of my cum in his ass almost made my dick stand right back up. Seth Walker was the only person I'd ever gone bare with and the only person who would ever wear my mark like that.

I reached over to run my fingers through his hair. Walker blinked his eyes open and stared at me.

"Please don't go," he whispered. "I'm scared you won't come back."

CHAPTER 31

WALKER

Walker,

Did you ever think about having kids? Now that I've told the navy I'm not re-upping, I've started thinking about the life I want back home. I want kids, Seth. I want a husband and kids and a good horse. Maybe a dog or some chickens even. I want to have space to ride and trees to sit under. I want to teach my children how to tack a horse and where to find the weeping willow tree we used to hide under. I want Grandpa and Doc to have more babies to spoil and for my brothers and sisters to bring their own children into the world so mine have cousins galore.

If only I could do all of those things with you. How are you, sweetheart? Wherever you are, I hope you're happy and thriving.

With all of my love forever,

Otto

(Unsent)

I'D BEEN RIGHT AFTER ALL. Otto stayed in Dallas well past the weekend. When I called him on it, he claimed to be helping his sisters paint one of their bedrooms. But I knew him better than that. He was avoiding me. He was avoiding me because of the damned arson cases, and it was pissing me the hell off.

Whatever it was he was hiding needed to come right out in the open, so I finally called him up on Wednesday morning and told him to get his ass back to Hobie.

"Just a few more days, Walker," he tried to say. "The girls need help rearranging their—"

"Do you hear yourself?" I snapped. "Do you hear your pathetic excuses for avoiding me?"

I was in the sheriff's office and my raised voice caused a couple of heads to turn, including my sister-in-law Beth and the kids who'd stopped by to bring Luanne some raffle tickets for one of the Hootenanny contests. I immediately lowered my voice to a hiss instead.

"Get your goddamned ass back here by sundown or I swear to god, Otto Wilde…"

His grin was obvious by the tone of his voice. "What? You gonna spank me, Sheriff?"

My face ignited. "Yes. If I have to."

"You gonna do it while I'm handcuffed, *Sheriff?*"

Now my face was red and my dick was stiff. He knew what that voice did to me. *Asshole.*

"Please come home." Okay, maybe that was more of a whine than I'd intended.

"Any updates on the case?" he asked softly.

"Not that I know of. Teri mentioned expecting some more lab results back but I don't know what they are."

"You going to come over and let me fix you dinner?"

"Why don't you come to my place?" I offered.

"Nah, Grandpa and Doc have been looking after Fire Kitten so I want to relieve them from duty."

"Okay. Text me when you're almost there and I'll meet you."

I hadn't been off the phone for five minutes when Teri and Chief Paige walked in. I knew right away by the looks on their faces, the news was bad. I walked up to the counter and said a quick goodbye to Beth and the kids before turning to Teri and the chief.

"What is it?"

"Do you know where Otto is? He was supposed to be back from Dallas on Monday," Chief Paige asked.

"He's still there, but he'll be back this evening. Why?"

"We got some lab results and have a few more questions for him, but we can wait till morning. I don't want to worry him while he's on the road. Will you ask him to come by the station tomorrow around noon? I've got training exercises in the morning I can't miss."

"Sure."

Teri shot me a sympathetic smile before the two of them turned to leave. I was desperate to ask them what the lab results were, but I knew they wouldn't tell me. They knew as well as anyone I wouldn't be able to keep from telling him.

When I settled back at my desk, I received a call from my mother.

"Hey, Mom. What's up?"

"Hi, Seth. Listen… your dad and I were hoping you could stop by and have dinner with us tonight. There's something we'd like to talk to you about," she said.

I didn't like the sound of her voice and wondered what was going on.

"I can't stay for dinner, but I could duck out of here early and come see you around five. That work?"

"Why can't you stay for dinner?"

"I have plans to see Otto. He's been out of town, but he's getting back tonight."

Silence on the line.

"Well… we can talk about that when you get here. See you after work."

The line went dead, and I spent the rest of my shift with the churning gut that usually accompanied getting judged by my parents and found lacking.

By the time I arrived at their house, I had the beginnings of a headache. My parents were sitting at the kitchen table, and I could see a crockpot steaming on the counter.

"Smells good," I said, leaning in to kiss Mom on the cheek.

"I made your favorite. I figured you could reschedule with your friend," she said, pursing her lips on the word *friend*.

I blinked at her.

"Mom, I'm not rescheduling with Otto. And he's a little more than my *friend*."

My parents exchanged a look before my dad told me to have a seat.

"That's what we wanted to talk to you about, son," he began. "We've been hearing plenty of rumors around town and we feel your association with the Wilde family needs to come to an end before this nonsense goes any farther."

He said Wilde family as if it tasted like horse shit in his mouth.

I tilted my head and studied them, realizing I'd spent my whole life knowing there were two sides to them. There was the loving devoted parent side—the parents who'd supported Jolie and me in Tisha's early years and gave us a house to live in when we arrived in Hobie—and there was the homophobic, bigoted side—the side I tried so hard to pretend didn't exist.

"By nonsense, do you mean the *gay* nonsense?" I asked, suddenly knowing for sure this conversation had been a long time coming.

My father's nostrils flared. "Among other things. Surely you know Otto Wilde is the primary suspect in the fire that almost took our family home."

"Surely you know Otto Wilde is the man who discovered and put out the teeny-tiny fire that didn't even touch that house," I corrected with a growl.

Before my father could say another word, I continued. "You have known since I was a teenager that I was both gay and in love with Otto Wilde. You also know that I've spent the past ten years trying to forget about him and prove my devotion to this family. This is not a phase. This is not going away. Regardless of what happens about the fires, Otto will be in my life as my partner for the rest of my days. If you have a problem with that—with Otto, with gay people, with the Wilde family—then you are the one who will lose out. You won't see Tisha and you won't see me. So before you say anything else about Otto Wilde, think about what you want in your life."

I stood up and leaned forward, resting my weight on my hands on the wooden table.

"I respect and love the hell out of you both for everything you've ever done for me, and I will be grateful till my dying day for the love and support you've given Tisha. But I will no longer sit back while you spew your bigotry to that girl or anyone else I care about. You've already lost one son, and I know how hard that's been for you. But I can't continue to pretend like I don't die a little on the inside every time you put down the man I love or pass judgement on the way I am. You stole me away from him ten years ago, and I'll be damned if I let that happen again."

My mom's voice was shaky when she spoke. "Seth, wait. You can't expect us to—"

I interrupted her. "To respect me? To love me? To respect and love the person who means more to me than anyone? Yes, I can."

Her jaw tightened and her arms crossed in front of her chest. I looked over at my dad and saw his gears turning.

"I don't appreciate being threatened in my own home, Seth," he said in his deep voice. "We raised you better than that."

"What exactly will you do with Tisha if you don't have us around to help you?" Mom asked with a sniff.

"I've already spoken to Otto's sister Sassy about babysitting. West and Nico would go in with Jolie and me to share her. Tisha loves their baby Pippa, so you don't need to worry about that anymore," I explained.

I saw the minute my mother realized how serious this was.

"Wait. Wait, Seth," she said. "Let's... can we maybe take some time to calm down and talk again about this tomorrow? None of us want to lose you or that precious girl. Just... just give us some time to come to terms with it, okay?"

I looked over at my father and saw the concern laced in his expression as well. "Okay," I said with a nod. "Thank you for listening to what I had to say."

I turned to exit the house, feeling freer in a way I hadn't felt for a very long time.

After making my way to Otto's, I thought maybe this would be a turning point in my life in Hobie. But my optimism was short-lived.

That night, for the first time since we'd reconnected, things were awkward between Otto and me. It started when he answered the door to his place but wouldn't let me in. It was as if I'd surprised him.

"Oh, hey," he said, closing the door to his cabin behind him so he was standing on the front porch with me. "You're early."

"I'm actually late," I corrected, holding out a bouquet of daisies. "I told you I'd be here at seven and it's seven thirty. I stopped to get you these flowers but Lee Edwin wouldn't shut the fuck up about how the streetlight out front of his house needed a new bulb. As if I'm the damned maintenance department around here."

"We should... we should go for a horse ride," he said quickly. "Come on. I'm sure Gulliver's antsy after I've been gone."

"What's going on with you?" I asked, moving past him to open the door so I could at least put the flowers down.

He lurched between the door and me to stop me. "Uh, nothing. What makes you think something's going on?"

I stared at him. "Really? Because you're acting like a mouse in a snake house right now."

Otto reached out his hands and cupped the sides of my neck before pulling me in for a deep kiss. I might have dropped the flowers by accident and sprung a boner right there on the front porch.

"Come ride with me, Seth."

Fuck. He knew what that damned growl did to me.

"Fine. Let me just put these in water first," I said, holding out my empty hand before realizing the flowers were on the ground. I looked up at him with a grin.

"Leave them, let's go. We'll be back super quick. C'mon."

He dragged me off the porch and over to the barn where we saddled up the horses and mounted up for a ride. Out of habit, we headed toward one of our favorite spots where a creek ran across part of the ranch and there was a giant weeping willow tree that leaned across the water.

Otto didn't say a word while we rode. It wasn't unusual, really.

Sometimes he was a very quiet guy. But I could tell something was bothering him and it didn't take much to figure out what it was. His life was in limbo. He didn't know when and if he'd be able to return to work, and he didn't know when and if he'd be charged with a crime he had no way of defending himself against.

The situation made both of us feel helpless.

Once we got to the creek, we dismounted and let the horses drink. I reached for Otto's hand and pulled him over to sit with me under the tree the way we'd done when we were younger.

"Talk to me, baby," I begged. "I hate it when you're stressed like this."

"I'm fine," he lied, trying to give me a shitty fake smile. I rolled my eyes.

"You're a fucking liar is what you are. Try again."

"Seth, you already know what I'm stressed about. Hell, at this point, part of me wants to cop to the damned fires just so we can move on from this. Plea down the jail stint and start serving my couple of years."

The idea of him pleading guilty to a crime he didn't commit made my blood boil.

"That's not happening, so shut your mouth right now," I told him. "And fuck you for even thinking about leaving me when I just goddamned got you back."

He blew out a breath and leaned into me, laying his head on my shoulder and clasping my hand in his. "You know I'm not going to do something that stupid. If nothing else, I wouldn't be able to be a fire-fighter anymore if I plead guilty to arson. Kinda sure that's a deal-breaker right there."

I snorted. "I think you might be right."

"Let's change the subject. Tell me how things are going with Tisha and Jolie. How's Jolie adapting to working full-time?"

"Good, I think. I had dinner with them while you were gone. Jolie seems happy. I think having a job outside the home has made her more confident. I can tell she enjoys dressing professionally and being around people all day. I mean, I think it's tiring too, but overall it seems like it's been good for her."

"And Tish?"

I felt my cheeks tighten in a grin when I thought about her sweet face and plucky personality. "She's having a ball. Spending tons of time with Cody and Eliza. Beth's taken them to the pool a bunch this summer already, and John's been a lifesaver in making sure they always have dinner together as a family even if Jolie and I get caught up with work. If it wasn't for that kind of stability in my family, I wouldn't feel as okay about the divorce, you know? But my family's really come through for Jolie and me with Tisha. As much as they seem to be upset about the split and about me being with you... they've proven they're committed to Tisha at least. And that means the world to me. I think even my parents might come around to accept me and you, if you can believe it."

Something strange came over his face for a brief moment before he smiled at me and straightened up. "That's great, Walker. I'm really glad things are working out with them."

"It's about time. After losing Ross, and then John going into a tailspin of depression, I thought my family was going to be struggling for a long time. But now that we're all settled together here in Hobie... it's really starting to feel like a fresh start. Like it's finally our turn to have an easy time of it."

I didn't tell him about overhearing John and Beth's conversation about Otto's parents' house. There was no way I could bear to see the expression on his face when he learned that there were people, my own fucking brother included, out there who were hoping to profit off of his family's misfortune.

Otto fell quickly back into his silent self, claiming a sudden headache and the desire to head back. When we brushed and fed the horses, he turned to me and said something that both surprised me and planted the first seed of doubt I'd ever had for him.

"I'm afraid I'm not feeling well, Walker. Would you mind if I just went home alone tonight?"

He left me standing in the yard in front of the barn staring after him as his jean-clad ass moseyed on home without me to his cabin. I stared after him like it was some kind of joke, too stunned to say a word.

First, he hadn't let me into his cabin, and then, he hadn't wanted me to stay the night. What exactly was he trying to keep me at arm's length for?

Or was he actually hiding something and the Otto Wilde I thought I'd known my whole life truly had changed in the ten years we'd been apart?

CHAPTER 32

OTTO

Otto,

I still can't believe it. The powers that be in Hobie have offered me the interim sheriff's position. Supposedly the last guy left amidst scandal, and they're desperate for someone Hobie locals know and trust, someone with ties to the community. Here and I never thought I'd see the day my family's ancient Hobie legacy ended up coming in handy. They said it's mine if I want it, so I said yes.

I'm coming home, Otto. Please god find a way to get out of the navy and come home to me.

Until we meet again,

Walker

(Unsent)

IT WAS DECIDED. I was not going to do anything at all to implicate the Walker family in those fires. If having Seth's family safe and stable was important to him, then by god, that's what was going to happen. But I'd be damned if I was going to let some teenaged arsonist think he could light a fire whenever he damned well wanted to. If I found out

Hal had set those fires, I'd give him a piece of my mind without holding back.

In the meantime, I'd totally lied to Walker.

I'd told him I was painting walls at my sisters' place when in reality I was working on an idea I'd come up with on the drive to Dallas.

When Walker and I were ten years old, our elementary school had gone on a field trip to the Museum of the American Railroad in Frisco. We'd both fallen head over heels in love with the place and spent hours and hours after that creating the elaborate model train setup we were going to have in our house one day.

Because there was never a question that we were going to be together forever. Even in those early days, we just said we were going to be roommates and to heck with any girls. The two of us knew right away there would be no wives involved. Obviously, we didn't know there would be husbands or lovers instead, but we knew we wanted to share our lives together and that included a mega-impressive model train collection.

Oh, and Oreos. Lots and lots of Oreos.

So I'd spent the weekend in Dallas with my sisters gathering the supplies I'd needed to start our model train village. It was a miniature Hobie complete with a sheriff's office, the Pinecone, Sugar Britches, Ritches Hardware store, and several of the other places lining the town square. Winnie had also squealed like a pig when she'd found the perfect little gazebo that looked just like the Hobie one in the square.

Hudson had been like a kid in a candy store. He'd even spent the night over at MJ's apartment with me so we could work on the project late into the night. With his OCD tendencies and attention to detail, we'd had the storefronts painted and the landscaping all glued before Seth had called me back home.

But I'd lost track of time after unloading it all from the car when I arrived home from Dallas. It had all been sitting out on my table in the middle of the cabin when he'd arrived. It was too important of a gift to have ruined by him seeing it in unassembled piles like that, so I'd lied and said I had a headache. My hope was to find out if Jolie had an extra key to Walker's lake house and would let me in so I could set it up later in the week and surprise him.

But that all went to shit later that night when someone set fire to my own damned cabin.

Luckily, after Walker had left, I'd lost track of time again working on the train project. I may have been a bit of a train geek myself because four or five hours went by in a flash. It was around two in the morning when I finally realized I truly did have a headache. I'd been squinting at tiny pieces and parts in the light of only one dim lamp for god knew how long when I realized how late it was.

I remembered having gotten up to use the bathroom at one point and turning out all the lights before double-checking the locks on the door. I'd changed into sleep shorts and then decided to check one more thing on the train set. Next thing I knew, it was the middle of the night and my head was killing me. That's what I got for working so long with only one dim lamp.

I dropped my face into my palms and rubbed my face while giving myself a mental lecture on staying up so late. That's where I was when the kitten came tearing out of the bedroom toward the front door just as I heard the sound of glass breaking. I followed the sound quickly toward my bathroom where I saw a sudden blaze of light and heard the muffled *whomp* of flames. I quickly backtracked to the kitchen and found the extinguisher under the sink, grabbing it and racing back to the bathroom to douse the flames. Towels and the shower curtain were igniting each other, lighting up the room like it was the middle of the day. The heat rushing from the tiny space pushed me back, but I was able to direct the hose of the extinguisher and put out the fire faster than I expected.

When I was sure the fire was out, I grabbed the cat and tore out of the cabin, searching around wildly. Orange spots danced in my vision in the dark night air, and I was grateful there was close to a full moon so I at least had a chance of spotting my arsonist.

There.

I saw a figure bolting across one of the pastures, straight toward the corner of the ranch that used to house my parents' house. While I may not have had my shoes on, I knew someone who did.

It took me all of three seconds to deposit Fire Kitten into an empty barn stall and grab Gulliver out of his stall before slipping a bridle over his sleepy face. I explained the situation to him in a fevered hush, knowing he couldn't understand a word I was saying. Maybe it was me just letting my adrenalin escape, but I couldn't seem to keep my mouth shut.

As I gathered a hank of his mane to help me mount up, I noticed a porch light come on in the main house and Grandpa step out on the front door.

"Cabin bathroom was on fire," I yelled. "Double-check it's out."

I didn't wait for his response, just tore out of there on Gulliver's bare back riding hell for leather toward my old house.

Gulliver had been reading my cues for years and had ridden between the barn and my parents' house a million times over the years. The strength of his huge body under my thighs was familiar and energizing and my mind raced with what I was going to say to the culprit when I caught him.

Sure enough, the kid ran out of steam about fifty yards shy of the burn site. I overtook him easily and turned Gulliver around to face the heaving, panting teen. His hands were braced on his knees, but when he looked up at me through Bieber bangs, his eyes were defiant.

"You can't prove it was me," he spat.

"Like hell I can't. Sit your ass down and take a breath. We're going to have a talk."

I hopped off the horse and winced as my bare feet landed on some gravel in the dirt. The only thing I had on was a pair of loose cotton sleep shorts, and for once I was glad for hot Texas summer nights.

Hal stood there glaring at me as if his scrawny thirteen-year-old self was any match for my twenty-eight-year-old firefighter's build.

"I said sit," I commanded, pulling on all my years listening to commanding officers barking out orders to put weight behind my words.

His ass hit the dirt before I could take a breath. I squatted down a few feet away from him and locked eyes with him.

"Tell me what the hell you think you're doing," I said.

"Nothing. I'm not doing anything," he said.

Lie.

I blew out a breath and sat all the way down, crossing my legs and leaning back on my hands. "Well, if you won't tell me, I guess you'll have to tell Chief Paige and your dad."

"He's not my dad," the kid mumbled.

"All right, then how about your mom? What would she say about her son being a three-time arsonist? Or maybe it's more than three?"

Hal's nostrils flared and I realized he looked more like Beth than I'd originally thought. I remembered hearing that his dad had died shortly after Beth had gotten pregnant with Cody, but I wasn't sure I'd ever known how. It was clear from his reaction, I'd hit a sensitive spot.

"You're going to tell the chief anyway, so what the hell's it matter?" he said.

"Who says? The way I see it, this conversation stays between the two of us."

He rolled his eyes. "Yeah, right. You're going to go blab about it to clear your name. I'm not an idiot."

"Hal, when I saw you teaching those kids at the lakeside park about toilet-roll fire starters the other night, I knew you were most likely the one who'd done all this. But I didn't say a word. Not to Walker, not to the chief, or the investigator, and not to your parents. And do you want to know why?"

He huffed, but I could see the curiosity in his eyes.

"Because I love your uncle too much to let you get in trouble with the law. Right or wrong, I'm not going to be the cause of his suffering. And if that means I wind up being pegged for these crimes, then so be it."

"I don't believe you."

"Listen, all I ask in return are two things. The first is that you never, and I mean never even think about setting fire to anything again. If I so much as hear about you offering someone a match for a birthday candle, I'm blowing the whistle. Do you understand?"

His eyes narrowed as if he still didn't trust me. "What's the other thing?"

"You tell me why you did it."

"Fuck you, you're just trying to get me to confess."

I shook my head, but I certainly couldn't blame him for thinking that. "No. I promise it's not that. As you can see," I said, holding out my arms, "I'm obviously not carrying a listening device of any kind. So even if I did tell someone what you said, which I won't, it would be hearsay. Which is inadmissible in court."

"Still. How do I know you're not pulling something?" He dug the back of his tennis shoes into the ground and picked at a long stalk of grass next to his hip.

"You don't. You have to trust me. If you can't trust me as a navy vet or a Hobie firefighter then maybe you can trust me as family, because whether you like it or not, I'm going to be one of your uncles someday in the future. Whether that comes before or after a couple of years in jail for arson remains to be seen, but I promise you, it will happen."

Hal looked off in the distance toward the site of where my childhood home had sat. I tried not to resent the kid in front of me for everything inside that had been lost, but it wasn't easy. That's why I desperately wanted to understand *why* he'd done it.

"My mom's never wanted anything in her life more than to stay home and raise her kids." His voice was quiet when he finally began speaking. His eyes moved around like he was checking out our surroundings for hidden microphones or cameras.

"She gave up her chance at college when my dad wanted to start a family, but then when he died, she lost the house. He didn't have any insurance and there she was, pregnant and raising a three-year-old with no job and no house. Her parents, my other grandparents, took us in and when the baby came, the three of us shared one tiny room. Me and mom slept in a single bed and Cody slept in a portable crib. That went on for over two years. Eventually Mom got a job cleaning houses and she'd have to leave me and Cody with our grandmother during the day.

"I remember when she met John. My grandparents had made us start going to church regularly, and there was a picnic social mixer thing there on Saturday. A group of local college students were in charge of kids' games or something. She told me later that John gave her unlimited tokens for me to toss rings at the glass bottles.

"She deserved that, you know? Someone who was sweet on her. I don't remember much, but I remember being thankful that John took us away from my grandparents' house and put a smile back on my mom's face."

"When we moved down here, it was all finally going to come together. The Walkers told John and my mom we could move into the main ranch house. We lived there for almost four years, Otto. Happy as could be. Eliza came and we had a huge yard to play in and a creek to walk to, plenty of space for our toys and games and family dinners. But then the rest of the family decided to move back and suddenly, we had to find our own place to live. John and my mom were shocked when the Walkers said they were giving the little house to Uncle Seth and Aunt Jolie."

What he was telling me finally started putting the pieces together.

"So you were angry," I prompted.

"Hell yeah I was angry. John and my mom deserved that house more than them! And then Uncle Seth freaking left! And now Jolie and tiny Tish have that place all to themselves. It's not fair. Meanwhile, because Grandpa Walker took my dad's promotion out from under him, all we can afford is a crappy little rental house. All our stuff is jammed in corners, and Cody and I have to share a room. Poor Eliza basically lives in a big closet. And there's Aunt Jolie, living rent free in a Walker home when she's not even technically a Walker!"

The fact that he'd referred to John as his dad during his passionate speech was not lost on me.

"Why start a fire at the little house?"

Hal laughed at himself and closed his eyes in embarrassment. "I just wanted to scare her off a little. I thought maybe if there was a little damage to the house, she'd move in with Uncle Seth and they'd get back together. Seth loves that lake house. Once they were all living there, I figured the little house would be free for us to move into. But then you showed up out of the blue and I freaked."

"And when the fire didn't work? What made you target my parents' house?"

His eyes stayed glued to the ground between his knees. "I overheard them talking about trying to buy that property. But John said they couldn't afford it. I thought it wasn't fair. I mean, there was this huge family house just sitting there empty, and it already bordered the Walker land. It seemed perfect, you know? But he told Mom even if they could afford it, he wasn't sure the owners would sell it."

"So, you got to thinking," I said gently.

"Yeah. I thought if there wasn't a house on it anymore, it'd be cheaper. And what did it matter if it burned down? No one was there, nobody would get hurt."

He looked at me with wide, imploring eyes. "I didn't know all your stuff was still in there! I swear I didn't know anything was still in there. I thought it was empty. Lots of the blinds were down and it was dark."

I nodded but didn't say anything in hopes he'd keep talking. When he didn't, I prompted him again.

"And tonight?"

That's when he started crying.

"I didn't think you were home," he wailed. The reality must have hit him then because he began sobbing so hard, he almost hyperventilated. "I could have hurt you real bad. I didn't know! I swear, Otto, I thought you were at the lake house. Uncle Seth was on the phone earlier telling you to meet him at the lake house. I could have sworn it! I just wanted Uncle Seth to stop seeing you so he could get back together with Aunt Jolie!"

I moved a little closer and rubbed circles on his back, trying to murmur advice on slowing his breathing down. Once he seemed to catch his breath, he looked up at me. Tear tracks caught in the moonlight and the look of devastation came over his pale face.

"After I threw the bottle in the bathroom window, I saw the litter box on the floor."

I squeezed the back of his neck. "She's okay. I put her in the barn after I put out the fire. But I hope you learned your lesson real well, Hal. Even if I hadn't been home, that poor kitten would have been burned to a crisp."

Yes, my words were harsh, but so was the reality of what he'd done. That was nothing compared to the guilt he would have felt if Seth and I had been asleep in my bed when it had happened. I shuddered to think of how close we'd come to that scenario.

Saved by a goddamned model train set.

Hal let out a long, tortured sob again and seemed to curl in on himself. We sat together in silence until I realized the barest flicker of red lights could be seen dancing against the trees between us and my parents' old yard.

Someone had called the damned fire department.

CHAPTER 33

WALKER

Seth,

I'm on my last leg home from Hawaii. Saint and I are trying to get to the ranch in time for Christmas dinner. I can't wait to see my family, but then I'll have to figure out what the next stage of my life is going to look like. There's a firefighter job waiting for me in Dallas, but I'm going to try my best to find a way to stay in Hobie. After all this time overseas, Walker, I miss my family. I need time on the ranch. Time to relax and reacquaint myself with life in the fresh air and sunshine.

But know this: after I get settled, I'm booking a flight to Minneapolis and starting my search for you. If you're still single, you'd better have a damned good reason you aren't sleeping in my bed every night, Seth Walker. I'm sick and fucking tired of waiting and wanting.

You belong with me.

Otto

(Unsent)

THIS TIME when the middle of the night call came in about Otto and a fire, I was overwhelmed by a feeling not only of deja vu, but also of inevitability.

It was like my subconscious knew something else was coming down the pike. Either that, or Otto had been right and bad things, like fire, really did come in threes.

I hustled out of bed and raced to the scene. When I heard the location of the fire, I damn near shit myself. Before I could even draw breath to ask the seriousness of the blaze, the dispatcher stopped me.

"He's fine, Sheriff. No casualties."

Thank fucking god.

When I pulled up, however, Otto was nowhere to be found.

"Where is he?" I asked as I approached a group of people including my deputy, Shayna, Grandpa, Doc, and the fire chief.

It was Doc who answered first. "Took off on Gulliver." His face was pinched with concern, and I noticed he was gripping Grandpa Wilde's hand for all he was worth.

"What?" I asked. "He went for a horse ride?"

It was like three o'clock in the damned morning.

"So, wait. He doesn't know his cabin was on fire?" I asked. "I don't understand."

Chief Paige stepped forward. "From what we can gather, there was another portable incendiary device thrown through his bathroom window. He must have been aware of it, because he was able to put it out with a fire extinguisher and escape the house. He headed toward the barn, which is when Mr. Wilde here," he said, nodding toward Grandpa, "heard a commotion in the barn and came out to see what was going on."

Grandpa took over. "He told me the bathroom had caught on fire, but that he'd put it out. Then he asked me to check to make sure it was all the way out. That's when he took off on Gulliver."

I spun around on my heel, looking in all directions. "Which way?"

Doc met my eye and seemed to be sending me a silent message. But there were too many places he could be. His parents' house, the weeping willow, a clearing where we used to build forts.

I looked back at the fire chief. "Who called it in?"

"Alarm company. Apparently when Felix originally built this place, he put in a high-end fire detection system both here and in his glass workshop because of the gas furnace. When it sensed the fire, it called it in automatically."

I began walking back to my vehicle. "I'll go find him."

Before I got to the car, the chief called out. "You'll bring him back here, won't you, Sheriff?"

I felt my teeth press together in annoyance at the implication I'd skirt the law. "I'm gonna pretend you didn't ask that, *Chief.*"

When I pulled up in his parents' driveway, I saw him sitting alone in the far edge of the front yard. Gulliver was snacking on some long blades of grass and meandering around close to his favorite guy.

I got out and approached him.

"You pulling a Paul Revere on us?" I called out softly.

He turned to face me, revealing deep creases on his forehead.

"You know I always did like a midnight ride," he said with a smirk. "Good for what ails you."

"And did it work?" I asked, looking around for signs of anyone else. I'd hoped and prayed he'd lit out of the barn in pursuit of someone else, but it looked like he just wanted to return to someplace meaningful.

"Not so much, no."

I sat down next to him and put my arm around his bare shoulders. He looked to be in his damned underwear, but upon closer inspection I saw they were baggy shorts of some kind.

"What happened, Otto?" I asked.

He leaned his head on my shoulder and I could make out the smell of smoke in his hair.

"Bathroom caught fire."

"Yeah. Yeah, I heard." I pressed a kiss to his forehead. "I want to know how."

He looked up into my eyes and lied right to my face. "Dunno. Maybe I left a candle burning."

I closed my eyes and counted to ten to keep from ripping into him. And then I did it again since ten wasn't nearly enough.

"Unless you've started using liquor bottles as candles, that isn't what happened. Care to try again?"

Suddenly he looked up at me with worry on his face. "You didn't go in there, did you?"

"In where?"

"My cabin."

"No. I came out here to find you. Why?"

He seemed relieved, and it reminded me he'd been hiding something from me earlier that night.

"No reason. I just don't want you going in there."

"Dammit, Otto. What the hell are you hiding? Fucking talk to me, baby," I cried. "You're deliberately being obtuse. Why won't you let me help you?"

He stood up and brushed off his shorts before grabbing a handful of Gulliver's mane and hopping up on the big horse's back. "I'll meet you back at the barn."

And that was that. He didn't look at me, touch me, or say another word to me.

"Fuck," I muttered. "Who the hell are you protecting?"

I hopped in my patrol car and made my way back to the barn where Chief Paige didn't even wait for him to put Gulliver away before he directed my deputy to take Otto into custody.

Poor Shayna looked at me for direction, and I looked at my boyfriend standing there in the dark in his fucking pajamas. I felt like my heart was being shredded all over again like it had when I'd left him for Minnesota. We'd been standing right by this same stretch of fence when I'd told him.

There must have been something awful and desperate on my face because Otto walked right up to Shayna with his hands out to the sides and lowered to his knees so she could cuff him. The sight of him turning himself in to prevent me from having to authorize his arrest made me want to vomit right there in front of everyone. Instead, I began to step forward, to stop this from happening, when I felt strong arms around me from behind and Doc's soothing voice in my ear.

"Let him do this. You can sort it out afterwards, but let him do this."

"I can't," I breathed, feeling on the verge of panic. I was the fucking sheriff, and I couldn't help him. "He didn't do it."

"I know. But he'd be devastated if you lost your job because of him, Seth."

I turned like a coward and let Doc pull me into a hug. There was no way I could watch the love of my life being arrested in my own damned jurisdiction for a crime I knew he didn't commit. Now I knew why families of criminals proclaimed their loved one's innocence till their dying breath. When you loved someone, it was impossible to think them capable of a crime.

Jesus, I was acting like all those idiot families—the ones my buddies and I would roll our eyes at in court when they sobbed and swore their lover or mother or brother couldn't have done such a thing. Now here I was, in the same damned denial.

Otto was careful not to look at me as Shayna cuffed him and followed protocol to place him in her squad car. After they pulled away, Grandpa and Doc both squeezed my shoulder before rushing off to follow the squad car to town.

I looked at Evan Paige. "What's the evidence to justify his arrest?"

The pity in his eyes was impossible to bear. "I'm not charging him yet, Seth. But he needs to explain some things. This is just the straw that broke the camel's back."

"What was on those lab reports?"

"Trace evidence found on the toilet-roll fire starter at Jolie's house showed the lint had been sprinkled liberally with a specific mineral spirit sold for use in painting toy models."

"So? What does that have to do with Otto?"

"We found the exact same kind of mineral in Otto's cabin."

"You couldn't have known that before tonight. Plus, all kinds of people build model shit. Hell, my nephews and I build model trains. That doesn't prove anything."

"We didn't know before tonight. That's why we just wanted to talk to him about it—to question him. But, Seth, you have to see that the evidence is only pointing us in one direction here. I know it's hard to accept. Believe me, I don't want to accept it either. But we can't let our personal feelings stop us from doing our jobs."

"Fuck!" I snapped. "This doesn't make any damned sense. Tell me why! Why would he do this? Why would he wreck his own damned place, Evan?"

He sighed and shrugged. "Firefighter arson maybe. Plenty of firebugs become firefighters and vice versa. Or maybe he has some kind of PTSD left over from what happened in the navy that's having a negative effect on him of some kind. Maybe there's a psychological explanation. We simply need to ask him some more questions, Seth. That's all."

I pulled out my phone and dialed Otto's brother, West. When he answered in a sleepy voice, I started talking right away. "Hey, it's Walker. Listen, I need you to come keep an eye on Otto's cabin. There's been another fire. He's fine, everyone's fine, but I don't want to leave his place unprotected."

"What? Wait… what?" His groggy voice came over the line, and I heard Nico in the background asking who it was.

"The lab techs are coming here and I think your family might want some, ah, representation here when that happens. You know, like maybe a lawyer or something?"

"Oh, right. Okay. I'm up. I'm coming. Where are Grandpa and Doc?"

"Headed to the sheriff's office. They took Otto in."

"Who did?"

I sighed and raked my fingers through my hair. "My deputy did it, but it may as well have been me. He's at the county jail, West. I've got to get over there and make sure he's okay."

"Shit, Walker. Fuck."

"Yeah. So… I'll leave the ranch in your hands?"

"I'll be there in five minutes."

I lit out of there without saying another word to Evan Paige. I was at my office in less than ten minutes and quickly made my way to the back room where our two jail cells sat. They were usually empty, but tonight everything had changed.

There, in a pair of scrubs, bless Doc's heart, sat my other half. On the wrong damned side of the bars.

His face lifted when he heard my footsteps, and I noticed Shayna had been nice enough to let Doc and Grandpa sit on the bench against the wall opposite the cells so they could visit with him.

"Hey," I said, walking up to the desk where Shayna sat filling out reports. My eyes stayed glued on Otto while I removed my gun belt and emptied my pockets, leaving everything remotely controversial on the desk with my deputy. Once I was unencumbered, I asked Shayna to let me into the cell.

Otto's eyes had tracked me with confusion while I'd halfway disrobed, but when I entered the cell and came straight for him, he seemed to finally understand. He stood and walked into my arms.

God, he felt so good. Even though he smelled like smoke, he still felt like my Otto. He turned his face into my neck, and I held him even tighter. I knew we were on display for anyone to see, but I didn't give a shit. I felt like I'd truly just gotten him back after all these years and now was going to have to watch while the same justice I'd fought for in the police academy and in my job as a peace officer was used against the one person I felt didn't deserve it.

He pulled back and took my face in his hands, forcing me to look at him.

"I am not going to fight this, Seth."

I opened my mouth to argue with the idiot, but he stopped me.

"This is a state jail felony since no one was targeted or hurt. The most I'll get for that is two years. Instead of spending god knows how many more months fighting this, I'd rather just start my time."

I barked out a laugh. "That's ridiculous. I've never heard something more insane in all my life. You're pulling my leg."

I could tell by the look on his face, he was not, in fact, pulling my leg.

"No," I growled. "No fucking way. You're insane if you think I'm going to let you plead guilty to a crime you didn't commit."

"Baby—"

"No!" I shouted. Out of the corner of my eye, I saw Doc and

Grandpa jump, but I kept my gaze locked on the motherfucker in front of me. "No martyr bullshit, Otto. Over my dead body."

He let out a sigh and then smiled at me, fucking *smiled*. "You have to trust me, Walker. I'm doing the right thing here. Please trust that I know what I'm doing."

I ran my fingers down the familiar planes of his face. "Who are you protecting?" I whispered.

His smile only deepened. "You once sacrificed a whole lot to give a kid a strong start in life. I don't know if I ever told you how proud I am of you for being such a good man, Seth Walker."

"Stop," I begged. "Please, stop. *Please.*"

I could feel myself losing my cool. As if I'd still had it to begin with.

Otto pulled me in for another hug and cradled the back of my head in his big hand. His mouth landed near my ear and he began murmuring words of love one after the other like a prayer.

"Do you have any idea how much I love you? You left here when you were still a kid and you had to grow up so fast, sweetheart. But you did it. You went to college while you had a newborn and then you graduated from the police academy and now you're the county's youngest sheriff. You're an incredibly devoted father and uncle and son and boyfriend. Hobie locals love you, and I love you. So, so much."

"Otto…" I breathed against his skin. "This is stupid. You're not going to jail for these fires. Forget it."

I pulled back and tried to shake off the sadness he was rubbing off on me. A couple of discreet swipes of my face, and it was like it wasn't even happening.

"No," I said, taking in a deep cleansing breath. "I'm calling Honovi Baptiste, and we're getting you out of here."

I turned to leave the cell, but Otto reached for my hand and pulled me back against him, my back landing against his chest. "When I get out of here, I have a surprise for you."

My eyes closed at the sound of his low rumble. "You gonna give me a hint?" I asked.

"Nope. Just wanted you to have a reason to wait for me."

I turned to him and gathered the fabric of the front of his shirt up to yank him closer until we were eye to eye. "I will never, ever leave you again as long as you draw breath on this earth. And if they send you to the farthest jail from Hobie, I will move there while you serve your time, jackass."

Otto just grinned and looked at me with those gorgeous green eyes and his face full of freckles so faded, you could only see them from up close. In that beautiful face I saw it all—my past, my present, and my future.

When I stepped out of the cell and turned back into the sheriff, I breathed easier.

Because I did trust Otto Wilde. And if copping to a crime he didn't commit was something he felt compelled to do, then I would make sure he went through the process as smoothly as possible.

But I'd be lying if I said I didn't want to find the bastard who set those fires and wring his goddamned neck, and no amount of Otto's good intentions were going to keep me from searching for the real arsonist.

Little did I know, the call was coming from inside the house.

CHAPTER 34

OTTO

Otto,

I found you in the barn today and thought I'd never seen anything more beautiful than your face. Touching you, kissing you, going down on you... all of those things were both familiar and new, comforting and exciting as hell.

Until I fucked it up.

The ring. The goddamned ring. I'm sorry I didn't tell you first. I'm sorry when I saw you, my brain went completely off line so I could touch you. But know this: you are mine Otto Wilde. And I'm done with trying to do the right thing. From this moment forward, I will do everything in my power to give you the life you always wanted and the love you always deserved.

You've waited ten years for me, baby. And you shouldn't have to wait a minute more.

I am yours forever,
Walker
(Unsent)

WHEN MORNING CAME, Honovi was able to spring me from the pokey. At least that's what I kept calling it. Hon wasn't quite as impressed with my lingo as I hoped he'd be. Instead, he was cursing me up a storm for "cavorting with the enemy," which I was pretty sure was his way of saying the sheriff.

"I think you mean 'sleeping' with the enemy," I mumbled while he signed some paperwork at an empty desk near Walker's in the main office area.

"Zip it," he said.

Walker had gotten up to get me a cup of coffee now that I was no longer in the cell. I was, however, handcuffed until the final whatever had been completed.

It was the handcuffs that led to my freedom in the end.

I was holding them up and joking about my fancy new jewelry when Hal Walker came racing through the front doors ahead of his parents.

"He didn't do it! He didn't do it! I did! I set the fires."

The entire office went still, and I heard the sound of a ceramic coffee mug biting the dust. I looked back to see Walker with his jaw open and coffee stains on the lower part of his uniform pants from where it had splashed when the mug hit the cement floor.

Hal's eyes were riveted on my cuffs, and it was obvious to me the reality of his actions had finally thrown him for a major loop.

"Hal, shh," I snapped. "Beth, John, get him out of here."

"Wait," Seth called from behind me. "Wait a minute. What are you guys doing here?"

Hal rushed forward, pulling out of John's and Beth's attempts to wrangle him back through the front door. Clearly they hadn't known what he was going to do.

"Uncle Seth, he didn't do it," Hal said urgently. His voice was shaky and hoarse and his eyes were red-rimmed. "You have to believe me. He didn't. He wouldn't have."

Seth looked up and around at all of us sitting in the sheriff's office before realizing what needed to be done.

"Hal, stop talking right now for just a minute, okay? Honovi, can you give me the name of a guardian ad litem or family attorney who can handle this for us?"

Hon nodded and pulled out his phone. In the meantime, Doc and

Grandpa walked back into the sheriff's office with armloads of pastries and coffees from Sugar Britches.

"What's going on?" Grandpa asked Doc.

"Don't know. Something is, though. That's for sure."

They made their way to the front counter and handed off half their spoils to Luanne, who accepted them as if this was all part and parcel of her regular workday.

Which, in a way, maybe it was.

I shook my head at them as a way of telling them to sit tight and not interfere. They took their seats in the reception area in two waiting chairs and began drinking their coffee.

"But, Uncle Seth," Hal began.

Seth held up a hand before using it to tilt Hal's chin up so he could lock eyes with him. "If you never listen to another word I say, Harold Covington Walker, listen to this. Do not say another word. Nod your head to agree."

Hal's eyes shifted to me, and I nodded emphatically at him. "Listen to Seth, Hal. He knows what he's talking about."

I ignored Hon as he shot me a dirty look for opening my own mouth.

Hal nodded at Seth and took a seat in a chair next to Shayna, who had resumed her reports at her desk in the open office rather than the jail area in the back.

Once my own paperwork was completed, I was free to go. They hadn't charged me with a crime in the end. Their intention had been to question me, but Honovi had arrived and put a quick stop to that instead. Now it looked like maybe I wouldn't get charged after all. But did that mean Hal would?

I didn't stick around to find out. Honovi basically booted my ass out of there as fast as possible and told me to go home to the ranch and sit tight.

Considering I hadn't slept at all, he didn't need to tell me twice. I looked back for Seth before walking out the front doors, but found him entrenched in a conversation with John and Beth. I could tell from their body language, Seth wasn't getting out of there anytime soon.

I let Grandpa and Doc take me home, and I fell into the bed in their guest room without even taking off my scrubs.

When I awoke sometime later, I was under the covers with a man attached to my back.

Oh, and I was buck naked.

"What the hell?" I mumbled, turning over.

Seth Walker was buck naked too and had been spooning the hell out of me for lord only knew how long.

"Hey, beautiful," I said with a smile, reaching out to run my fingers through his hair. His eyes opened and looked so sad, all the memories of the previous night and subsequent morning came rushing back. "Oh, honey, I'm so sorry about Hal."

"No, I'm the one who's so sorry. I should have seen it. I should have known."

"Baby, how in the world could you have known?"

"All the clues were there. I just didn't want to see it. I thought it was John, but then he had an alibi. I thought it was John, Otto."

His eyes filled and began to spill over. I thumbed them off before leaning in and kissing his lips softly. He let me kiss him for a little while, our mouths moving slowly together while our bodies moved closer to intertwine naturally. My hand landed on his warm back, and I moved it up and down to feel the swell of his bare ass and the dip of his lower spine.

"I'm sorry," I breathed into his mouth. "I tried to keep him from being found out. I didn't want him to get in trouble."

The tears came faster now. "That's why I'm so fucking pissed at you," he groaned, ducking his head under my chin and sniffling. "Why? Why did you do that?"

"He was scared and confused, Seth. He's too young to realize the consequences of his actions. You know what it's like in the justice system sometimes. What if he got a bad deal? What if he got a super-strict judge? What if he got some juvie time and met up with some bad apples?"

"He's not your responsibility. Why do you always feel like you need to give everyone the benefit of the doubt? You did the same thing by not ratting out that bastard who set the fire on the *Poseyville.*"

That one was easy.

I pulled him off me so that I could look at him. "Because the one time in my life I didn't give someone the benefit of the doubt, you were gone for ten fucking years. If I'd trusted my instincts and given you the benefit of the doubt back then, I would have come to fucking Minnesota and found out what the hell was going on."

"And what difference would that have made?" he asked, clearly overwhelmed and exhausted.

I grinned. "We could have had ourselves a real interesting threesome marriage and diaper duty would have been much easier with six hands instead of four."

He smacked my chest, but a small smile appeared on his gorgeous lips. I considered that a win.

"Seth, when I thought it was John who did this, I realized you'd feel responsible for Beth and the kids. You'd add four more mouths to feed to your already full plate of responsibility. I couldn't let that happen. So when I found out it was Hal instead of John, I'd already accepted my fate. Plus, I knew there couldn't be enough evidence for more than the lightest of arson crimes which, honestly, is only a maximum two-year sentence. It wasn't like I took his spot in the electric chair or anything."

Walker's eyes narrowed at me. "Can we make an agreement no more taking the fall for people in my own damned jurisdiction?"

I thought about how many people I loved in his jurisdiction... Grandpa, Doc, Sassy, West, Nico, Pippa, Cal, Tisha... "Mm, nope. Sorry. Can't make that promise."

He rolled over on top of me and I felt his soft cock press against mine, instantly making it not quite so soft.

"How about a moratorium on guilty pleas for like... six months?"

I put my index finger to my chin for a moment before reluctantly agreeing. "Fine, but only if you tell your family to stop setting my shit on fire."

The look on Walker's face was priceless. Shock, outrage, and then finally a reluctant smile when he realized I was trying to lighten the moment.

"You're a great man, Otto Wilde," he said before leaning down to kiss me. I noticed his cock was now the opposite of soft.

I wiggled my hips back and forth to tease him a little.

"Did Hon find you a good attorney for Hal?" I asked, running my hands down to cup his perfect ass.

He thrust into me and nodded. "A guy in the next county. I've heard of him. Specializes in juvie crime. Honovi told John not to worry about Hal at all, but they'll know more after reaching out to Evan Paige. In the meantime, Evan texted me to tell me he was sorry and to tell you to show up Monday morning ready to work."

Hearing I had my job back was bittersweet. My arson ordeal might be ending, but Hal's was just beginning.

"He'll be okay, Otto. As a kid, he probably won't get more than shit tons of community service. Surely you knew that before you agreed to take the fall."

"It will still be on his record and give him a rougher start than others," I argued.

Seth shook his head. "That's where you're wrong, baby. It will teach him to be grateful for second chances and to be glad his biggest mistake happened when he was only thirteen."

"Let's hope," I said.

"Mm," he agreed, leaning down to tease my lips with the tip of his tongue. "Let's hope. And let's not think about it again until tomorrow. Or the next day. It'll take a while for them to change direction on the case and re-evaluate the evidence."

I gave in to the kiss and licked deeply into his mouth, savoring the ability to take my time with him as he ground his pelvis into mine. Our cocks rubbed up against each other until we were pretty much dry humping and necking like we'd done a million times as teenagers.

"Sometimes I forget we can actually fuck," Walker said with a laugh. "Wanna do that? Wanna fuck?"

His eyes were teasing and his lips were puffy and red.

"Hell yeah I wanna fuck. Have I ever said no to that?" I stretched to the side to reach for the lube when I realized we were in my grandparents' guest bedroom. "Shit."

Walker crawled across me and continued to open the drawer, actually finding lube there. "Bingo. Leave it to a family of gays to stash lube everywhere."

I shuddered at the thought of the number of people in my family who'd had sex in this room, including Doc and Grandpa.

"Oh shit, boner killer," Seth murmured, moving down to help me with my sudden problem. "Gonna have to suck this bad boy back into action."

He only needed to say the word *suck* before it plumped right up again, but seeing the top of his head going down on me was enough to make it granite-hard and jumpy.

"Suck me," I muttered under my breath. "Please suck me."

After a few quick but glorious slurps, Seth popped his head up and grinned at me. "Are you talking to yourself?"

He looked so cute with his hair all messy from sleep and his eyes twinkling with love and lust.

Bubbles of laughter came out of me before I could stop them, and it only made Seth grin even wider.

"What?" he asked. "Why are you laughing?"

"Because you're beautiful, you're here, and you're *mine*," I said.

He leaned in to kiss me again before speaking. "And you're the most dedicated, patient soul mate I could have asked for. You're more than I deserve, Ottawa Hubert Wilde, but I'm taking you anyway, and never, ever giving you back."

Right as I was finally about to slide my lubed cock into my soul mate's tight ass, the guest room door creaked open and froze us on the spot.

In walked a tiny orange-flamed kitten with all the sass and spunk of our goddamned pain-in-the-ass rooster.

Seth and I looked at the cat and then looked at each other and named that fucker at the exact same time.

"*Cockblock.*"

It was the following weekend when Seth was busy as hell with the Hootenanny that I was finally able to sneak over to the lake house and set up the model train set. He'd given me a key to the lake house and told me to move in since my bathroom was a complete disaster at the cabin. We both knew that once I was there, I wasn't ever leaving, and both of us were a thousand percent fine with that.

Doc and Grandpa had a field day helping me set everything up, and Jolie even stopped by to bring Tisha over to help. I'd run into them in town at the festival the night before and pulled Jolie aside to ask a favor.

"Do you have any photos of you and Tisha I could copy?" I'd asked.

She'd smiled and asked what I was up to. I noticed a new lightness to her I hadn't seen before and wondered what was going on with her these days. She'd come over a few more times to ride horses with Tisha, and I had to admit things were getting friendlier between us.

"I'm putting together a model train set for him as a surprise, and I built a little version of your house for the town. I thought I'd paste photos of you guys in the windows. Is that too corny or what?" I'd asked.

She'd reached out and squeezed my arm. "He's going to flip, Otto. I'll find something for you tonight and bring it over after Seth leaves for work."

Now that she was there helping me set things up, I could tell she was distracted.

"You okay?" I asked.

She looked up in surprise from where she was sweeping up some spilled grass particles from the town square piece. "Yeah, um... hey... do you think... I mean, do you think I could ask Seth to keep Tisha a few extra days next weekend?"

"Of course. He'd love it. And if he has to work, I'm around. I can always get Sassy to come help if you'd feel more comfortable—"

She held up her hand. "No, no. I trust you, Otto. It's just... I've been invited out of town for the weekend and feel a little strange telling Seth about it."

"Jolie, he'll be happy you're doing something for yourself. Trust me on that. You going to tell me where you're going?"

I'd noticed the blush on her face and wondered if I was being too personal.

"Daevon Hays and I have been seeing each other a little bit. You might have heard about it at the firehouse?"

I blinked at her in surprise. "No, not at all. Although, now that you mention it, he has seemed extra happy lately. But I only started back to work on Monday."

She flushed even redder and looked down. "Yeah, well, anyway... he and his sister invited me to go their family's condo down near Galveston to spend the weekend at the beach."

"That sounds like fun. I'm sure it's no problem for us to have Tisha. You guys go and have a good time. You deserve a break."

"Thanks. I really appreciate that. And thank you for what you did for Hal. I didn't get a chance to tell you but... that was really big of you. I can see why Seth cares about you so much."

"The feeling is mutual, Jolie. And thank you for trusting me with Tisha. She's a special young woman. You should be really proud of her. You and Seth have done a great job raising her," I said.

She met my eyes and beamed before shocking me with a big hug. It was over almost before it started, but it was heartfelt and marked a change in our relationship. After that, I felt like maybe the four of us plus our extended families could give Tisha Walker the best life possible.

When it was time for Walker to get home late that night, I had the train running and all the little town lights on. The lake house lights were mostly out and when his keys hit the table by the door, I spoke up so I didn't spook him.

"Surprise," I said softly.

His head snapped up in surprise. "What's all this?"

"This is what I've been working on for you and why I didn't want you coming into my place the night of the fire. When I was in Dallas, I remembered how you and I had always daydreamed about having a house with a model train set, so I figured it was time."

"Otto, look at it," he said in an awed hush as he approached it slowly. The little engine raced around, past Sugar Britches bakery, the sheriff's office, the Pinecone, and the post office. Then it turned down by Ritches Hardware and headed out toward the lake, which was on the floor over by the huge windows of the family room that looked out over the real lake.

"We can add to it as we want. This is just a start," I began, knowing I was probably going to babble nervously until I was sure he liked it.

His eyes flicked up to mine and that's all the answer I needed.

"This is the most amazing thing anyone's ever done for me," he said. "Thank you. Fuck, Wilde Man, you're gonna make me cry worse than when we read each other's letters the other night." He squatted down to look at the tiny buildings and details. "Look! There's Tisha's house and Doc and Grandpa's barn... Oh my god, there's Gulliver," he said with a laugh before looking back up at me.

"You like it then?" I teased.

He stood up and walked over to me, sliding his hands around my waist and pulling me close. "I love it. It really is the most amazing gift, Otto. The best thing you could have given me."

It was now or never.

Okay, that wasn't quite right. But it was now because I just couldn't wait any longer.

I reached in my pocket and pulled out the rest of his gift, presenting it to him on my open palm while his arms were still around me.

"Well, not quite. Maybe *this* is the best thing I could give you. My grandfather's ring. The one I've been waiting a decade to put on your finger. It's the real reason I went into the fire at Mom and Dad's house that night." Well, that and the letters, but he already knew about those.

I could tell he was torn between wanting to shoot me and kiss me. "Don't you know that your healthy body is worth more to me than any symbol you could ever give me? I don't need a ring nearly as much as I need your steady heartbeat next to mine in bed every night, Otto. How could you take such a risk?"

I could feel my tears coming but my jaw tried to remain firm while I spoke. "Because we've had too many of our dreams taken away from us, dammit. And I didn't want to lose this too."

I pulled back from our embrace and got down on one knee.

"Please."

It was all I said.

But from the look on his face, I could tell it was enough.

EPILOGUE

WALKER - THREE MONTHS LATER

My hands were shaking, and I couldn't stop cursing.

"Fuck."

Otto bit his tongue to keep from laughing at me. "Baby, it's going to be okay. You're going to survive it, I promise."

"Shit. Fuck. Goddammit," I muttered, looking away.

"Baby." This time it was Nico who muttered the word, and it wasn't an endearment.

"I'm sorry? Just because you're a human pincushion doesn't mean other people don't feel pain," I snapped. "Now get on with it before I change my mind."

Nico's eyes met mine. "Dude, I know how much a tattoo hurts. Believe me, I do. I'm healing one on my tit right now."

"Oh Jesus," Otto muttered, leaning back in the chair next to mine and closing his eyes. "Here we go."

It was West's turn to chime in. "Show it to him, Nico."

That was all it took for Nico to strip down and parade his boobs at me. The reddened area over his heart was puffy with fresh ink.

"What's it say?" I asked. "Is that a website address?"

"No, jackass. It's West's initials with the word Pipsqueak weaving

293

in and out of it. See?" He shoved his left pec in my face, and I couldn't help but notice the nipple piercings. I had to admit those were hot.

I turned to Otto. "Would you ever—"

He cut me off. "No."

"Dammit, you didn't even let me finish."

"You were going to ask me to get nipple barbells," he said, closing his eyes like he was relaxed enough for a nap despite the giant stranger pressing needles into his skin.

"I… but I…" I looked from Nico to West and back to Otto. "But I really want you to get some. They're hot as fuck," I whined.

"Then you get them," he muttered.

My eyes shot to Nico, who had a decidedly evil grin on his face.

"Don't even think about it," I growled. "The wedding ring tattoo is all I can handle right now. Whose idea was it anyway? I have a perfectly good ring right here that you walked into an inferno to get for me, remember?"

"These are for when we can't wear our rings when we're in a dangerous situation for work. And I'm sorry to be such a burden on you," Otto said. "If you were so opposed to marriage, why'd you do it so many times?"

"Twice, jerk face. Two times. That's my limit. If this one doesn't take, I give up," I promised.

"Then I guess we'd better make it work," he said with a wink.

I reached out my right hand to squeeze his shoulder. "I love you."

"I know," he said with his eyes closed again. "I'm still not getting the nipple piercings."

"Dammit."

Nico tried to distract me from the pain. "Hey, I heard the judge went easy on Hal. How's your family doing?"

I blew out a breath. "Yeah. The prosecutor was a single mom who really worked with us. Agreed to plead it way down to a Class C misdemeanor vandalism charge, which just carried a fine. John and Beth insisted he do community service too, so she included that. He'll do most of it through the youth center. I think the biggest help was Bill and Shelby, honestly."

West looked up and met my eyes. "Mom and Dad didn't want Hal to be hobbled by this, Walker. You would have done the same thing in their shoes. Plus, John and Beth are paying out the cost of the house in their financing of the purchase, so Mom and Dad didn't have to claim it on their insurance."

"Yeah. My parents are helping them. Dad leased out some of his pasture land to help pay for it. If you ask me, he should have been doing that all along since the family ranch hasn't been used for cattle in decades," I said.

Hudson spoke up from where he sat on a stool in the corner of the second-floor tattoo shop. "Mom and Dad sent me a copy of the letter Hal wrote to them. It was sincere and thoughtful. I'll send you a copy so you can show John and Beth. They'd be proud of him."

It was Otto's turn to chime in. "I'm so damned proud of him owning up to what he did. He even apologized to Tisha for making her lie about seeing me at Mom and Dad's house that night. It couldn't have been easy to spell it all out the way he did. Takes balls to confront your mistakes like that."

West looked over at Hudson. "Speaking of mistakes, did you tell Otto what you did to Darci?"

"Fuck," Hudson muttered, looking at his feet. "I don't want to talk about it."

"What'd he do?" Otto asked. "You have to tell us now."

"It's too embarrassing. Fucking rookie mistake," Hudson said with a put-upon sigh.

West turned to us with glee. "You remember how our geek brother invented some kind of special doohickey to improve the beer taps? It regulates the amount of foam in a pour."

We nodded.

West chuckled. "Well, it happens to be a little metal ring that attaches to the end of the tap. He wanted to present it to Darci on their one-year anniversary of dating as a kind gesture to her and her family since they're so into beer making."

Oh god.

"So he put the metal ring in a tiny box..." At this point West giggled too hard to continue. Hudson looked like he wanted to crawl under the stool he sat on.

Nico winked at me. "And then presented it to her in front of her family with a big production."

"Oh shit," I whispered.

"No," Otto gasped. "Hudson, fuck."

Hudson groaned and covered his face with his hands. "I didn't even think."

The big tattoo artist who was helping Nico looked sympathetic. "What did she do?"

"She saw the tiny box and freaked. Her mother screamed and her sister squealed and started videoing it," Hudson said. "I still didn't understand what the big deal was until Darci opened it and saw the head constrictor."

At the term "head constrictor" every man in the room burst into laughter. I thought Hudson Wilde was going to shrink into nothingness. His face was the color of pickled beets.

"Please tell me you nicknamed it the cock ring," Nico hooted.

"Jesusfuckingchrist," Hudson said.

None of us could stop laughing even though we all felt sorry for the guy.

"Hudson accidentally proposed to Darci with a cock ring?" Otto snorted, setting me off even more.

"Needless to say, we broke up," Hudson confessed.

"Crap. Sorry, man," I said.

He shrugged. "It's fine. I think I'm broken. I don't seem to get as much out of relationships as other people do. I think it's going to be easier to be alone, honestly."

West walked over and put his hand on Hudson's shoulder. "You just haven't found the right woman, Hud. I promise you that. When you find the right person, you'll finally see the difference."

"I really liked her. She was nice and pretty. Social, you know? I liked that she had lots of friends and always made plans for us. Otherwise, I'd be sitting at home alone with my nose in a book or tinkering with pieces and parts."

"Well," Otto said, "why don't you let the rest of us be your social life for a while? Walker needs to be introduced to nightlife in the big city anyway."

"Great, just what I need. A bunch of gay guys dragging me to dance clubs," Hudson muttered. "Been there, done that, got the rainbow T-shirt to prove it."

West held up an index finger. "I'd just like to point out that the last time you came to Station 4 with us, you got more dick than any of us did."

Hudson couldn't help but chuckle. "I didn't realize dancing with guys meant getting humped the whole time. That takes some getting used to."

Otto turned to me with a wink. "That's the best part."

"It's his eyes," Nico said, gazing at Hudson. "They're bedroom eyes. That's why the guys can't leave him alone."

Hudson blushed, and West came over to smack Nico in the shoulder. "That's my brother, asshole. My *straight* brother."

"Baby, he's a Wilde. How straight could he possibly be?"

UP NEXT: Hudson takes his odd invention to Ireland where he meets the most beautiful redhead he's ever seen. Only... it's not a woman. Grab *Hudson's Luck* now!

LETTER FROM LUCY

Dear Reader,

Thank you so much for reading *Wilde Fire*, the third book in the Forever Wilde series!

Up next is Hudson's story as he jets off to Ireland in search of redemption. What he finds there might surprise you. *Hudson's Luck* is available now.

Be sure to follow me on Amazon to be notified of new releases, and look for me on Facebook for sneak peeks of upcoming stories.

Please take a moment to write a review of *Wilde Fire* on Amazon and Goodreads. Reviews can make all the difference in helping a book show up in Amazon searches.

Feel free to sign up for my newsletter, stop by www.LucyLennox.com or visit me on social media to stay in touch. We have a super fun reader group on Facebook that can be found here:

https://www.facebook.com/groups/lucyslair/

To see fun inspiration photos for all of my novels, visit my Pinterest boards.

Finally, all Lucy Lennox titles are available on audio within a month of release and are narrated by the fabulous Michael Pauley.

Happy reading!
Lucy

ABOUT THE AUTHOR

Lucy Lennox is the creator of the bestselling Made Marian series, the Forever Wilde series, and co-creator of the Twist of Fate Series as well as the maker of three sarcastic kids. Born and raised in the southeast, she is finally putting good use to that English Lit degree.

Lucy enjoys naps, pizza, and procrastinating. She is married to someone who is better at math than romance but who makes her laugh every single day and is the best dancer in the history of ever.

She stays up way too late each night reading M/M romance because that stuff is impossible to put down.

For more information and to stay updated about future releases, please sign up for Lucy's author newsletter on her website.

Connect with Lucy on social media:
www.LucyLennox.com
Lucy@LucyLennox.com

WANT MORE?

Join Lucy's Lair

Get Lucy's New Release Alerts

Like Lucy on Facebook

Follow Lucy on BookBub

Follow Lucy on Amazon

Follow Lucy on Instagram

Follow Lucy on Pinterest

Other books by Lucy:

Made Marian Series

Forever Wilde Series

Aster Valley Series

Twist of Fate Series with Sloane Kennedy

After Oscar Series with Molly Maddox

Licking Thicket Series with May Archer

Virgin Flyer

Say You'll Be Nine

Visit Lucy's website at www.LucyLennox.com for a comprehensive list of titles, audio samples, freebies, suggested reading order, and more!

Milton Keynes UK
Ingram Content Group UK Ltd.
UKHW010716200923
429039UK00001B/63